Praise for the Melanie Hogan Mystery Series

Shear Fear

I love the Melanie Hogan series! I was so excited a month ago seeing that another one came out. I am about ready to start chapter for during my camping trip in Larkspur, Colorado and just can't put it down! Yet another incident that gets Melanie involved!

Shear Fear

"In this installment of the Melanie Hogan series some loose ends are tied up and new beginnings are on the horizon. It's a very good read; especially as a standalone."

Shear Camping Caper

"Enjoyed this short installment in the Melanie Hogan series. A complete mystery you can read in one sitting. Humorous characters in a beautiful setting. Hoping for more short stories like this one."

Shear Camping Caper

"I really liked this short book and that you didn't really need any background on the series of books. It all made sense and had great flow. I can't wait for the next Melanie Hogan book to come out!!"

Shear Madness

"Great story – Took a twist at the end that I hadn't anticipated! Rhonda writes in a way that helps the reader visualize the scene – makes it a very fun read and even more suspenseful. I'm ready for the next one in the series!"

Shear Madness

"It was an excellent read, caught your attention at the beginning and held it to the end. Likable characters that are well developed. Rhonda Blackhurst has a way of writing that is very visual."

Shear Madness

"Loved this cozy mystery and can't wait for the next one in the series. Melanie is a charming character, the dialogue is witty and funny, and the mystery has a twist I didn't guess."

Shear Madness

"The author of The Inheritance has a new book out and it's a start to a new series! Shear Madness is an engaging mystery novel … It reminded me of Scarlett Thomas' Lily Pascal series which I have also enjoyed. Just like

The Inheritance, I have enjoyed the characters and felt I understood them. I liked the suspenseful stalker introduced in the book and enjoyed trying to solve the mystery with Melanie Hogan ... I look forward to the next book in the series."

Shear Deception

"Wonderfully written, kept me in suspense!"

Shear Deception

"Once again Rhonda has written an excellent mystery. Her characters come alive, you feel you know them personally. She gets you interested from the first page and keeps you to the last page. A very good read."

Shear Deception

"Melanie Hogan's story continues in this next book in the series - and Blackhurst does not disappoint. All the lovable characters are back, and one that's not so lovable-a surprising foe to Melanie's sweet character."

Shear Murder

"Very enjoyable cozy mystery. The dialogue draws the reader into the story and helps to develop the characters and story development. I was drawn in from the beginning. The main character attended a reunion gathering of old friends when the unthinkable happens.

Great who-done-it with likable characters and a surprising ending. Highly recommended."

Shear Holiday Mayhem

"I love all the Melanie Hogan books and my favorite is always the last one I read - because they keep getting better and better. Take a trip to Minnesota at Christmas to visit Melanie and her friends and you will be able to feel the cold of the snow and taste the holiday cookies. The mystery has surprising twists and the romances are sweet. Best of all are the friendships and Melanie's special relationship with her Nana. If you want to get into the holiday spirit - read this now, though it will be a fun read at any time of the year."

Shear Holiday Mayhem

"Holiday Mayhem indeed. Melanie really didn't have to get involved in this mystery, but of course she does and it's quite an interesting read. I recommend it."

Shear Misfortune

A Melanie Hogan Mystery
Book 7

Rhonda Blackhurst

Books may be purchased in quantity and/or special sales by contacting the author at www.rhondablackhurst.com or rhondablackhurst@gmail.com.

Published by Lighthouse Press, Colorado
Cover Design by: No Sweat Graphics & Formatting
Edited by Jessica Cornwell Author Services

Library of Congress Control Number: 2022904057
ISBN: 978-1-7359393-3-9

First Edition
Printed in the United States of America

Also by Rhonda Blackhurst

- ➤ The Inheritance

The Melanie Hogan Cozy Mystery Series
- ➤ Shear Madness
- ➤ Shear Deception
- ➤ Shear Malice
- ➤ Shear Murder
- ➤ Shear Holiday Mayhem
- ➤ Shear Fear
- ➤ Shear Camping Caper-A Short Story

The Whispering Pines Mysteries
- ➤ Finding Abby
- ➤ Abby's Redemption

To Dan and Greg — Our lives will never be the same without you, but you both live on through your kids, grandkids, and the handprints you have left on so many hearts. Those who knew you were truly blessed.

And to Clint — you are my *one*. XO

1

I was dying. I was absolutely sure of it. My muscles strained like never before as I forced myself to stay upright, convinced cardiac arrest was imminent, and I'd never see another day.

I watched as Claire, my best friend, worked effortlessly on the rowing machine, her muscles glistening. Trying to keep up with her was going to put me six feet under, not make me healthier.

I looped a hand towel around the back of my neck, grabbed an end, and wiped my forehead as I headed over toward Claire. Sitting down, she was still almost as tall as I was while I was standing. Well, maybe not quite, but I didn't have to look down too far.

I hovered over her and waited, catching whatever cool air I could from the fan on the rowing machine. Small beads of perspiration glistened on her forehead.

"You do that on purpose, don't you?" I said, shaking my head as she came to a slow finish and set the rowing handle in the cradle.

She looked at me and laughed. "Do what on purpose?" she asked with ease, not in the least breathless. "And stop looking at me like you want to wrap that towel around my neck."

"I kind of do," I said.

"Why are you being such a hater?" She unhooked her feet from the machine, stood, and grabbed her towel from the floor beside the rower. Unlike me, who was still wiping my forehead, she merely dabbed at her brow and took a long drink of water from her multi-colored bottle.

"I love you. I just hate the fact that after a workout, you look better than I do after a shower. How is that fair?"

"As I tell Syd, life's not fair, my friend." She grinned and patted my back.

Syd was Claire's ten-year-old daughter. Ten going on twenty. That girl had attitude that was out of this world. But she's my favorite kid ever. Not to mention smart. I kept telling Claire that Syd would be the first woman president someday.

"You're the one who suggested we get the gym membership," she reminded me.

"'Cause I've gained ten pounds in six months!" I exclaimed. "I practically have to jump off a ten-story building to fit into my jeans these days."

Claire laughed loud. "You're so dramatic. And if you gained ten pounds—which I don't believe, by the way—you're still teeny tiny." I rolled my eyes, and she pulled my arm. "Come on. I need to get home to Syd."

When Claire and I work out together, we go in the evenings since she's arranged for her neighbor, Mrs. Carter, to stay an extra hour a couple of nights a week. Mrs. Carter meets Sydney as she gets off the bus and stays with her until Claire gets home, a transition that has worked marvelously. Mrs. Carter lives alone, her grandchildren are grown and live across the country, and she adores Syd.

When Syd goes to her grandparents' houses, we get to work out longer. Sometimes I go by myself early in the morning before anyone else is there. That is, except for one other person who always beats me, no matter how early I've gotten to the gym. While it piqued my curiosity, it had never bothered me enough to try to beat her. With the gym open twenty-four-seven, for all I knew, she could be there at three in the morning.

We grabbed our duffel bags out of our respective lockers and made for the exit, Claire waving to the front desk crew on the way out. "See you guys!" she called joyfully. I marveled at the energy she still had.

The cool air hit as I opened the door. For mid-March, it had been chilly, and there wasn't any indication of warmer weather for the next two-week forecast. "I can't wait to take a shower," I said over my shoulder.

"Take one here from now on," she said. "Then you won't have to wait."

I shrank back and wrinkled my nose. "Gross. Besides, no one else needs to see my business." My Nana and Granddad raised me, and we lived modestly. To this day, I'm not comfortable in front of anyone except Nana and Claire unless I'm fully clothed. And Levi, my fiancé. My heart fluttered at the thought of him. *Fiancé.* I loved that word.

"Who says anyone would even pay attention to your business?" she teased.

I snorted. "You make a good point."

"On a more pleasant topic," she said as we reached our cars, "what are we doing for your birthday this year?"

"Pretending it's not happening."

"Yeah. *That's* what's not happening. We're celebrating! Has Levi already planned something, though? Because I get first dibs. You were my friend first." She smiled and winked. "If he's made plans, tell him he'll have to reschedule for another night. You need to spend your birthday evening with Rubie, Jack, and me at Grizzley's for dinner and a birthday drink. We can't break tradition. Levi can join us, but he can't take you from us."

Jack and Rubie completed our friendship circle. "Shirley Temples? Maybe that will make me feel young again."

"You go right ahead and let me know how that works for ya," she said, laughing. "You can live dangerously by ordering one of those instead of your typical seltzer with an orange slice."

"I might surprise you and have an adult beverage," I said. "Like a glass of wine."

"You have a week and a half to prepare."

"Pshaw," I said, waving my hand through the air. "Done deal." I opened my car door. "See you tomorrow morning."

"Yes, you will."

4

Claire and I co-own a salon, A Cut Above. It's the perfect partnership. We excel in different business areas — me with the bookwork and anything that requires serious concentration, and Claire with the hands-on and creative things.

"Hey," she said right before I closed my car door. "I can't make it here tomorrow night. I have student-teacher conferences for Syd. And the next night, I can't either. Mrs. Carter has to leave early and can't stay."

"That works. I'll come early tomorrow morning by my lonesome."

"Take a day off, girl," Claire said.

"I want to find out who the woman is that beats me here every time I do come in the morning."

"That's still bugging you?" She shook her head. "Why?" She stood with her car door open, one foot on the ground and the other inside the car. She rested one hand on the roof of the vehicle and the other on the door handle.

"It's doesn't."

"Really?" she said. "Because the fact that you're still talking about it tells me it does."

"Curiosity is all."

"More like competitive," she said.

We both knew she was right, but I wasn't about to concede. I'm not sure which trait is stronger with me — sarcasm or stubbornness. "Not true," I said.

"True. See ya," she said with a wave. She slid into her car and closed the door before I could argue my side any further.

***

Claire turned into her driveway seconds before I turned into mine. She honked quickly as I drove by, and I answered with a quick beep of my own. My house is a small log home on one of Minnesota's ten thousand lakes. Claire owns a beautiful Victorian-style house across a field spotted with oak, maple, and birch trees. Hers is closer to the road without lake access. And hers is the only Victorian-style house in the entire community. One-of-a-kind. Just like Claire.

I parked in my detached garage, gathered my duffel bag and purse, and crossed the front yard. I climbed the steps and let myself into the house, breathing deeply as I opened the door. The pine-scented air freshener was subtle and welcome. I took one last deep inhale, slipped out of my shoes, and went upstairs to the loft where my bedroom was. I tossed my bag on my bed, stripped out of my dirty clothes, and started the shower. Just as I stepped in, my phone rang. I contemplated answering but decided it was nothing that couldn't wait. The shower had greater pull.

It rang again as I toweled off. I wrapped the towel around myself, scooped up my phone, and looked at caller ID. Levi. I smiled. "Hey, stud," I said.

"Hi, blondie. Guess what?"

His voice made me weak in the knees every time. And it wasn't until just recently that I finally stopped fighting it, stopped making excuses about why it couldn't work, about why *we* couldn't work. Stopped entertaining all of the *what-ifs*. And since then, it's never been better. I'd never been so happy in a relationship. Not that I'd had a lot. Trust wasn't exactly something that came easy for me. I pretty much trusted no one except my circle. And my circle consisted of Nana, Claire, Levi, Jack—mine and Claire's best friend—and Rubie, who is one of the stylists at the salon. And now my half-brother, Max, and his daughter, Daisy. My circle was growing, and as long as we stayed a circle, I was good. I'd once read scientists have proven that circles embody attributes that attract humans because they represent calmness, peacefulness, and relaxation. I have experienced that as a hard truth.

"Are you there?" he asked

"Oh, yeah. Sorry. What's up?"

"I can't come by tonight because Mona's bringing Jackson by. She got called into work."

A felt a pang of disappointment. But I understood completely. Jackson was Levi's ten-year-old son. And because of the failed relationship between my birth mother and me, and the fact that my biological father was absent from my life—a blessing, actually—it was an area of Levi's life I swore I wouldn't interfere with. His relationship with Jackson had to be first. I was determined not to be the cause of a broken parent-child relationship. And I loved Jackson. Almost as much as I loved Syd. Almost. Syd had stolen my heart from day one.

"Absolutely no worries," I said. "Enjoy your time together."

"Want to come by?" he asked, hopeful.

I mulled the idea over quickly. "Not tonight."

"Sure?" he tempted.

I smiled. "Yes, I'm sure. I just got out of the shower. Think I'll grab a cup of chamomile tea and call it an early night."

"See you tomorrow?"

"Definitely."

"Night, blondie. I love you."

"Love you too." Those words were something I swore I'd never say to a man ever again. And I fought them as long as I could with Levi, until common sense won out. And yet, still, those three little words held more weight than the Webster's dictionary.

2

My alarm bleeped far too early, and I groaned. I reached my arm from beneath the covers and fumbled for the snooze. I winced as my muscles stretched. Last night before I went to sleep, I insisted on seeing how many push-ups I could do without dropping. Not the girly-girl push-ups, but the real ones. "Why did you do this to yourself, Melanie Hogan?" I grumbled. "Because you're a masochist?"

I loved mornings more than any other part of the day. Today that joy was stolen because I couldn't move without hurting. And I hadn't even gotten out of bed yet. Maybe I should just work the same muscles every time so I wouldn't hurt. Or just stop altogether. But I knew I wouldn't. I wasn't even two weeks into the routine and knew it would take at least two to start feeling something good come from it. It was so important to me that I even moved my cherished morning devotional time to nighttime to accommodate this. I'd let myself get out of shape as I'd never been before. Not that I was fat, but I sported zero muscle tone. Not to mention I didn't feel the energy I once had. I'd been feeling sluggish. Typically, I was loaded with energy, and lately, I got tired too easily. In fact, some days, I woke up exhausted. Like this morning. Nana noticed and had been pushing me to see a doctor, but I kept putting it off.

"It's just because I've worn myself down, Nana," I had assured her. "I haven't been sleeping well." Which wasn't a lie. I had hoped exercising would help me sleep, but instead, it gave me enough of an energy boost to keep me from getting to sleep right away. *And they say exercise is supposed to be good for you*, I thought ruefully. Instead, it kept me up and made me hurt. Bah humbug. Getting something to help me sleep might not be a bad idea, but I'd always hated medication—much to Nana's dismay. "I don't know why you're being so stubborn, dear," Nana had said.

"It'll hurt the baby," I had teased her, to which she laughed, her cornflower-blue eyes crinkling at the corners. I'm unable to have children, which is why my ex-husband, Cain, left me after just five years of marriage. That and he had a wee bit of a problem with infidelity.

Nana was a retired nurse, which made her familiar with medication, and why she said I was stubborn for not taking it. "I guess I take after Violet in that area," I had teased her. It wasn't unusual to call my birth mother by her name. She lost the title of mother when she dropped me off with my grandparents when I was four years old because she wanted to go to Hollywood to be a big movie star. Not only didn't she make it in the movie business, but she also got mixed up with the wrong people, most notably my birth father, and got herself in a boatload of trouble. I'd only seen Violet once since she went to prison. I'd stopped hoping that she would love me and, in doing that, I'd almost managed to forgive her. Almost. After Granddad died, the bond between Nana and I deepened even more. There was nothing I wouldn't do for her and vice versa. Some of the best times of my life had been spent in her kitchen as we cooked together. Nana and her kitchen table had heard more secrets of mine than anyone else in the world. Good thing tables can't talk.

I forced myself out of bed and into my workout clothes before I gave in to the temptation of falling back into bed for another ten minutes. I brushed my teeth, threw my hair in a ponytail, grabbed my workout bag, and was out the door.

Twenty minutes later, at four forty-five, when I pulled into the parking lot, I was surprised at how empty it was. There were only five cars there, including one that looked like it had been there all night. The windows had a thick layer of frost on them. I looked toward the door. The last few early mornings I'd come here, there had been a man hanging out by the front door. He usually wore a black hoodie, hood pulled up, his hands tucked inside the front pocket. Yesterday when I'd tried to get a glimpse of his face under his hoodie, he ducked and went around the corner into the dark shadows. He didn't look like he'd just worked out because he wore jeans and didn't carry a workout bag. He could have been an employee, but I didn't think so. Regardless, I was happy he wasn't there to greet me today. He creeped me out. Maybe he'd moved on somewhere else.

As I got closer, I scanned the gym through the large front window and yanked open the door, eager to get inside. I took in the machines. So far, since I'd been coming, it was pretty much the same die-hard early morning stragglers whose time there invariably crossed with mine at some point: a young kid behind the desk who had a cup in front of him of what looked like coffee as he appeared lost on his cell phone; a man lifting weights off in the corner; a woman on a stationary bike; and two on the rowing machines. But today, one of them wasn't there. And then there was the mystery woman on the elliptical who'd caught my attention from the first day. She was tall and thin, had a single large tattoo of a dragonfly on her shoulder, and her long, curly red hair pulled high into a ponytail. I was fifteen minutes earlier than usual, and she still beat me. Geez!

I went to the locker room to dump my bag and jacket into a locker, put in my earbuds, found a true-crime podcast to listen to, and then hopped on a treadmill to walk and loosen up before hitting the circuit room. To my surprise, after five minutes, the mystery woman stepped onto the treadmill next to me. I stopped the podcast and took out my earbuds as she ramped up her machine to a fast-walking pace.

She glanced over at me and smiled. "Another early riser, huh? I've seen you in here a few times."

"Never as early as you, though. What time do you get here in the mornings?"

"Depends. Usually four-thirty."

I focused back on the treadmill. With my sore muscles, I wasn't exactly graceful this morning and didn't need to fly off the back like a cartoon character.

"My name is Andie Rose," she said, never missing a beat, clearly in much better shape than I was.

Where had I heard that name before? "Melanie," I said. "Do you live around here?"

"Only for a few more weeks. Then I'm moving to Spirit Lake to run an inn my grandpa left me."

I looked at her quickly. "Spirit Lake? That town is haunted, isn't it? Oh! And I'm so sorry about your grandfather." My face turned a shade of pink, not caused by exercise.

Andie Rose laughed. "So they say. About Spirt Lake being haunted," she added. "The jury is still out on whether I believe in that stuff yet. I mean, I believe in ghosts, yeah, and I've witnessed some out-of-the-ordinary stuff, but sometimes people see what they're hoping to. Know what I mean?"

I snickered. "Completely. So you get here at four-thirty?"

"Usually. I can run outside any time of day. I love it out there. But I'm not a fan of the gym, so if I'm using the machines and I don't get here early in the mornings, I won't go at all. And when I was working at my last job, I had to go this early, so it's become a habit. Besides," she said, dabbing her brow, "I'm staying with my cousin until I move. My house sold sooner than expected. So while I'm staying with her, I try to stay away as much as I can so I'm not in her way."

"Most people are still sleeping at four-thirty."

"Not my cousin. I swear, she never sleeps." She chuckled.

"Oh." I had nothing to add. Andie Rose talked some more, briefly mentioning a boyfriend between talk of the weather. She was far more talkative than I am in the mornings. Probably more so than I was any time of day, for that matter. But I already liked her. Odd for me to take a liking to someone so quickly. There was something strangely familiar about her, though. In a comfortable sort of way. "My grandmother's name is Rose," I said. She looked at me like I'd said the moon was green.

"Yeah?"

"Your name being Andie Rose. Reminds me of my grandmother."

"Oh," she said and laughed. "I was confused for a minute there about why you'd be telling me your grandmother's name."

I chuckled. "Do you go by Andie or Andie Rose?"

"Whatever people call me. The Rose part adds a little femininity to a man's name, so it depends on the day." She laughed.

14

"I get it," I said. "Well, I'm going to head to the circuit room. Nice to meet you."

"You too." She looked at her fitness tracker. "Time for me to hit the shower and head home. Well, to my cousin's home, that is. This homeless stuff is humbling."

"See you again, I'm sure."

"If you're here in the next few weeks, you can count on it." With a quick wave, she was off.

The machines in the circuit room added insult to injury with my already sore arm muscles, but I forced myself to continue. If I was anything, it was stubborn. And determined. Not following through on something I set my mind to wasn't what I did.

Thirty minutes later, I snatched my water bottle from the corner of the room and headed to the locker room. The gym was empty except for a man working with the free weights and a woman on a stationary bike. The guy behind the desk was still on his phone with one cheek of his behind resting on the counter. The man and the woman from when I arrived were now gone. As I turned the corner into the locker room, I nearly smacked into Andie Rose. Her hair was still wet.

"Have a good one," she said. "Probably see you soon."

"Looking forward to it," I said. And I was. It would be fun to have someone familiar to work out with. At the same time, anyway. Even if it was only for two more weeks. I wondered if the weird guy was trolling outside the door yet and wished I would have said something to Andie Rose just in case he showed up again.

I stepped back out and looked toward the door, but she was already outside. I went back into the locker room to grab my bag and jacket, deciding to hit the restroom first. I had to pee—again—and fifteen or twenty minutes until I got home was a long time to wait.

As I passed a mostly hidden nook in the locker room— I assumed for the modest women who wanted privacy—I noticed a thin red trail snaking from the corner. Blood? *Gross!* I shuddered and continued before deciding to backtrack a couple of steps and peek around the corner. I gasped and stifled a scream, my hand flying up to cover my mouth. Lying on the floor in a pool of blood was the woman who had been absent from the morning's usual group.

3

"Coming in!" a young male's voice called. Within a second, the kid that had been engrossed in his phone stood behind me. "Oh man!" he exclaimed as he saw the body. "What did you do?" he asked me.

"I didn't do this!" I said, taking out my phone. "I came in to use the bathroom, is all."

"Well, someone heard a scream. You're the only one here still alive."

"It was me that screamed," I explained, unaware until then that I'd done so.

"Stuff like this never happens in my life. Just in the movies."

I glanced at him and gasped as he could barely contain his excitement. "This isn't something you *want* to happen in your life."

"Did you call 911?" he asked, ignoring my comment.

"That's what I'm doing," I said, showing him my phone before quickly putting it back up to my ear. I scanned the area around the body, committing to memory anything out of the ordinary.

"911, what's your emergency?" came the voice on the phone.

I was getting too good at giving them the exact information they needed. The past three years had brought more dead bodies into my life than a coroner's. And it all happened since I'd decided I wanted more excitement in my perfectly consistent, somewhat boring life. Instead, I had cursed myself.

As I stayed on the line as instructed, I noted anything odd, including drops of what looked like coffee by her hand, but no cup anywhere. Her left hand clutched what appeared to be a torn and crumpled piece of paper peeking out between two fingers. The 911 operator assured me units were on scene, so I hung up. It took a second to realize the guy hovering over me was speaking.

"...then who?"

I shook my head. "What?"

"I said if it wasn't you, then who? Who did this?"

"How would I know?" I snapped.

"You didn't see anyone else in here?"

I heard Levi's voice as he approached, and I inhaled, holding it briefly. Of course, he would be the one to show up. He was one of two homicide detectives in Birch Haven and the one who lived the closest, not to mention the one on call. Still crouched down, I looked up as he approached. Our eyes met, and he exhaled, closed his eyes briefly, and shook his head.

"I should have known," he said through a groan.

"What's that supposed to mean?" I asked, eyes narrowed.

"You know exactly what it means," he said, sounding more resigned. "What happened?" he asked as two officers came up behind him.

"I don't know. I finished my workout, so I came in the locker room to get my stuff and found—this." I jerked my hand toward the body.

"You have the absolute worst timing and luck of anyone I know."

"Umm...exactly how many people would that be?" I asked, twisting my lips.

"Sir," Officer Anderson said, "I'll go look at the electronic log at the front desk. See who's all checked in this morning."

Levi nodded. "Check on the security cameras too. We'll see if they're as state-of-the-art as they claim on their commercials. I want footage." He looked at me and the front desk dude. "I need you both to leave the room." Then to me, "Melanie, don't leave the gym."

"Like I would," I said. I looked at the time on my fitness tracker—six o'clock. "But I have to leave by seven so I can shower and get to work. I have a client at nine."

He glanced at me and shook his head. "Unfortunately, you know all too well how these things work. I can't make any promises."

I put my hands on my hips and faced him head-on. "And I know enough to know that you can't keep me here without cause."

I saw the corner of his lip curl up ever so slightly. "Don't I know it."

"You two know each other?" the front desk kid asked.

Levi looked at me, and I quickly diverted my attention. I looked at the young man and, for the first time, noticed his name badge. Sean. "Come on, Sean. Let's stay out of their way and let them do their job."

"Now there's a novel idea," Levi said.

"I just need to grab something from my locker first."

Levi looked at me. "Melanie, this is a crime scene. You can't 'just grab' anything at all."

"My locker isn't a crime scene. Detective," I added.

"This entire locker room is," he argued. "I'll let you know when you can get back in." He looked at Officer Pinter, who stood guard. "Pinter, block off the door, please. After Ms. Hogan and the gentleman leave. In fact, please see them out."

I narrowed my eyes at Levi.

"Go," he mouthed with a wink. A wink so brief I wondered if I'd seen it at all.

"I still haven't used the restroom," I said.

"Go in the men's."

"We have a unisex biff," Sean said. "Right on the other side of the men's locker room."

I trailed behind Sean and Officer Pinter, and when I was out of Levi's eyesight, I stopped and scanned the second row of lockers to see a wet white and blue towel with droplets of what looked like blood, as well as an opened notebook. I snapped a quick photo of each with my phone and hoped the camera on my new smartphone was sophisticated enough to zoom in clearly. I needed to see the pattern of the blood as well as what was written on the open page of the notebook.

"Ms. Hogan," Officer Pinter said, "come on."

As soon as I was out, Sean pointed toward a single door that I'd never noticed before. "Over there," he said.

"Sean," I said, "do you know the woman in there?" I jerked my thumb toward the women's locker room.

"No. But I've seen her in here. Fact, she was in yesterday morning, but not this morning. Alive, anyway." He swallowed and paled, the reality apparently setting in.

"Does everyone have to have a membership to come in here, or can they pay per visit?"

"We allow people one free visit to try it out. And then they either have to buy a membership or come with someone who has one."

"So she had a membership, then?"

"Yep."

"Can I see her information?"

His neck tinted pink. "I can't show you anything. That's confidential. We're not supposed to give out anyone's information."

"That is kind of the confidential part," I muttered, disappointed this particular young kid would be such a rule-follower. I looked around the gym, the yellow and black machines and lighting looking eerie now instead of welcoming. I shuddered. Death can sure change the look of a place.

I inhaled deeply and closed my eyes to think about the morning. I replayed everything from the moment I pulled into the parking lot until now. The strange man out front—strangely absent after being present four days in a row; Sean, too preoccupied with his phone to notice anything going on around him; the man on the weights; the woman on the rowing machine; and the woman, now dead, who had been on the rowing machine on prior mornings but absent today. I thought about Andie Rose hopping on the treadmill next to mine and the man and woman who'd come in after I'd begun the machines in the circuit room. And then it struck me—Andie Rose. Her hair was wet, and there was the damp towel with blood on it on the locker room floor not far from the body. And Andie had come out of the locker room right before I'd gone in and found the body. I had to tell Levi. Or did I? I wished I could talk with her first. But I didn't have her contact information. Just that she was living with her cousin. I wished I'd gotten her cousin's name.

***

I was released from the gym at a quarter past seven, just in time to fly home, shower, dress, and head back into town. And at eight-thirty, I was flying to work, accompanied by such horrendous nausea I was barely able to keep the protein shake and toast I wolfed down from coming back up. Apparently, the body affected me more than I'd expected. I had to reroute my thoughts; otherwise, I'd see the dead woman's face again in my mind's eye. At the first stoplight, I shot Levi a text to call me as soon as he could. To which I got an immediate response, *I can only imagine why you want me to call.*

To tell you I love you, why else? I texted back.

Right. Just remember this is an open investigation. I can't discuss it.

I'm crushed.

I waited for a response. Nothing. Which was good because I ran out of stoplights at which to text. I turned into the parking lot, grateful for the distraction my salon would no doubt bring me for the day. I unlocked the door and let it fall shut behind me, the door's bells merrily ringing and then falling silent. I breathed deep, willing my mind to be still. I loved it here. The smells of nail and hair chemicals, the sounds of blow dryers running, the good old-fashioned hair dryers for roller sets — of which we still did a few — voices chatting about nothing and everything, laughter, and phones ringing. Although, the phones were probably my least favorite. It was a pet peeve of mine when I was working on someone's hair, and they insisted on answering their ringing phone. It's so inconsiderate to talk on the phone while making people wait for you.

I thought about calling Nana since I'd put it off so far. She can tell whenever anything is wrong, and I didn't know how to tell her that I had come across yet another dead body. I hadn't even told Claire yet.

We opened at nine, and I had unlocked the front door with fifteen minutes to spare – just enough time to put my makeup on before my client arrived. The rest of the ladies would be zipping in at any minute, except for Babs, our nail tech. She started at ten every day except Saturdays when she started at nine, or when she had a special early appointment. I looked at my watch. Claire must be running late. She was usually here by eight-thirty.

"Claire?" I called toward the back. Maybe Cole had dropped her off, and she was here already. Cole was her boyfriend and worked patrol at the Birch Haven PD. He was also Levi's best friend. When she didn't answer, I strode toward the office in the back across the hallway from the restrooms. The doors were closed, and I shuddered. Being alone right after finding a body, I didn't like the closed doors so much right now. Apparently, murderers killed in public places. I was alone in this one at the moment, and I wanted to be sure of it.

I reached for the door handle at the same time the little bell hanging above the front door jingled. I startled, then crept toward the salon and called a bit quietly, "Claire?"

"Yep," she called back.

I exhaled my relief. "I'm in the office. I'll be right out."

"No hurries! I'm going to make a quick trip to the grocery store," she said. "Want anything?"

My stomach flipped, then flopped. The residual effects of the morning were taking their toll. "No, thank you."

"Not even a blueberry danish?"

"No," I said, my stomach queasy at the mention of what had always been my favorite. Instead, I kept seeing the dead woman in my head.

The doorbell jingled again, followed by more voices—Connie and Rubie's. I'd be smelling Rubie's Loves Baby Soft perfume any minute now. As soon as she turned the corner into the office, I gasped. "Did you bathe in that stuff again, Rubie?" She was all girly-girl with a pink long-sleeved silk blouse and white skirt. Her blond curls were pulled into a ponytail, one curly tendril lying beside her pink rouged cheek. Pink gloss coated her lips.

"Maybe," she said, smiled, and winked. "What's it to ya?"

"Babs called," Connie said. "She has company who's apparently pretty shaken up about something. She's going to be a little late today. Said she'd try to be here by eleven. She asked if someone could squeeze in her first client. I guess it's just a pedicure."

I shuddered. "Eww! Count me out." I ended up doing all the walk-in men's flat-top haircuts but steered a mile clear of any pedicures. Touching people's feet was not it for me.

25

The ladies giggled knowingly before Connie said, "Babs said it's a new client, so she shouldn't care."

"Who shouldn't care?" Rubie asked. "Babs or the client?"

We all looked at Rubie, speechless. I finally shook my head and went to my station to get my equipment ready.

"Did you go to the gym this morning, Melanie?" Connie asked.

My head swam a little bit. "Yes."

Thankfully, before either of them could ask another question, my nine o'clock client walked in. Once I got busy working on her hair, the rest of the morning flew by before I knew it. It was eleven fifteen by the time I looked up, and Babs was walking in the door. Someone trailed behind her.

"Bringing people in off the street for—"

I stopped dead in my tracks and stared.

"Melanie, this is my cousin, Andie Rose. Andie," she said, extending her arm toward me, "this is Melanie."

4

A ndie Rose and I stared at each other in surprise, and then she laughed.

"Hey, Melanie. Nice to see you again so soon."

Babs, Connie, Claire, and Rubie looked from me to Andie Rose and then back to me again. They reminded me of puppets with the puppet master keeping them all in tandem.

"I know the two of you talked on the phone a couple of months back about something, Mel, but I didn't know if you'd remember her," Babs finally said.

Of course! That's where I'd heard her voice before! Andie Rose worked on the deceased's hair and makeup at Birch Haven Funeral Home. And since that *something* Babs referred to had been a murder, how could I forget? "I sure do," I said, trying to read Andie Rose. "I found a body in the locker room right after you left this morning."

The sound of glass shattering broke the moment. Claire had dropped her Barbicide jar that held her combs and brushes. Her milk-chocolate skin turned a shade of milky white.

"A b-body?" she stammered. "For God's sake, Melanie, what is it with you and bodies? Dead ones!" She sat down on the chair, staring absently at the mess on the floor. Babs' gaze was stuck on me, jaw slackened, then she looked at Andie Rose.

"It's hardly my fault, Claire," I said. Even to me, it sounded like a pathetic attempt at making sense of something that wouldn't make sense to *anyone*.

"I am so sorry," Andie Rose said. Her blue eyes were wide. She was either genuinely empathetic or a better actress than Violet could have ever hoped to be. "Did you recognize who it was?"

"No," I said, still trying to get a read on her. I couldn't. She truly appeared concerned, but she hadn't denied knowing about it, either. "But I think it was the woman missing from the usual small group of exercise enthusiasts this morning."

"The woman from the rowing machine?" Her brows furrowed. "I noticed she was gone this morning too."

"The police will probably contact you. If they haven't already," I said. "They got everyone's name from the computer as well as memberships. It shouldn't take long because it was pretty dead this morning — pardon the pun."

"Oh, Melanie!" Claire exclaimed, mouth open, eyes closed a moment. "That was a terrible play on words."

Babs twisted her mouth, her nose ring askew. "Yeah, it really kind of was."

"Sorry," I murmured. "It wasn't intentional."

The door opened, and I glanced over to see Max, my newly discovered half-brother, walk in. "You're early," I said.

"Better than late," he answered in his usual monotone. "I have to leave town for a few days and was hoping to hit the road a little earlier if I can."

"What about Daisy? Do you want me to watch her?" Daisy was my new niece, who I'd fallen completely in love with.

"My mom's got her covered since she's staying with us for now."

I shrugged and swallowed my disappointment. "All right. We're just catching up on murder talk. If you don't mind listening to that, I can quick squeeze you in now."

"Murder talk?" He frowned. "Maybe now isn't a good time."

I grabbed his arm and led him to my chair. "Sit."

"Didn't know what you were getting into with that one as a sister, did you, Max?" Babs asked. I looked at her, then at Andie, whose gaze was glued to Max. I glanced at Max, who returned her gaze before I socked him in the shoulder, leaned in close to his ear, and whispered, "She's got a boyfriend, Romeo. Cool it."

He jerked his head away and frowned again. "I didn't do anything."

"Right," I scoffed. Andie Rose turned her head away slightly, her cheeks a shade closer to her hair color. I said to her, "So are you the one who was upset, causing Babs to come in late?" I shook out my cape and fastened it around Max's neck.

She looked at me sheepishly. "Yeah, sorry. I didn't mean to cause trouble for anyone."

I watched her in silence a moment. Since they found the body after she'd left, she would have had no way of knowing until I told her, unless...

"No," Babs said, shaking her head slowly.

"No?" I was confused. "No, what?" I walked Max to the shampoo bowls and leaned him back.

"No, Andie Rose didn't do it," Babs said. "Don't look all innocent there, missy," she told me. "I know exactly why you asked that."

"Anyone wanna clue me in?" Andie Rose said.

"And me," Max said, raising his head slightly, water shooting down his back. "Hey!"

"You're the one who did it," I said. "Stay still."

Claire and Rubie only shook their heads. They knew full well about the information I sought from Andie.

"The fact that she was upset had nothing to do with the body," Babs said. "It was personal."

"I've been at the receiving end of your suspicions, and it's not fun," Max muttered. I gave him a threatening look. "Just sayin'."

The salon grew quiet, and shame threatened to swallow me whole. My cheeks not only burned, they oddly pinched. I finished rinsing Max's hair and towel dried his coal-black locks before leading him back to my stylist chair. I forced myself to look at Babs to see that she'd forgiven me completely. I briefly closed my eyes and took a breath. *Note to self—stop looking at everyone as suspects, or you'll be a lonely old cat woman.* I took a deep breath, bumping my mental attitude to another plane.

"I'm sorry, Andie. It's nice to finally meet you in person, this time knowing who you are," I said.

"That's better," Max whispered. I discreetly pulled a strand of hair at the nape of his neck as I pulled the towel off. "Ouch!"

I smiled sweetly at him. "I hadn't realized Babs was the cousin you'd referred to at the gym," I said to Andie Rose as she snuck another glance at Max. *Geez!*

"I told you I had family staying with me for a while," Babs said.

"Well, yeah, but I didn't put two and two together. Especially you two," I said.

Babs looked at Andie Rose. "Yeah, we don't resemble each other much, do we?"

"Much?" I said. "How about not at all. Except for your voices."

Both had smokey, sultry voices. I didn't know about Andie Rose, but in Babs' case, it led to a lot of men asking for her to be their stylist when they called for an appointment if she happened to answer the phone, disappointed when she'd told them she's a nail tech. But it led to an accumulation of male manicures and pedicures.

Babs had several piercings on her face and ears and at least as many tattoos. She was completely the opposite of what one would expect a nail technician to look like. The nail tech position hadn't had the best luck over the past few years. Thank goodness Babs changed the bad-luck streak. Her hair was short, now blond, and a classic spiked pixie. The only thing she and Andie Rose had in common—other than their voices—was the square, strong, yet feminine jawline.

"The grandfather that's leaving you the inn in Spirit Lake, is he both of yours?" I asked.

They looked at each other, and Babs shook her head. "Long story."

"Family drama," Andie Rose added.

Connie's client walked through the door. Connie had been so quiet through all the commotion that I'd forgotten she was even in the salon. Rubie too, for that matter. And if there's one thing Rubie typically wasn't, it's quiet.

"Hey," I said to her, "as soon as I finish with Max's hair, wanna walk down to the grocery store with me? I should only be another two minutes." Our salon was on one end of a strip mall, the grocery store on the other. The businesses and additional stores in between included a bail bonds agency, a liquor store, an attorney's office, and an insurance business. One-stop shopping. I think we could support the bakery at the grocery store all by ourselves, though. And now that the shock had worn off—somewhat—I was suddenly hungry.

"I don't know," she said. "Being with you appears to be hazardous to one's health."

The summer before last, Rubie went with me to a reunion of sorts with my beauty college buddies. It included an unexpected murder investigation of which I was the lead suspect.

"That's why I come here to get my haircut," Max said. "There are witnesses if anything happens."

The ladies laughed, but only Andie Rose appeared thoroughly amused. Maybe she was simply smitten.

"Suit yourself," I said. "But don't drool all over my blueberry croissant." I finished rubbing the pomade through Max's hair and picked up the blow dryer.

"Fine. I'll come with." Her blond ponytail flipped over her shoulder as she turned toward the office for what I assumed was to grab her wallet—a pink one with rhinestones.

I finished drying Max's hair, and he headed to the coat rack by which Andie Rose happened to be standing. I watched as they glanced at each other; she moved from his way, he reached past her with one arm to get his coat. No words were spoken, but none were needed. I was certain that if Andie Rose lived in town, there would be a connection here. I couldn't decide if I'd wanted that or not. Not that it was my decision to make. But she had a boyfriend already, and Max was newly divorced. *Very* newly. And neither of them struck me as the impulsive type. But what did I know? I still had a lot to learn about both of them.

"You'd better get going," I told Max. "And drive safe." After he left, I said to the others, "Do you all want us to get you anything?"

Each, except Andie Rose, gave me their order.

"Andie Rose?" I said. "I'm buying."

She shook her head and gave a half-hearted smile. "No, thank you. My stomach's not feeling so great."

Bab's studied her cousin. "When did that start?" she asked. "You were feeling perfectly fine on the way here."

Andie Rose shrugged. "I'm not sure. I guess the whole dead body thing is gnawing at me."

Connie glared our way and swiveled her stylist chair, turning her client away from us. I looked at Andie Rose and whispered, "Why?"

Claire looked at me as though I'd lost my mind. "Why do you think?"

Connie turned and glared our way again, this time with a scowl. *Sorry!* I mouthed. I looked at Claire again. I wasn't used to her without a smile on her face. It happened so infrequently that it threw me off my game when it did. "I admit it's unsettling, to say the least. I just thought maybe there was more to it." I held my breath, waiting for her to reply, but she didn't.

"Like what?" Bab's asked.

I put my finger to my lips. "Shh. I don't think Connie wants her client to hear us talking about dead bodies," I whispered.

"Wonder why," Rubie quipped. She looked at her watch. "I'm not going to be able to go with you, Mel. My next client is due in five minutes. She's always late, but," she nodded out the window, "this is the one time she's here early." She tucked her wallet inside the top drawer at her station. It was such an array of pink it hurt my eyes to look at it. Pink brushes, pink combs, pink blow dryer, pink curling iron, pink everything. Even her cape was pink. It was nauseating. She had about as much pink as I had black.

Another woman was a few short steps behind Rubie's client.

"Claire," I said, "here's your next one, too."

"You go ahead, Mel," Babs said. "I'll hold down the fort here."

I slipped into my jacket. "I'll be right back."

"I guess I can walk down there with you," Andie Rose said. "And then I need to get home to Aspen."

"Aspen?" I said.

"My dog. He's used to going everywhere I go. When I leave him home—or in this case at Babs'—he gets a little out of sorts."

With everyone's pastry order in my head, we began the short walk toward the other end of the mall. "What do you do with him when you're at work? Doggy daycare?"

"No, he came with me."

I swiveled my head to look at her. "But you work in a funeral home." Andie Rose was the one who prepared the deceased for viewing by making sure their hair and makeup was done to perfection.

"Aspen's a good boy." She smiled, her eyes revealing her love for the dog. "He stays right by my side. I like to think he brings comfort to the deceased." She shrugged. "Besides, I only worked there part-time. And I had permission to bring him with me to the hotel I worked at."

I shivered and tucked my hands in my jacket pockets. "How did you ever get into that line of work? Funeral home stuff."

"When my grandmother died, I did her hair and makeup. I wanted to give others the tender care I wanted for my grandmother. And other reasons," she added quietly. "But I'm jobless temporarily because I'm moving. When I'm running the inn, I'll focus on that instead. I'm also a life coach, so I'm hoping to nab one of the rooms as an office to do that. Even if it's the broom closet."

I snickered. "People might not be comfortable coming out of the closet in public." I thought of Jack and his journey in that area, and it warmed my heart.

I glanced at Andie Rose, who was smiling, yet looked troubled. I focused in front of me, kicking a stone out of the way. "You're used to working with dead people. Why did finding out about the body in the gym this morning bother you?" I didn't want to think she could have killed the woman.

"The people I worked on at Birch Haven Funeral Home were strangers."

My breath caught in my throat. "Did you know the woman who was killed this morning?"

"No!" she answered quickly. Too quickly. "But as you pointed out earlier, there aren't a lot of us there so early in the morning. You get to know who the regulars are. And to think that someone was exercising one day and dead the next—well—" This time, Andie Rose shivered and tucked her hands in her jacket pockets. "What if one of us would have been the one to walk in the locker room at the wrong time?"

We walked in silence for a few seconds before I asked, "What was that with my brother?"

"What do you mean?"

I glanced at her, and she quickly looked away. "I'm not blind. He just got a divorce. As in just last month. I don't want you to be a rebound."

She laughed aloud. "Oh my gosh! Trust me, you have nothing to worry about."

"That's not what it looked like."

She stopped and turned toward me. "Melanie, I have a boyfriend. But it can't be lost on you how gorgeous he is. Those eyes!"

"Yeah, yeah, I know about the eyes. But he's my brother. Gorgeous isn't a term I'd use. Annoying, maybe."

She laughed again, and we continued walking. "You sound just like a sister. And he probably says the same thing about you."

I wasn't sure how to respond to that. Max and I had only known each other for a few months, and I was still getting used to having him around. I tried to change the subject; unfortunately, the only thing I could think of was—again—the murder. "What if it wasn't random? The murder. They rarely are, you know."

"Spoken by one who knows. I bet you hear a lot with your boyfriend being a homicide detective."

"Sometimes too much." *But not from Levi.* If she only knew. "Wait! How did you know he was a homicide detective?"

"Babs told me."

"Oh, of course."

"Maybe you can get some information on this murder."

I shook my head. "It's an open investigation. Since I found the body…" I shook my head again, this time more forcefully. "No, he can't tell me anything." I remembered the notebook lying open and pulled out my phone.

"What's that?" Andie Rose asked.

"When I left the locker room this morning, I saw a notebook lying open by one of the lockers. I snapped a picture of the page that was lying open."

Andie Rose gasped. "No, you did not!"

"It was practically begging me to," I said. "It was just lying there. It's not like I touched anything."

"Let me see!" she exclaimed. We'd reached the doors to the grocery store; we stopped and huddled over my phone and the photo of the notebook page. I stretched the image with my thumb and forefinger, making a logo on top of the page easier to read: *Lakes News and Reviews*. Suddenly Andie gasped, her face paled.

5

"What is it?" I asked, staring at her, my eyes wide. "Now I know why the woman looked so familiar to me. I tried to remember where I knew her from and then decided she must have been a family member of a deceased at the funeral home."

"But?" I prompted. "She's not?"

"I don't think so."

"You don't think so?" I squinted as I looked at her.

"The woman who was missing from the gym this morning—*was* it her? Blond hair, black streak—the streak is new from when I saw her before, and I think that's what threw me off."

I tried my hardest to remember. "I can't say with a hundred percent certainty. I was a little shaken up."

"I can imagine," she said with sympathy. "Who wouldn't be shaken up after that?"

With the way my life had been going lately, I would think I'd have been used to it by now. "There were other things I noticed, though."

"Like what?" she asked, nearly breathless at the new revelation. "Something about the body?"

"About the surroundings. But first, how do you know this woman? Who do you think she is?"

"Maggie Thompson." Andie Rose looked off across the parking lot, avoiding my eyes.

"How do you know her?"

"Because we argued a couple of months ago over a bad review she wrote about the inn." She combed her fingers through her hair. "Oh man, Melanie, this doesn't look good for me."

I exhaled long and slow. "No, it doesn't. At all. How did you not see her when you went into the locker room?"

"Why would I? You said she was in the privacy nook. I don't give two hoots who sees all this." She swept her hands down her figure. "So I haven't used that while I've been here. All I did was take a shower and boogie out of there."

"Where did you leave your towel?"

"I bring my own, so it was in my gym bag. The hand towels the gym supplies for the workouts, I tossed the one I used into the dirty towel bin."

"But you're sure you took your wet towel with you?"

"Yes! I emptied my bag into the washing machine as soon as I got home. I know it was in there." Her hand flew up to her mouth, and her eyes grew huge. "Oh, sweet baby Jesus! Was she killed when I was in the shower? Was the killer in there at that time?"

"Maybe Levi can tell me the time of death at the very least. I'll ask him. All he can do is say no. Which he probably will, along with 'stay out of the investigation, Melanie.'"

"As much as I don't want to cause problems for you guys, it sure would be nice to find out the time of death. It'll either freak me out because I was in there at the same time — and make me a suspect, if I'm not already — or it will clear me. Hopefully the latter."

"Come on," I said, "I need to get this stuff so I can get back to the salon."

"Yeah. I need to get back to Aspen."

As we strode back to the bakery, a thought occurred to me. "Do you still have connections at the funeral home? Maybe you could do some digging and see if you can come up with anything."

"That would be a good idea, but there are two funeral homes in town. It's not guaranteed that she would go to Birch Haven Funeral Home. Also, I'm done there. I thought I would be in Spirit Lake already."

"But you still have contacts there, yeah?"

"Yeah. But the body doesn't go directly to the funeral home. They need to contact the next of kin and find out where they want her after an autopsy. They do them on all unattended deaths. Especially if it looks like murder."

"How soon will they do the autopsy?"

"Homicides are typically within a day or two," she said.

One of the women standing behind us gasped.

I turned toward them. "So sorry."

Her friend gave me a look that could literally kill. I thought the first might get sick. *Geez!* Sensitive people. But then, not everyone had been exposed to dead bodies as often as I had been lately. Fortunate for them. Unfortunate for me.

***

Andie Rose left as soon as we got back to the salon, claiming she needed to walk Aspen.

"That girl doesn't go anywhere without that dog," Babs said. "Her boyfriend even gets jealous of the attention she gives it."

"Sounds like he has an insecurity problem," Rubie told her. "The boyfriend, not the dog."

"Yeah, that's just one of the problems he has," she grumbled.

"Meaning?" I asked.

"The guy is boring as heck. And his job is always first, no matter what. I don't know what she sees in him," Babs said.

I felt a wave of gratitude for Levi. There wasn't anything boring about him. I looked at my left hand and the vintage rose gold princess cut solitaire diamond it sported. I'd finally said yes, much to my grandmother's delight.

"Let him make an honest woman out of you," she'd said, more than once.

"Nana, I couldn't be more honest," I'd replied every time. She'd always laughed, her cornflower-blue eyes dancing.

Speaking of Nana, I still hadn't talked to her yet today. I didn't want to tell her about the body, but I didn't want her to find out from somewhere else, either. But since I always talked to her by this time of the day, she was probably worried anyway. I picked up the phone as soon as my client left and before the next arrived. All of us except Claire had some blank space in the appointment book. Unusual, to be sure. It must be something in the air today.

Nana answered on the second ring. "Melanie, dear, I was just beginning to worry."

I looked at my watch. Two-thirty. "You were only starting to worry now?" I teased.

"Come by for dinner tonight. And bring that man of yours."

"I'll ask him, but he might be working. Or sleeping. It depends how his day goes."

"Meaning?"

"You're too smart for your own good."

"I may be old, but I'm not slow, dontcha know."

I chuckled. "Oh, I know that."

"You didn't answer my question."

"Didn't I?"

"Melanie Hogan!" she scolded playfully.

"I'll fill you in tonight, Nana. I promise."

"All right, dear. Six-thirty?"

"I'll be there at six. I need to be home early and get some sleep."

"Tired again, are ya?"

Some days her Minnesota accent was heavier than others. Today was one of those days.

"Let's just say it's been an interesting day. But nothing that seeing you won't make better."

"See you at six then. Bring your appetite."

My stomach turned a bit. "Not too much for me, Nana. I can help cook when I get there, so don't work yourself crazy."

"You just come and relax this evening. We'll cook together another night."

"Okay. See you in a few hours."

After we hung up, I thought about her and how lucky I was to have her in my corner. What I once thought of as a curse, Violet not wanting me and all, turned out to be a blessing. Nana and Granddad were angels in disguise. Tears sprang to my eyes, and I pushed them away.

***

Levi showed up as I finished my last client of the afternoon. There had been a heaviness that seemed to hang in the air all day, but as I saw him, the proverbial clouds parted, and my knees weakened. The man made my bad days good and my good days better. His shaved head shone, his black leather jacket fit his muscles just so, and his tactical pants looked absolutely perfect.

I nodded my head, smiled, and held up five fingers briefly, letting him know I'd be five minutes. He winked and struck up a conversation with Claire, who had just rung out her last client at the front desk. I caught Rubie and Babs giving him an appreciative look. Connie just walked into the back room, and I heard the dryer door close. She must have felt the weirdness in the air today too.

As soon as my client left, I took Levi by the hand and led him to the office.

"PDA, Ms. Hogan?" He said, amused. "What's that about?"

As soon as we turned the corner into the office, I stood on my tiptoes and kissed him. "Are you complaining?" I said, grinning.

"Not even a little." He pulled back and met my eyes. "But just so we're straight, it won't get you answers about this investigation."

I feigned surprise. "Whatever are you talking about?" I began to nuzzle his neck.

He chuckled. "Melanie Hogan, you're the devil. It's not going to work."

I pulled back. "Levi, you have to tell me something. Anything."

"No, Melanie, I don't." He kissed my hand and sat down. "But I do have a few questions."

"How about you ask one, I ask one."

"How about you let me do my job," he said, raising an eyebrow.

I sighed and sat down in the chair next to him. "Fine."

He smiled. "You're kind of sexy when you pout."

I stuck my bottom lip out and looked at him, batting my eyelashes. "Yeah?"

He chuckled and shook his head. "You're impossible."

"Can you tell me the time of death?"

"No."

"Cause of death?"

"No."

"Any leads?" I tried again.

"No."

I exhaled loudly and groaned. "You're so frustrating. I could help you, you know."

"You can help me by not getting involved. There's a killer out there, Melanie. Let me find him."

I sat back and slouched in my chair. "Fine."

"You're pouting again."

"Only because I know it's getting to you. Eventually, you'll wear down and give me something to work with."

"Or you will eventually realize I'm serious about you staying out of the investigation."

"Have you talked to Babs' cousin yet?"

"Babs' cousin?"

"Andie Rose. The woman in the locker room right before I went in there. She was going to call you."

"She did. Walker was going to meet her at her house at four. Babs' cousin, huh?" as if trying to find the familial resemblance.

Walker was the second detective with Birch Haven PD and one with whom I'd gotten far too familiar. "Hmm. So that's why Babs left early."

"Did she say anything? Or hear anything?"

"No. She said she had just taken a shower. She didn't go into the privacy nook of the locker room at all," I said. "What I think is weird, though, is that she's staying at Babs' apartment until she moves to Spirit Lake in two weeks. She's not even working right now. Why would she take a shower there instead of going home to take one? It's not like she had to go somewhere after working out. But then it's not like I know her schedule, I guess. We only spoke briefly."

"Do you think she did it?"

"No," I answered quickly.

"Why not?"

"I just don't. How do you police guys say it—I don't *like* her for it."

Levi laughed lightly. "Why? Because she's Babs' cousin?"

I guffawed. "Come on. Am I that shallow? I have a sense about people."

"I hate to break it to you, blondie, but you really don't."

"Rude," I scoffed, then smiled. Despite the heaviness of the topic, it felt good to be with him no matter what we were doing.

"Walker is going to have to talk to you. You know that, right?"

I scowled. "Why him?"

"Because I can't be the lead on this one. Again. Not where you're concerned anyway. And you're the one who found the body, Mel. Statistics show that—"

"The one who finds the body is usually the one who did it," I finished for him. "But you don't believe that."

"And that's exactly why. I'm not coming into this without bias. We have to play it by the book. Especially because of your involvement. Which, by the way, you seem always to do. I might as well apply in another town so I have some work to do."

"I'm not *involved*. Geez, Levi. You make it sound like I had something to do with it." He quietly watched me. I inhaled deeply and rested my head against the back of the chair. "Fine. I'll talk to him. I've got nothing to hide."

He leaned forward in his chair and rested his elbows on his knees, hands fiddling with a pen. "Got anything else for me?"

"Yeah. Andie Rose knew the victim."

6

"Uh, back up a minute there. What do you mean Andie Rose knew the victim?" His eyes narrowed, and he tilted his head slightly.

"Just as I said. She knew the victim."

"I heard that part just fine. I want to know how?"

"Shouldn't Walker be asking me these things?"

His eyes pierced mine. I felt one side of my mouth curve upward.

"Mel, I don't know how your grandmother didn't swat you one when you were growing up."

"Granddad did once." I chuckled at the memory. However, it wasn't fun back then.

"Yeah?" Levi chuckled. "Just once? What did you do to deserve that one?"

"What makes you think I did anything to deserve it?"

"I can only imagine."

I laughed softly at the memory. "Granddad used to teach me how to work on cars. He had a special old one. A blue and white 55 Chevy BelAir with a 350 rebuilt engine. She was a beauty." Levi's eyes softened as I told him about it. "Well, Granddad told me once he finished it, I could drive it. I was fourteen and thought just a quick spin that evening after he retired to his room for the night wouldn't hurt." I wrinkled my nose. "Except it did."

He raised his eyebrows. "Did you crash it?"

"No. Granddad wouldn't have been mad about that. He would have been worried but not mad."

"Then what?"

"I had a crush on this kid in my math class, so I thought I would impress him. By letting him drive it."

Levi clenched his teeth together. "Ooh. Not good. How did he find out?"

"The boy told his buddies. One of them told his dad, who then told Granddad. And the rest is history."

"Bet you never did that again, did you?"

"You know what the worst part was?" Levi just looked at me, waiting patiently. "The disappointment I saw in his face. The punishment was nothing compared to the pain of that." I looked away and blinked rapidly. Tears were far and few between with me, but they sure seemed to be happening today.

Levi reached for my hand. The love in his eyes warmed me.

"Getting back to why you're here."

"I'm here because of you." His voice was soft. "The case just gave me an excuse."

Claire poked her head around the corner. "I'm leaving, Mel."

"Me too!" Rubie called out.

"Are Babs and Connie still here?" I asked.

Claire grabbed her purse and jacket. "Babs left a long time ago."

"Duh! That's right. What about Connie?"

"Connie left a bit ago. Hey, Levi," she said, turning to face him. "Are you going to share Mel with us on her birthday?"

"That's up to Mel," he said, smiling at her, then at me. "I learned from day one that I don't tell her what to do."

I laughed. "I thought we'd already discussed this, Claire."

"We did," she agreed. "But as I remember it, you said you had to talk to Levi first."

"I was teasing you. I would never stop our tradition. We always celebrate our birthdays together."

She clapped her hands. "Okay then. Levi, you're more than welcome to join us, you know. Just let me know if you are because I'll invite Cole, too."

Having so many close friends who were police officers always made me feel safe, and Cole was one of the best. I thought for sure Claire and Cole would be married by now. Claire's husband, Tyler, Sydney's father, died on active duty. Claire had many a man try to get her attention, to no avail. Until Cole. But she was in no hurry to get married for fear of how it would affect Sydney. I told her to let Sydney come live with me, and the problem would be solved. But I knew Sydney loved Cole, and it wouldn't take much for her to be okay with him marrying her mom. Still, I'd lightly left open the option of Sydney living with me—to which Claire had scoffed. Not being able to have kids had always been a source of pain for me. Claire's daughter, and now Levi's son, have become extra special to me. And, of course, Daisy.

"I'll let Mel tell me if I'm going." He looked at me and then Claire. "If she wants it to be just the girls, we can celebrate another night."

Just when I didn't think I could love the man any more than I already did. My heart melted. As much as I loved being with him, I missed spending time with just Claire. Our lives had gotten so crazy lately, our time limited since both Cole and Levi had entered into our lives. Other than Nana, it had only been Claire, Jack, and me for so long. The three of us had been inseparable for years. And then, all of a sudden, there had been an explosion of other people populating my life. First, Rubie wiggled her way into our circle, then my new brother, Max, and my niece, Daisy. Not that I'm complaining. I loved all these beautiful people. It's just that Claire, Jack, and I didn't have time alone anymore. And my heart ached for that.

"I'll call Jack," Claire said.

"Tell him he can stay at my house, so he doesn't have to worry about driving home."

"Like he doesn't always stay at your house," Claire said, giggling.

"It's easier at my house since you have Syd. Besides, that's the only chance we have to talk about you," I teased.

She laughed, a beautiful sound I never tired of. "Whatever."

"Bryce has finally moved on for good," I told Levi. Bryce had been Jack's longtime partner. It ended in a nasty split, Bryce being the nasty one. And then he had the nerve to try to get Jack to go back to him shortly after. He'd waffled for a while, much to my disapproval. Finally, he'd said a firm, 'No.'

"It's about time," Levi said.

"Okay, enough," Claire said, slinging her purse over her shoulder. "See you kids tomorrow." She stopped and peeked her head back through the door. "Hey, Mel? No more bodies, okay? Half the role of being your friend is keeping your skinny little butt out of jail."

I made a face at her. "Go!"

As she left, Levi said, "She does have a point, you know."

"No. I don't know," I said. "Back to the subject of earlier. As it turns out, Andie Rose recognized the victim as someone who wrote a bad review about her grandparents' inn. The one here in Minnesota, not the one in Colorado. Babs told me there were two of them. But I digress; Andie Rose had just exchanged words with the victim a couple of months back."

Levi scribbled notes on his pad. "Did she run into her somewhere? How did she know it was her that wrote the review?"

"The woman worked for a magazine or newspaper. They're famous for doing reviews of hotels, inns, and restaurants. Apparently, there weren't enough clean towels in the room, and it didn't come equipped with toothpaste."

"She wrote a bad review for that?" Levi asked. "People actually pay attention to that stuff?"

"Apparently."

"Where did Andie Rose run into her? And again, how did she know it was her?"

"Andie Rose went to the magazine. To confront her."

Levi tipped his head back and groaned. "That doesn't look good for her. It makes her look like the aggressor."

"She said nothing happened there."

"That you know of. This Andie Rose probably wouldn't have told you if there had been."

"I disagree with you."

"Melanie," he said as if he were talking to a child, "you're talking about a person of interest in a murder. Someone of whom you know very little. I hardly think you should accept her word as gospel. In fact, after this bit of news, she's even more of a suspect."

"I thought you said 'person of interest.' This bumps her up to suspect?"

He ran his hand over his head, running it back and forth for a moment. "Tomato tomahto."

Levi's phone rang. He looked at the caller ID. "I have to get this." He put the phone up to his ear. "Yo, Walker. What's up?"

I watched as his facial expression turned from one of interest to one of doom. My stomach turned.

Finally, he said, "Damn! Thanks, man." He hung up and looked at me in disbelief.

"What is it?" I asked.

"I think we have much bigger problems than we'd thought."

7

A ndie Rose looked at her watch.

"It's the same time it was ten seconds ago when you checked," Babs said. "Try to relax."

"Easy for you to say. It feels like I'm on my way to my own funeral."

"Look," Babs said, her hands on Andie Rose's upper arms, "you didn't do anything wrong, right?"

"Nothing that includes murder," Andie Rose said.

"Well, at this time, that's all that matters. But I do want to hear about the other stuff you did wrong."

Andie Rose smiled stiffly at her cousin.

"Why isn't Brad here for this? Doesn't he realize you could use his support right now?"

"He had to work," Andie Rose said. "Important client in town. Besides, he knows I have you."

Babs stared at her and shook her head. "Did you know when you talk about Brad, your voice is about as flat as he is?"

Andie Rose rested her cheek against Aspen's head and rubbed his neck. "What do you mean?"

"Meaning the guy has literally no personality. I don't know what you see in him. Never have."

"He's a good guy, Babs. Give him some credit."

"I think you stay with him because it's comfortable."

Andie Rose chuckled. "You make him sound like an old shoe."

"He's about as exciting as one," Babs said.

"Well, it's a good thing you're not the one dating him, then, isn't it?" Andie Rose nuzzled Aspen's neck. "Your cousin Babs just has no accounting for good taste, does she, boy?"

"Gag me," Babs said. "Seriously, cuz, you could do so much better."

"He's good to me, Babs. That's all that matters."

Babs shot her arms up in the air. "Are you flipping kidding me?"

At a knock on the door, Andie Rose jumped as if someone had poked her in the backside with a stick pin. Even though she expected Detective Walker, she didn't know what to *expect*. Would he arrest her on the spot? Would he even try to find her innocent? Or was his mind already made up?

She went to the door, took a deep breath, and opened it.

"Are you Andie Rose Kaczmarek?" he asked in a baritone voice, one that didn't fit the person she was looking at. He had a tall, thin build with short, cropped hair that appeared to be prematurely silver.

"I am." She stepped back and toward the side, extending her arm. "Come on in."

He scanned the room, his gaze settling on Babs. "You are?"

"Babs. Andie's cousin. This is my apartment."

"I believe we may have met before at a local hair salon. Anybody else here?" he asked as he scanned the room.

Andie Rose stiffened at his abrasiveness. No warm fuzzies here, thank you very much. "No. Just the two of us." She looked behind her and started walking toward the other room, motioning for him to follow her. "We can talk in the kitchen."

"Right here works fine," he said.

She turned back toward the living room. *Hardly a surprise,* she thought. *He probably thinks I'm a killer.* Her eyes went to the gun attached at his hip.

Babs sat down on the sofa, having no intention of leaving Andie Rose. Andie sat down beside her, finding her presence comforting. She'd wished Brad would have been able to get out of work tonight, but he said he couldn't. What she hadn't told Babs was that he was charged with taking the *important client* to a Timberwolves basketball game. 'Andie, if I have any shot at all of getting this promotion, it will be because of taking this guy to the game,' he'd said. What could she say?

"Thank you for calling me back," Detective Walker said. "For a while, I thought you were trying to dodge me."

Andie Rose frowned. "Why would I do that?"

"You tell me." He sat with pen poised above his notepad.

"Since I wasn't dodging you, I can't tell you. I didn't know who was calling and assumed it was those stupid robocalls."

"Yup, well, you need to empty your voicemails so I could have left one. Several of the missed calls weren't robocalls."

"Yeah. I think we've established she knows that now," Babs said. "And we also established she didn't know it then. So here you are."

Andie Rose placed her hand on Babs' knee, applying some pressure.

Babs squirmed. "Ouch," she whispered.

The last thing Andie Rose wanted was to make this detective angry. Easy for Babs to tell her not to worry. It wasn't her future hanging in the balance.

Detective Walker looked at Babs with what appeared to Andie Rose as amusement.

"Thank you for that clarification," he said. He looked back at Andie Rose. "Tell me what happened."

Andie Rose started at the beginning. "When I got to the gym—"

"What time did you get there?"

"About four-thirty. Around there."

"Okay." He jotted something on his notepad. He drew a line and then another one so that it made a T. Babs craned her neck to see, but Detective Walker sat back further, tipping his notepad up just so. "Then what?"

"I looked for the creeper who had been there probably for the past week or so. I've seen him about four times, and I try to steer clear of him if he's there. But he wasn't there this morning."

"Have you called the police?"

Andie Rose frowned. "Well, no. He hasn't done anything wrong, and you guys would be swamped if people called because of *vibes*." She wiggled her fingers in the air.

Detective Walker tipped his head, then shrugged slightly. "Better safe than sorry, as they say. I'll ask the guys to keep an eye out for him. Did you recognize him?"

Andie Rose shook her head. "No. I just think it's odd because he's never dressed to work out and doesn't carry a gym bag."

"If he's not dressed to work out, then how is he dressed?"

"Plaid shirt hanging beneath a hoodie, jeans, black hair slicked back. And sunglasses. That strikes me as odd and is probably what weirds me out about him the most. There's not exactly any sun that early in the morning. All but one of the times I've seen him, he had the hood up on his sweatshirt. I just figured it was because it's cold that early. And it's been colder than normal this year. A brutal winter." She waited for him to stop writing.

"Go on."

"I got in the gym, went to put my stuff in a locker, and—"

"Did you notice anything unusual?"

In her mind, Andie Rose returned to early that morning, trying to remember the details. "No. I—I—" She blushed. "I, um, used the facilities, and there was nothing out of the ordinary."

"Which locker did you use?"

"One in the middle bay. Third one in, I believe."

"Okay. Then what?"

"I took my locker key, a hand towel from the locker room, and my phone and went to work out. There was hardly anyone there. But there usually aren't too many that early anyway, just a few usuals. The woman who was dead, she's one of the usuals from the past week, but she was gone today. She looked familiar when I'd seen her but just assumed it was from the funeral home."

"The funeral home?" He stopped writing and looked at her.

"I worked there temporarily."

"Office work?"

"I did the hair and makeup of the deceased. Gave them that extra touch that I would want if it were me."

"Interesting job," he mumbled as he wrote something on his pad. He looked up again. "What else do you do?"

"I managed a hotel in a nearby city. At least I did. I'm in the process of moving to Spirit Lake."

He quirked an eyebrow. "Why not work at a mortuary in your home city?"

Andie Rose shrugged. "Because I like the one here in Birch Haven, and it wasn't a far drive. Right now, I'm staying with Babs until I move to Spirit Lake. My boyfriend lives—"

Babs cleared her throat. "Boy Wonder," she mumbled as she ran her hand through her short spiked blond hair. Andie Rose kicked her. "Ouch!"

Detective Walker attempted to conceal his amusement, closed his eyes momentarily, and shook his head slightly.

"What does all this have to do with the investigation of the woman at the gym?" Babs asked.

"Just trying to establish why she drives to Birch Haven instead of staying in her home city."

"She told you why. And she doesn't live there anymore. She's living with me right now." The protective cousin's voice reared, and Andie patted her leg.

"I've always liked Birch Haven," Andie Rose said. "And given it's a small town, I only needed to drive back and forth about once or twice a week. And it allowed me to see Babs more often."

"Business has kicked up a bit the past few years," he mumbled. "This woman that you recognized. Tell me about her."

She shrugged and lifted her hands. "There's nothing to tell."

"Can you not talk with your hands?" Babs whispered. "You've almost smacked me in the face twice now."

Detective Walker smirked as he wrote more. "Was it someone from the funeral home then?"

"No. But I didn't realize it until later this morning."

"I want to hear more about that, but let's focus on the gym this morning first."

"I saw a woman come in that I've seen several times. She went into the locker room and came back out a couple of minutes later."

"Was the woman you recognized earlier still in the gym at that time?"

"Yes—no—" Andie thought back and shook her head. "I don't remember seeing her this morning at all. But the other woman came out of the locker room and hopped on a treadmill. Since we're frequently at the gym at the same time, I went to introduce myself to her. You can never have too many workout buddies. Especially for the days you just don't feel like getting out of bed. We chatted briefly, and then I left to take a shower. I guess I was in the locker room for about twenty or twenty-five minutes. About ten minutes of that time, I was on my phone with my boyfriend."

"That'd be Boy Wonder I referenced earlier," Babs muttered, quickly ducking away from Andie Rose.

Andie Rose was sure she heard Detective Walker snicker. "When I came out of the locker room, the woman from the treadmill was walking in. We practically ran into each other as we turned the corner. And the rest you already know. Or at least I can't tell you anymore because I left."

"Who was the woman you introduced yourself to? The one going into the locker room as you were leaving."

"Her name is Melanie Hogan. She owns A Cut Above hair salon, where Babs works."

Detective Walker's head snapped up, and he groaned. "Oh yes, I know Ms. Hogan. Was she still in the locker room when you left the gym?"

"I don't know. I would imagine she was. I left right away."

"Was the man with the hoodie outside when you left?"

Andie Rose shook her head. "No. I didn't see him, anyway. I guess he could have been around the corner there to the left of the doors."

"Tell me about the woman you recognized at the gym. The one you decided you must have met at some point at the funeral home."

Andie Rose looked at Babs, then at Detective Walker. "This is going to make me look guilty as sin."

"Might as well tell me and get it over with."

Andie Rose hesitated before explaining. "She's a reporter from a magazine that does reviews on hotels, inns, B&Bs, that sort of thing, as well as big news stories. Well, she did a bad review on my grandparents' inn. It was so stupid and uncalled for. Bad reviews can irreparably damage a business, so I went to talk with her and we kind of — umm — we kind of got into an argument."

Detective Walker cleared his throat. "You're right. That isn't helpful for you." He paused a moment. "Ms. Kaczmarek," he met her eyes, "this is very important. Can you give me definite times you were in and out of the locker room?"

"Within five minutes, probably. I get to the gym at four-thirty. Give or take five minutes."

"Why so early?"

"Habit and staying on a routine. Used to be the only time I could go when I was working my jobs. Until I get re-established, it's easier."

He nodded. "Go on."

"I went directly to the locker room and put my stuff in a locker. I'm already dressed out, so I'm only in there for about two minutes. I finished working out around five-thirty and was out of the locker room before six."

Detective Walker flipped through the pages of his notebook, tapped his pen on a page, and looked at Andie Rose.

"Well, Ms. Kaczmarek, if anyone can vouch for your timeline, I may have some good news for you. Did anyone see you?"

"I'm sure they saw me, but it's not like anyone pays that close attention. Because I get there so early, there isn't anyone at the desk unless they happen to be there early. They usually get there minutes after I arrive, though. But customers have twenty-four-seven access by unlocking the door with a member card. They have cameras everywhere, so it's not like there's anything to worry about. Except in the locker rooms, obviously."

"Obviously," he said.

"The employees start at five, but sometimes they get in a little earlier or later. Not real consistent. They're just kids. They're on their phones more often than not. Occasionally, they fill the paper towel dispensers and sanitizer spray bottles."

"I'll check around. If your timeline is accurate, you'll be cleared. According to the victim's fitness tracker, her heart stopped right after you'd left."

Detective Walker gave her a form to write her statement down, and as soon as she finished, he shook her hand, took one more look at Babs, then Andie Rose, and he left. Andie Rose closed the door behind him.

Babs said, "Well, that's great news, huh? You're in the clear." She hugged Andie Rose.

"Yeah. But you know who's not?" Andie Rose said as she pulled back, frowning. "Melanie Hogan."

8

"What do you mean I'm the lead suspect?" I asked, standing so suddenly I almost fell back down.

Levi leaped to his feet and grabbed hold of my arm. "Are you okay?"

"I'm fine. I got up too fast and got dizzy. What do you mean I'm the lead suspect?" My heart raced. "Oh no! I'm due at Nana's house for dinner. How on earth am I going to break the news to her? My existence is going to be the death of her. And yes, that was a bad statement at a time like this." I knew I was rambling but couldn't stop.

"Melanie, sit down and take a breath." He stood beside me, one hand on my shoulder, the other rubbing small circles on my upper back. "I'll call your grandmother if you want me to. I can put off work for a while and come with you."

I leaned into the comfort he offered. "She would love that."

"The question is, would you?"

"Yes, I would. But we have to go now. She'll be waiting for me. And I don't want her to worry before she has to." I slipped my arms into the sleeves of my black leather jacket and grabbed my handbag in one bunch of fabric. "Besides, it might be my last supper with her," I groused.

"Don't get yourself worked up for nothing. You know you didn't do anything. The process will clear you."

"I'm not as sure as you are."

"I'll drive," he said. "You're in no shape to be behind the wheel right now."

He placed his hand on the small of my back and steered me across the parking lot to his car. He opened the door for me and closed it after I was in.

"Levi," I said after he got in and closed his door, "this is going to destroy Nana."

"She's stronger than you give her credit for."

"Detective Walker won't show up over there, will he?"

"He's going to call you first thing in the morning."

"He'd better not come to the salon. I don't need that kind of talk going around town. Talk of the police at my salon again, I mean. If this keeps up, I'll have to move to another town. Maybe I'll move to Spirit Lake with Andie Rose."

"Chin up. We'll get you through this."

He rested his hand on my thigh. "Well, Nana will be happy to see you. That will help."

We drove in silence until we got to my grandmother's house, his hand protectively on my thigh the entire time. I stared out the window, the streetlights illuminated the street and sidewalks as if it was daylight. We pulled into my grandmother's driveway, her front yard lit up by the porch light. I stayed seated after Levi pulled the key from the ignition. Finally, he said, "Come on. You're already late."

We strolled up the sidewalk to the front door. I reached for the doorknob as she opened it from the inside. She hugged me, then Levi.

"Well, isn't this a nice surprise," she said, her smile reaching her eyes. "Come in! Come in! I made extra, dontcha know. Just in case my Melanie convinced you to come with her. Work will always be there. You have to eat." Food was my grandmother's love language. She beamed at Levi and then looked at me. "Oh, dear." The smile left her eyes. "What's wrong? What happened?" She took my arm and led me to the kitchen table. The table that had heard years of conversation not meant for anyone else's ears besides mine and Nana's. I tried swallowing the lump of emotions in my throat.

I looked at Levi, and he sat down on the other side of me.

"For goodness sakes, people," Nana said. "Someone tell me what's going on."

I placed my hand on top of hers. Her skin was so soft and yet so worn and weathered from years of gardening. Even though she wore gloves most of the time, it had taken its toll. "Sorry we're late."

"You look exhausted," she said. She looked at Levi. "Make sure she starts getting some sleep."

"I'm a grown woman who can make sure I get some sleep, Nana. Levi doesn't have to do that for me." I winced; I hadn't intended it to sound so harsh.

"Simmer down, why dontcha," she said with a frown. "I must say, you're not doin' a very fine job of taking care of yourself."

I took a deep breath, filled with shame that I'd snapped at her. "I'm sorry. Remember when I told you that I would fill you in tonight on what happened earlier today? Why I was late in calling you?"

"Yes." Her brows furrowed.

I looked at Levi then back at my grandmother. "I was at the gym early this morning, and someone was—uh—well—someone was found dead in the locker room."

Nana gasped. "Who was it?"

"Her name is Maggie Thompson."

"We think," Levi interrupted. "Detective Walker hasn't gotten a positive ID yet."

"Detective Walker?" Nana asked, looking at Levi. "You're not investigating?"

"It started as mine, but I had to conflict out. Again." He squeezed my hand a little tighter.

Nana's eyes were wide, and confusion swam in them.

"I'm the one who found the body, Nana."

Nana gasped again, and her hand flew to her chest. "Oh, my sweet stars! Again?"

"I'm afraid so."

"Are you okay?" She lay her hand against my face. I reached for it and sandwiched her hand between my own, resting them on the table.

"I sure hope so," I murmured. Levi put his hand on my back.

"I'll make sure she's okay, Rose. I promise." Levi laid his hand over the top of mine, which was still on Nana's.

"There's one more thing," I said. "I'm a suspect."

"*Again?*" Nana exclaimed incredulously. "But that's ridiculous."

"I know that, and you know that. We just need to convince the police."

"Can't you do something, Levi?" she asked. "Surely you don't think—"

"Of course, she didn't, Rose. But this isn't my investigation. And because it's Melanie—well, because of our relationship, the department must be sure everything is handled by the book. All *t*'s crossed and all *i*'s dotted, as they say. But the good part about that is they'll find out positively, not to mention quickly, that she's innocent."

"Well, not quick enough," Nana said, worry creasing her forehead. "She already has a hard time sleeping. How is she supposed to sleep with this hanging over her head?" She turned to me. "Melanie, it's time you go see that doctor of yours and get something to help you sleep."

For the first time, I agreed. In fact, I hoped the good doc would give me something to make me sleep until this whole nightmare ended. Or gave me something to wake me up from the nightmare. I wasn't picky.

"I'll start taking melatonin again, first. If that doesn't work, I'll go see Dr. Madden. I promise."

"Thank you, dear. If you don't do it for yourself, do it for me."

"I would do absolutely anything for you, Nana." I tried to smile, but it felt wooden.

"I don't suppose anyone is hungry," she said.

"Actually, I *am* hungry," I said, surprised. Now that I had spilled the beans, I didn't have the stress of having to tell her the news, so my appetite returned. I sniffed. "Is that goulash I smell?"

"An old favorite," she said, smiling again. "It sounded like you were having a tough day—but I hadn't realized just *how* tough until a moment ago—so I thought I'd make you some good old-fashioned Minnesota comfort food. Now I'm glad I did."

"Me too." I got up and got the plates down and the silverware from the drawer. I reached three glasses from the cupboard and filled them with ice and tap water. As I walked past the stove, heat radiated. I doubled back and opened the oven door slowly. "Oh my gosh!" I said. "You're baking banana bread?"

"Walnut chocolate chip banana bread," she said.

"Good thing I don't have to wear a duty belt. I wouldn't be able to fit it around me after spending too much time over here," Levi said. His phone rang, and he looked at it. "Speak of the devil. Work calls." He briefly flashed the screen toward Nana and me. I struggled to see the display but without luck. "If you ladies will excuse me, I need to take this. Hello?" he said into the phone.

My heart started racing. *Dear God, please don't let them come arrest me tonight.* Again, my appetite disappeared, but I didn't want to let on to my grandmother. I took a deep breath and exhaled slowly, then turned toward her. "Come on, Nana. He could be a while. Let's eat."

9

I got up the following morning and bounded out of bed immediately. For the first morning in a long time, I didn't hit the snooze button. Levi couldn't discuss the phone call from the night before with me, and I'd lain awake, turning over every possibility. When I finally fell asleep at midnight, I had decided that I would go to the gym again. If I was the suspect in a murder investigation, I needed to help the police find out who the real murderer was while I still could, before I was tagged for something I didn't do. I planned to help even if the police didn't know I was helping. Besides, avoiding the gym would only serve to make me appear more guilty than I already did.

I threw on my workout clothes and tossed an extra set into a gym bag as I always did. For what, I had no idea. Claire had asked me that question, and all I could come up with was, *what if something happens on the way to the gym?* My grandmother always said to wear clean underwear in case of an accident. I just went beyond and brought a whole new set of clothes, the overachiever that I am.

I made my bed, placed my pillows just so, brushed my teeth, pulled my hair up into a ponytail, and headed downstairs. A cup of coffee to go, and I was out the door. I had investigative work to do before getting down to business on the machines. I wished Claire could have come with me, but it wasn't possible with Syd home. Tyler's folks were, however, coming to stay for a couple of days but wouldn't get there until later this afternoon. That would help for the next couple of mornings but did nothing for today.

When I pulled into the parking lot at four-thirty, several cars had beat me there. I didn't know what kind of car Andie Rose drove, so I had no idea if she was one of them or not. I scanned the lot closer, paying attention to anything at all that appeared out of the ordinary. I desperately wished that I'd paid closer attention yesterday, especially since there had been so few cars then. But who would have guessed that a dead body would have entered into the picture? And that I would be a suspect? Again? I either had the worst luck in the world or was getting punished for something. Or tested. Nana once said that God tests us but always provides a way out. *I need fast access to that door out.*

As I neared the door, I looked for the odd man that had been hanging out, but he wasn't there for the second morning in a row. Thankful he'd moved on, I peeked around the corner to be sure. It was dark, but I could see well enough to know no one was there. Truthfully, I wasn't sure whether I was relieved or disappointed. I was on my game and wanted to know who he was and what he was doing hanging around here. Andie Rose and Claire both said they had noticed him too. His absence now was peculiar. I doubted it was coincidental. I'd never believed in coincidence.

I thought about the photo I'd taken of the notebook page yesterday. Inside the first set of double doors, I stopped and pulled out my phone to look at it again. I unlocked it with my fingerprint and tapped on the app that held my photos. I tapped on the picture and used my forefinger and thumb to make the image larger. I pulled it closer to my face and studied it. A man walked out of the gym, and I took my attention from my screen and memorized everything about him as he walked out. *Navy workout pants, red t-shirt, Nike tennis shoes, short red hair and short red beard, five-ten, one hundred eighty pounds.* I watched what car he went to. *Red Jeep Wrangler.* I typed his license plate into my phone.

Another person walked out, this time a woman. *Long blond hair, blue eyes, false eyelashes, makeup applied as though she was attending a ball, perfume strong enough to wake the dead, leopard print leggings and matching top, five-four, a hundred and ten pounds soaking wet.* I watched what car she went to. *White BMW.* I typed her license plate into my phone, too. I stopped, shook my head in disbelief, and deleted the numbers. As skeptical as I was about the people in the gym, sadly, I was the one who appeared to be the creeper.

Once again, I looked at the photo of the notebook page. It appeared to be a story of some sort for *Lakes News and Reviews.* It was unclear. I tried before to make sense of notes jotted down and bullet-point lists. This particular gym was part of a corporation. Maybe she was doing a review, and that's why she was here in town. I couldn't imagine she worked in Spirit Lake and lived in Birch Haven.

The door flew open, nearly knocking me over, as someone hurriedly left. I tucked my phone away and entered the second set of doors. I scanned the entire gym before going to the front desk to scan my check-in card. A different young man worked the desk this morning. The one from yesterday was probably in therapy today. Poor kid. This one behaved the same, though, with one hip hoisted up on the counter, tapping away at his phone. Must be a job requirement to work here.

I scanned my card and said, "Have a good day."

"Thanks," he said. "You too."

"I'm kind of surprised you guys are open today," I said. "I mean with what happened yesterday and all." He looked up, appearing annoyed that he had to engage in conversation.

"Yesterday?"

"Yeah. The dead body yesterday morning."

He nodded. "Oh, yeah. That. We closed the rest of the day, but today it's business as usual."

His lack of enthusiasm was chilling. "It doesn't freak you out at all? That someone in here could potentially be a killer?"

"Nope."

I stared at him for a minute and tilted my head slightly. "Huh." Today's generation sure was different. "Thanks," I said, tapping my hand on the front desk. "Have a good day."

He looked at me and forced a smile. "You, too." He looked around the gym briefly and went back to his phone.

"One more thing," I said, causing further annoyance. "That paper towel dispenser and sanitizer bottle are empty." I pointed toward the station closest to the front desk, then turned and went about my way.

As I walked in a bit further, I spotted Andie Rose over by the circuit room. I turned into the locker room to drop off my bag before heading her way but stopped. It felt weird to go in there. Almost disrespectful to the dead woman. I shook off my heebie-jeebie feeling, attributed it to lack of sleep, and forced myself forward, my legs feeling a bit Jell-O-y.

I opened a locker and looked around, stuffed my bag inside, and slipped out of my jacket.

"I thought that was you."

I jumped and stifled a scream. "Andie Rose," I said.

"I spotted you coming in here. You doing okay? I know for me, it felt a little creepy."

"But you worked with dead bodies all the time."

"It's different. Those people weren't murdered."

"That you know of," I said.

She shrugged. "True. But they weren't killed in a building I frequent. What if her spirit is still in here, and she's angry?"

"I thought you weren't a believer in all that ghost stuff," I said. "Or did you change your mind? Did something happen?"

"I'm not sure what I believe. I'm on the fence. I'm skeptical, but there seems to be evidence. If you can trust what people say is real and not their imagination. Guess I better figure it out soon since I'm moving to Spirit Lake." She gave me a nervous smile. "But they're friendly ghosts there, they say."

I shivered. "No, thank you. I would stay far, far away."

"If you don't believe in them, you'd have nothing to worry about."

I shrugged a shoulder and chuckled. "You could be right." I tucked the sleeve of my jacket that poked outside the locker inside, shut the door, and put the lock on, tugging on it to be sure it latched into place. "You heard I'm a suspect, right?"

"Babs and I figured it out yesterday after Detective Walker left. That you would probably be a suspect."

"Are you, too?"

"I was. But Maggie's fitness tracker cleared me."

"What do you mean?"

"They can tell when her heart stopped beating by her tracker."

I processed what she'd just dropped on me. "That's why I'm the lead suspect. I must have been there when her fitness tracker stopped."

"That, and you found the body that I didn't see when I was in there. He hasn't talked to you yet?" Andie asked, surprised.

"He called my boyfriend, Levi, last night. He's also one of the homicide detectives for the police department. He started on this case but had to conflict off because of me. But Walker either didn't tell Levi why I'm the lead suspect, or else he did, and Levi didn't want to tell me that detail for some reason."

My first reaction was irritation with Levi, but if he knew and didn't tell me, I had to believe there was a good reason for it. I was startled at that revelation. When did I become so trusting? Even if it was Levi? I shook my head. Times, they were a-changin'.

"I didn't do this; you know that, right?" I said.

"Yes, I know that." She waved her hand dismissively. "Babs told me you don't have it in you. But the fact that you've been a suspect before isn't going to play in your favor."

I sighed. "I know. But I was cleared every time. That oughta count for something."

"I sure hope so. I've been looking at everyone in here today like they might be a killer. It's unnerving."

"Me too. Even though more than eighty percent of them weren't here yesterday. It's like word got out, and everyone wanted to come see for themselves."

She touched my arm gently. "What can I do to help?"

"I need to look through this locker room in case the police missed anything."

"You said it was Levi that was here, though, right? Do you think he would be so careless as to miss something?" I shifted from foot to foot, a bit uneasy.

"He only did the initial matters. When he found out I was quote, *involved*," I did air quotes with my fingers, "he called in Detective Walker."

"Is Walker incompetent? I sure hope not because your freedom depends on it." She inhaled sharply and put her hand up to her mouth. "Oh, sweet baby Jesus! That came out totally wrong. What I meant is don't you think he would have combed through this locker room?"

I shook my head slowly. "Don't worry about it. I know you didn't mean anything by it. And I'm sure he did comb through the locker room, but there's always room for error, right? I mean, after all, he is human. What did you think of him when he interviewed you?"

"I was so nervous that I didn't think anything at all. Except he was quite smitten with Babs."

I chuckled. "Wouldn't that be ironic if another employee of A Cut Above began dating an officer from Birch Haven PD?"

"That'll never happen," she said.

"How do you know that?"

"Because Babs is hung up on Nate." I had never met Nate, but as much as he and Babs did together and as often as they 'hung out,' she insisted they were best friends and nothing more.

"You're kidding me! I thought they were just friends."

"That's what she'll tell you and everyone else. But only because she's afraid."

"Of what?"

"That it'll ruin their friendship if it doesn't work out. But I'm telling you, she won't even so much as look at anyone else."

I mused over that for just a moment before turning my attention back to my future and whether it would be on this side of the bars or, God forbid, the other.

"I'm going to look around in here for a bit. Feel free to go finish your workout."

She snorted. "Yeah, right. I don't know about you, but I'm looking forward to moving. I'm going to buy myself a treadmill and a rowing machine, maybe a few free weights, and start doing my own thing at home. When I can't get outside to run, that is."

"Yeah, I've decided this working out stuff is overrated too. It's dangerous for my health."

Andie Rose laughed. "I hear ya, sister! You run?"

"Used to. Lately, the only time I run is if something's chasing me."

She laughed again, and it made me feel better. I was sorry she was moving. If she stayed in Birch Haven, I could see us becoming friends. "Maybe I'll come visit you in Spirit Lake sometime," I said.

"And risk the ghosts?"

"Some risks are worth taking," I said.

10

The locker room was small, but Andie Rose and I split up anyway. We scoured every inch of the space, between and under the lockers, in the unoccupied ones, and even on top of them. And it was there I hit the jackpot. Behind the metal ledge that rimmed the top were miscellaneous items I couldn't fully see. Andie had an advantage over me in height.

"Hey, Andie Rose?" I called out. "Come here!"

Within a second, she was standing at my side. "What'd you find?"

"I don't know for sure, but it's something. I'm not tall enough to see what it is."

Two women walked in. "You ladies lose something?" one of them asked.

"Uh...I lost a contact lens," I blurted.

The other woman laughed. "On top of the lockers? What exactly were you doing?"

"She lost her contact down here somewhere," Andie Rose said. "While we were looking for it, I lost a nail, and it flew up. On top of the lockers. I was hoping just to glue the sucker back on." She shook her hand and winced as if it still hurt.

"But you don't have false nails," one of the women said, narrowing her eyes.

Andie Rose looked down at her hands, "Well, by golly, that's why it hurt so badly. It was my real nail."

Both women shook their heads. "Crazy," one of them muttered to the other.

"Sandwich short of a picnic," the other muttered back.

We waited until they put their things in their lockers, making a big production of letting us know they locked them and left. Andie Rose and I both sputtered with laughter the minute they turned the corner.

"Broke a nail? And it flew up? What, it sprouted wings when it broke?" I said, barely containing my laughter. "You're not even wearing false nails." I laughed then, unable to stop.

Andie Rose laughed too. "Well, I had to come up with something quick when you said you lost a contact up there."

We both stopped when a woman came in, went to her locker, and took out her gym bag. I turned away as she began stripping down. Andie Rose tapped my shoulder. I turned just as the woman turned the corner into the showers. As soon as the water started running, Andie Rose and I resumed our search. She stepped up onto the bench that ran in front of the lockers.

"Yup, there's some stuff up here, all right. But I can guarantee not everything is connected to this case. Geez! Don't they ever clean up here? This is disgusting!"

"Maybe I'm glad I'm short."

"Trust me," she said, "you are." She reached for something then handed it to me. Socks. With blood on one of them. And a pair of undies—minus the blood, thank goodness—that appeared to have been there a good long time. So gross! I shuddered. "Dang, Melanie, we need gloves for this."

"Who knew." I grabbed the socks—leaving the undies—between two fingers and tossed them into an empty locker in front of me. "Hurry before someone else comes in and before the woman is out of the shower."

"Oh my stars!" she exclaimed, seemingly out of breath. "I found—" she poked at something a bit, attempted to reach for it, and shrank back.

"What is it?" I said in a harsh whisper. "Is it alive?"

Andie Rose was motionless for a moment as she stared at the mystery object.

"Andie Rose!" I said. "We need to hurry. What is it?"

"I don't know for sure, but—"

Laughter reached the door before three women came in, wiping their foreheads with towels, one taking a swig of water from a bottle.

"I can't believe you did that!" the one dressed all in yellow and black squealed. She looked like a bumblebee. How could I not have spotted her when I walked in? Given the gym's decor, she would have blended right in if she were standing next to the walls or the equipment. The one standing next to her was a ball of pink. She would have made Rubie feel right at home. On numerous occasions—

okay, more than numerous—I'd teased Rubie about all the pink she wore.

Bumblebee hit Flamingo on her shoulder. "You are such a clutz! You fell right into that guy."

"Like it was an accident," the third in the trio scoffed. "She's had the hots for that guy since I've been coming here with the two of you."

All three seemed entirely unaware of our existence until Andie Rose stepped down from the bench.

"Hi, guys!" Flamingo chirped.

"Hey," I said with a wave of a hand.

"You three all done for the morning?" Andie Rose asked, her tone blending with theirs. "Great feeling to get it out of the way early, huh?"

"Just taking a break," Bumble Bee said, then poked her finger at Flamingo, "That one embarrassed us so bad we had to leave for a minute."

"Both of you kind of made a scene," the third said. She was the most mature of the three and didn't seem so flighty and boy-crazy. While Andie Rose interacted with them, occupying their attention, I studied her. *Black leggings, longish gray t-shirt of fancy sweat-wicking fabric, UnderArmour tennis shoes, black hair pulled up in a loose ponytail, wireless earbuds, one in and one out. Long, slender nose, closely set together deep brown eyes, bangs touching long black eyelashes.* She reeked of money.

"How do you all know each other?" I asked, interrupting the small chit-chat.

"We're friends," Bumble Bee said. "And that one's my older sister." She pointed to Moneybags. "She's from Spirit Lake."

Andie Rose's head snapped toward Moneybags. "You're from Spirit Lake?"

She nodded. "Just visiting Birch Haven for a spell."

"What do you do there?" I asked.

"A little of this, a little of that," she said.

"Don't be shy," Bumble Bee said, then looked at me. "She's a big-time news reporter. Right now, she's working on a massive story covering the entire state."

Moneybags shot her a visual arrow. It appeared Bumble Bee said too much, and my curiosity was piqued.

She shook her head. "I'm not a news reporter, I'm an investigative journalist. My employer is the Minneapolis Post, but they send me other places to get the rest of the story, as Paul Harvey used to say. This time I'm lucky enough that it's in my hometown, and I'm collaborating with another journalist there." She waved a hand. "Besides, the story isn't as huge as she," she jerked her thumb toward the blabbermouth, "says it is. All news is something people have a right to hear."

"Isn't that a long way for you to have to drive every day?" I asked.

"Most of it is remote these days, thank the good Lord. You know, with the changes the world has experienced lately. We've reached a new normal," she said as though trying to explain to a first-grader.

"Unfortunately, the cosmetology industry isn't something we can do remotely."

"I'll have to watch for you," Andie Rose said to Moneybags, obviously impressed. "I'm moving to Spirit Lake in a few weeks."

The woman's face registered surprise. "Really? A lot of people visit there hoping to catch a glimpse of the ghost thing. Wooooo," she sang, wiggling her fingers in the air. "But not a lot of people *move* there. Although, no one so much moves *from* there, either. The locals are pretty loyal."

"So I guess I might be a little interested in seeing the town," I said to Andie with a smile. "I think I've just invited myself to stay at your place."

"Where will that be?" the woman asked Andie. "Your place. Where will you be living? You buying?"

"The Spirit Lake Inn."

The woman was even more surprised. "I read a review of that place a few months ago. I hope you can turn it around."

Andie Rose bristled. "That review wasn't accurate."

She shrugged. "Well, let's hope other people don't believe it. I've always thought it was the cutest place. And the whole story about it supposedly being haunted adds to its appeal. Of course, what *isn't* supposedly haunted in Spirit Lake?"

I could tell by listening to her that the haunting part made her almost giddy with excitement. Andie, on the other hand, wasn't so impressed with her any longer.

SHEAR MISFORTUNE

"It's a tourist attraction, that's all. I'm sure it earns the town money."

"You don't believe it's haunted?" Her shoulders slumped, and she exhaled her disappointment. "I haven't seen anything yet, but I believe it is."

"My name is Melanie Hogan," I said, extending my hand toward her as I tried to relieve Andie Rose from the hot seat.

"I'm Natalie Wood," she said, shaking my hand firmly.

"I'm Andie Rose Kaczmarek." Andie shook Natalie's hand next.

"This is Sonia Vega," Natalie said, pointing to her sister, and her friend here is Patty Wilson."

Andie Rose and I shook their hands next.

"Well, ladies," Patty said, "are you ready to finish up? The dude is probably gone by now."

"Or not," Natalie said. "How about you guys go on out? I'm going to call it done and good."

The two girls shrugged. "Suit yourself," Sonia said. "But when you end up fat and jiggly, I'll remind you of your lack of dedication."

Somehow, I had a hard time believing that Natalie would ever turn out to be fat and jiggly.

"Whatever," Natalie said. "You just want to go flirt with your lover boy some more." She poked her thumb toward her chest. "This chick isn't interested in looking like a teenage idiot. Go embarrass yourself. I'm going to shower and head out."

Andie Rose and I exchanged looks. We wanted the locker room to ourselves so we could finish investigating. Now we would have to wait even longer. Or move quickly while Natalie showered.

"It's no wonder you're still single," Sonia said. "You're boring."

"And remember you're not," Natalie shot back with surprising force. Then she looked at Andie Rose and me. "I may be single, but at least I'm not making an ass of myself for everyone to see." She looked at Sonia and Patty. "Go. I'll see you girls at Sonia's."

Sonia and Patty left, and Natalie said to Andie Rose, "It was nice to meet you. I'll look forward to seeing you in Spirit Lake."

"Likewise," Andie Rose said. "I'd like to ask that you not judge the Spirit Lake Inn until you've tried it for yourself, though. I read that review. It was unfair and not true."

Natalie smiled. "Well, I look forward to trying it out myself someday."

"Thank you," Andie Rose said. "I'll even give you a discount."

Natalie smiled, grabbed her gym bag, and went to the showers.

I highly doubted the woman needed a discount, but who wouldn't accept one if offered? As if reading my mind, Andie Rose looked at me and said, "You'll get a discount too. That goes without saying."

"You'll run yourself right out of business if you give everyone discounts."

"At the hotel where I just left, we always gave unsatisfied customers special treatment. It works like a charm. But I'm sure you know that from having your own business."

"Yeah, but I'm not an unsatisfied customer." I nodded my head toward the lockers. "Come on. Our time is limited; let's get the rest of whatever's up there." I pointed to the top of the lockers.

"Yeah, I need a closer look."

"What was it?"

"I'm not sure. But it was narrow and thin and had a lot of dark red."

I screwed up my face. "Gross! Probably a feminine product."

"Melanie!" she said, trying not to laugh as she stepped back up onto the bench. "If that's what it is, we're calling this investigative thing done."

I nabbed a tissue from my pocket and held it up to her. "Use this."

She either didn't hear me or ignored my request because she reached for the mysterious object, emitted a small scream, and dropped it. My arm shot out, and I instinctively opened my hand to catch the falling item. It bounced off my hand, fumbling until I clumsily caught it just before it hit the floor. Without thinking, my fingers wrapped around it.

"Oh no," I cried out in a whisper, unable to take my eyes off my hand holding the now contaminated object. Andie Rose stood still, breathless, eyes huge.

"Melanie, that's so not good."

"Um, no, it's not," I said, staring, unable to blink. "I think we might have found the murder weapon. And now our fingerprints are all over it."

11

I looked at the object in my hand, covered in blood — a ballpoint stick pen. I frowned and looked at Andie Rose.

"This can't be the murder weapon. How does a ballpoint pen kill someone? Unless you're a professional killer, knowing exactly where to stick the pen, how could that happen?"

"Luck?" Andie Rose answered. "If someone was angry enough to kill, they might have grabbed the closest thing available, even if it was just a pen. Maybe they didn't intend to kill, just to injure. That would have been very *un*lucky," she added quietly. "But I've heard of stranger things."

"I'll bet you have," I murmured as I studied the object. Writing showed beneath the dried blood, but I couldn't decipher what it said. Wiping the blood off to read it would just add another charge onto my already growing list of felonies — obstructing a legal process or evidence tampering. Finally, I snapped myself out of my frozen state.

"Andie Rose, call Detective Walker."

"Not your boyfriend?"

"I don't want him getting in any trouble. He's not supposed to touch this investigation."

She took out her phone. "Especially now, I would imagine."

As Andie Rose called Detective Walker, I stood holding the pen. I finally decided to wrap it in a paper towel when Natalie came out of the shower, her towel wrapped tightly around her ample chest. She looked and gasped. The color drained from her face.

"Is that blood?"

I didn't know how much to reveal, then decided playing dumb was the best course of action. "It sure looks like it."

"Oh my God. I need to sit down," she said.

"Are you okay?" I asked.

"I don't do so well with blood. Pass out every time I even get a blood draw. They've gotten to where they lay me down now right off the bat."

I wrapped it up quickly in the paper. "There, out of sight."

She took slow, deep breaths, with her eyes closed. I sure hoped Detective Walker got here fast in case she passed out. An ambulance too. "The police will be here soon," I said. "Are you going to be okay?"

"I'll be fine." She looked at the paper towel and shuddered, then looked down at her towel.

"Good God! I need to get dressed if some guy is going to be coming in here."

"Good idea," I said.

In record speed, she stood and dressed, including slipping into her jacket, paused and took another deep breath, then smiled. "Okay, then. Thanks for the adrenaline rush this morning. You ladies have a good day."

"Detective Walker is on his way," Andie Rose said as she hung up the phone. "He's in the area, so it will only be a couple of minutes." Strands of curly red hair worked their way loose from her ponytail holder. She blew a strand out of her face.

"I'm sure I'll run into you in Spirit Lake," Andie Rose said right before Natalie left. "And, please, take me up on my offer about staying at the inn. I know you won't be disappointed."

"I'll do that. And thanks again. I hope you ladies solve this thing." She pointed to the paper towel and shuddered.

After she left, I told Andie Rose, "I sure wish you still worked at the funeral home so we could get the inside scoop on Ms. Thompson."

"There are two things wrong with that wish. I told you before that it's not a given that she would even be at the Birch Haven funeral home. There's another one in this town. And we're not the morgue. By the time they get to our place, everything is pretty much done and over."

"Yeah, but you have to hear things, don't you?"

"Not usually, no. If I wanted to hear things, I had to look for them and ask around. And even then, it's not a guarantee. Typically, we didn't know things at our business that you'd want to learn in an investigation."

I crossed the small area and sat down on the bench, leaning against the lockers. "So much for a workout today."

"I was just thinking the same thing. But at least I got in a short one."

I shook my head. "Andie Rose, I am so sorry. I totally wouldn't fault you at all if you wanted to head out and finish up. I'll stay right here and wait for Detective Walker."

She shook her head vigorously. "Nope. No way. I'm staying here with you. We women need to stick together."

Again, I was sad she was moving. I wished Claire could have gotten to know her better. They would hit it off fabulously. I looked around the room, convinced that when this whole thing was done, I wouldn't set foot inside of here again. That's if I even had the opportunity. I might be looking at a gym behind bars.

I looked down at Andie Rose's shoes, cute black boots that snagged my attention, and spotted something under the rim of the bottom row of lockers, tucked ever so perfectly under one of them.

"Andie Rose, by your foot." I got up, walked toward her, and knelt on the floor. She moved and bent over to see what I was looking at. I grabbed another tissue and used it to pull the corner that peeked out from under the locker, then used the tissue to pick it up.

"What is it?" Andie Rose asked.

I looked at one side, then the other. "A hotel key card."

"For which hotel, does it say?" she asked.

"Rest Awhile."

"Coming in," called a male voice. "Police. Everyone decent?"

"As decent as we're going to be," I called back. "Detective Walker?"

"Yes."

"It's safe," I said, quickly sliding the key card into the waistband of my workout pants. Andie Rose gave me a look that questioned my judgment.

"Where's the object in question?" Detective Walker asked.

"Right there." I pointed to the paper towel-wrapped pen. "You'll find my fingerprints on it because I touched it."

"I'm sure you did." He shook his head slowly, his face grim. "Ms. Hogan, you're not helping yourself here."

"It's my fault, Detective," Andie Rose said. "I dropped it, she grabbed it in midair before realizing what it was."

"You know what frightens me?" he asked, looking from one of us to the other, quickly continuing before either of us could answer. "That you two are hanging out together, here of all places, and bonding over a possible murder weapon. You're both suspects. It just doesn't look good."

"I thought I've been cleared," Andie Rose said.

"No one from a crime scene is a hundred percent cleared until we find the suspect." He looked at me. "Look, Melanie, I have nothing but the highest regard for Levi, and you're going to get him into a lot of hot water with this."

Shame crept up my neck and into my cheeks. Heat was taking over my body like logs on a bonfire. Sweat began to trickle down the center of my back.

"I didn't ask for this, Detective Walker."

"You never do. It just follows you." He took a deep breath before giving me a look of what appeared to be pity. That was the last thing I ever wanted from anyone; it was enough to set a fire beneath me. "Look," he said, "I'm not trying to be a jerk. I just don't want this to come down on Levi from the corner office."

I knew what he meant by 'the corner office.' None other than the chief himself. I cringed. "I don't either."

He pulled a set of latex gloves from his bag and pushed his hands into them before unwrapping the weapon. He studied it, rolling it slowly between two fingers. He squinted and held it closer to his eyes, trying to read the writing.

"I'll have to get this to the lab. Where did you find this?" he asked Andie Rose.

"Up there," she said, pointing to the top of the lockers.

"Did either of you see," he looked at me, "or touch," back to Andie Rose, "anything else?"

"No," I answered quickly before she could. She shot me a look. I prayed she'd keep silent. There were a few beats of nothing that hung in the air as I held my breath. Andie Rose shifted her feet and looked at the ground.

"Ms. Kaczmarek?" Detective Walker asked.

"No. Nothing, sir."

He looked at her over the top of his glasses, then at me. "If you're sure, then." He stepped up onto the bench and looked for himself. "Looks like they don't clean up here."

Andie Rose and I both stayed silent. *No talking unless you're spoken to, Melanie. Keep your mouth shut.*

"Find anything?" I blurted. So much for keeping my mouth shut.

He reached his left hand as far as he could, picked something up, studied it a moment, then put it back down. "Nope."

He stepped back down and said, "Appears the CSI that was here had his upcoming nuptials on his mind instead of collecting evidence." He shook his head and exhaled slowly. "I'll have the other one come back out here." He pulled out his phone and punched in a number. "Yeah, Jenny?" he said. "Get me Jonas." After a few moments, he said, "Yeah, Jonas, I need you to get to the gym to—what do you mean which one? We only had a homicide at one," he barked. "Jensen missed some pretty crucial evidence." He waited a moment as he listened, then barked, "Like the possible murder weapon! I need you out here now!"

A gasp came from the doorway, and we all three turned. Detective Walker said to the woman, "You need to leave. Didn't you see the 'do not enter' tape across the door?"

"There's been a murder?" She held a hand towel up to her chest with both hands as if it would protect her. "*When?*"

"Ma'am," Detective Walker said, a single word laced with impatience, "please. I'm asking you to leave. This room is closed for now."

"But I have to get to work," she complained with a bit of attitude. "I can't do that without my clothes and keys, can I?"

Detective Walker took a breath, closed his eyes, and pinched the top of his nose with his thumb and forefinger. "Hurry it up, please."

Detective Walker would have a stroke if he didn't learn some relaxation techniques. Andie Rose and I exchanged a look. I patted my waistband to ensure the key card was still in place and secure. The last thing I needed was for it to fall onto the floor.

"You two can leave. I'll wait here for Jonas. Melanie, do me a favor. Be sure the 'do not enter' tape is still secured."

"Sure thing."

We grabbed our things from our lockers and walked out into the parking lot. The air was cold for late spring.

"That was the easiest but hardest workout I've ever had," I said. "I need to call Levi before Detective Walker does."

Andie Rose blew air through pursed lips. "Oh, yeah. That'd be good. I think I'm going to jog home. Run off some negative energy. I'll come back later and pick up my car."

I nodded. "I'm sure I'll see you soon."

She trotted over to her car and dumped her gym bag into the front seat. I watched as she took off into a jog toward the large expanse of field behind the gym that led to a path through the woods. There was a trail of stamped-down grass and weeds from others taking the same way. I took my phone and punched in the quick dial number, then held my breath. He picked up. "Hey, Levi? Um, yeah, I have to tell you something before Walker does." And I told him about Walker's most recent visit to the women's locker room.

12

"What do you mean you found the murder weapon?" Levi asked after I briefly explained the morning's events, his voice filled with concern. I may have left out a few little, teeny-tiny minor details. Like withholding the key card. But I couldn't make him complicit in my shenanigans. "Where are you now?"

"Just leaving the gym."

"Geez, Melanie, I don't even know what to say."

"Thank you?" I asked sheepishly.

"Thank you?" He repeated incredulously.

"Yes. If it hadn't been for us *girls* looking, you *boys* wouldn't have found the murder weapon."

"Honestly, I can't believe the CSI tech missed that. As much as he's been off his game, I can't believe Chief hasn't fired him. Should have been Jonas on the case, to begin with."

"Well, you're welcome," I teased lightly. "As has become the usual lately, I'm finding myself in a position where I have to clear myself because no one else will."

He cleared his throat. "That's not a fair statement."

Guilt riddled me. "No, it wasn't. But I wasn't referring to you. I was referring to the system."

"I am *part* of the system, Melanie. And the system works if people don't get involved where they're not supposed to be."

I looked at the key card in my hand; my fingers folded around it.

"Now your prints are all over the murder weapon," he said. "It's just not a good situation all the way around."

"And Andie's. But someone else's prints will be on that pen too. Now they can find out who else is involved instead of focusing on me."

"No one believes you did it, blondie. And they're trying hard to find concrete proof to clear you. But your meddling isn't helping."

"Do you trust Detective Walker?"

"With my life. He's good at what he does."

"Hm. Not as good as you, though."

"You're biased." A little of his charm crept back into his voice.

I switched him to speaker, enabling me to open the photos on my phone. I looked at the picture of the pen I'd been able to snap before wrapping it in the paper towels. I zoomed in to try to read the words. *L* something. *La*? I could make out the word *News* followed by an *R*. Maybe it was *Lakes News and Reviews* to match the logo on the notebook? But I couldn't be entirely sure, and at this point, I didn't want to assume. I would have to do a search on what I had and try various combinations and hope something popped up.

"Melanie, you there?"

I snapped back to my conversation with Levi. "Yeah, sorry."

"Where'd you go?"

"I'm here. Just thinking. Trying to figure this stuff out so I can dig myself out of the hole I'm burying myself in."

"Then stop digging said hole. We'll get through this."

"Easy for you to say," I said. I knew pouting wasn't very becoming, but it was all I had at this point.

"We will, Melanie. We'll get through it together."

"Jackson's going to have a felon for a stepmom."

"What are you doing tonight?" he asked. "I can take off work if you need me to."

"No, don't do that. I'm going to ask Claire and Rubie to drop by. And Jack. I need a girls' night."

"Okay. That'll be good for you. It will help take your mind off all of this."

"Hey, Levi?"

"Yeah?"

"It's not too late to get out of this, you know. It's looking like this could be your life if you stay with me."

He groaned. "Tell me you're kidding, and we're not back to this nonsense." It took me a while to accept Levi's proposal out of nothing other than sheer fear of getting hurt again. Now that I'd accepted and we'd gotten engaged, I managed to dodge setting an actual date. When I didn't say anything, he added, "Melanie, I'm not going anywhere. And you're done running. I'm much taller than you, and my legs are longer. You can never outrun me. Besides, the engagement ring on your finger won't come off. I made sure of it."

"I wouldn't blame you for running. Just sayin'."

"Well, stop talking. Just sayin'," he mimicked me. "Now get home, get ready for work, and have a good day. I'll talk to you later."

I was quiet. I didn't have anything to say for a change.

"Hey, Mel?" he asked.

"Yeah?"

"I love you."

I felt a bit of relief in the earnestness I heard in his voice. "Love you too."

After we hung up, I sat in my car for a few moments and looked at the entrance to the gym. I knew in my heart this would be my last time here. Working out was even less appealing to me now than ever. Here, at least. Spring was just around the corner so I could run outside. Or walk. Whatever I chose to do. But I didn't have to do it here. And I had no intention of it. I had promised Claire I'd work out with her, but she would understand.

I started my car just as Detective Walker came outside. He waved as if trying to get my attention. I took a deep breath and rolled my eyes. If he interviewed me now, at least it would be done and out of the way, and I could get on with my day. At least, that was my hope. But he had permitted me to leave.

I turned off the engine and rolled down my window as he neared. "Detective," I said, voice flat.

"Good to see you too, Ms. Hogan," he said. "As long as you're still here, got a minute?"

"No more than that. I have a job I need to get to."

"It'll only take a minute for now." He must have caught my vibe because he said, "Look, Melanie, I know you didn't do this. It's not my first day on the job. But the evidence points in your direction."

"So it's a toss-up between trusting me or the evidence. We know which of those will hold up in court." I shook my head slowly and looked off over the field. "Fine. Let's get this over with. And quickly, please."

Quickly was precisely what it was. Answering his questions without elaborating on anything was all it took. And rather than get irritated with my blunt, to-the-point answers, offering up nothing more, he seemed content. And somewhat...relieved?

"That wasn't so bad, was it?" he asked as he closed the notebook in which he'd jotted notes. "I mean, I know I'm not as good as Levi in your eyes, but if you didn't do it, Melanie, I *will* clear you. Trust me."

I sighed. "You cleared Andie fast, so do the same for me, okay?"

"I'm doing the best I can. But it would go faster if you steered clear of the process."

"I'll do my best." When I mentioned Andie Rose, the brief look in his eyes hadn't escaped me.

***

Andie Rose left Melanie when she called Levi so Melanie could talk privately. Andie started at a jog around the side of the building, then stopped momentarily to call Babs. Texting would have been easier, but her AA sponsor had drilled into her head the importance of phone calls for so many years, so she usually did that. This was hardly the same thing, but all the same. When she didn't get an answer, though, she hung up without leaving a voicemail and tapped out a text after all. Babs was probably in the shower and would get the text as soon as she finished.

Decided to go for a run so I'll be gone awhile. Will get my car from the gym later. Didn't get much of a workout in. Long story. Can you please let Aspen outside 4 me? c u in 30.

She didn't bother putting in her earbuds but instead left them tucked in her pocket. Enjoying the sounds of nature was much more appealing this morning. The noise of the morning was overwhelming, and her mind was on overload. She longed for peace from blue skies, grass that was getting greener by the day, and trees with their bare branches reaching toward the sky as if praying for a covering of leaves soon.

The worn path through the weeds to get to the trail in the woods wasn't her ideal choice due to her insane fear of snakes, but she chose it today anyway. Hopefully, it was still too cold for the slithery little demons. She kept her eyes to the ground just in case, nearly screaming when she happened upon a narrow brown stick that crossed the path. She stopped, touched her hand to her chest, and ran the other over her hair. She bent at the waist and rested her hands on her knees. It was just a stick for crying out loud. The events of late had made her jumpier than usual.

She straightened and began jogging at a slow pace, regaining her normal breathing as she reached the edge of the woods. She glanced up to see four or five turkey vultures circling the air above the forest canopy. Their little bald red heads had always grossed her out. *Dumb decision,* she thought. *I should've just driven home.* Her heart picked up its pace once again. As much as she loved the outdoors, she wasn't what one would call a country girl. She loved small towns, but that was as country as she got or wished to be. Stumbling upon a dead animal wasn't in her plans this morning. Of course, helping solve a murder hadn't been either.

She kept an eye on the vultures, hoping with all her might that they recognized she was moving. She waved her arms above her head to prove it, making a spectacle of herself should anyone see her. She'd heard they wouldn't attack living animals, much less humans. But she didn't exactly want to be the one to prove that theory wrong, either.

Pacing along, her breath light, she glanced upward again through the thick, bare entangled branches, then back down. Just in time. She stopped dead in her tracks. A leg clad in denim was lying across the path, a black tennis shoe partially off. She wasn't sure if she should take off in a sprint and get to the sidewalk alongside the street or tiptoe past, hoping she didn't wake up the man. He'd obviously had a rough night, and she didn't want to startle him. Ever so slowly, she started tiptoeing past him, stepping over his leg, careful not to bump into him. She looked at him, lying on his stomach, a black hooded sweatshirt with the hood over his head. Could this be the man that had been hanging out in front of the gym? Maybe that's why he hung out there. If he was homeless and slept out here, nights got darn cold at this time of the year. Her heart went out to the man. Should she get him a cup of coffee or a warm breakfast?

As she contemplated what to do, out of the corner of her eye, something glistened, making her catch her breath. She jerked her head in the direction of the object and saw a bottle of nail polish lying beside the man's hand. Not just any old nail polish, but what appeared to be the same color as that on the pen used to murder Maggie Thompson. Blood red. Except she was almost positive what was on the pen was blood, not nail polish. But as quickly as she'd dropped the pen, she couldn't be sure. Her breath caught in her throat. Had this man killed Maggie?

Realizing this could be the murderer, she readied to take off at a run before calling the police when she saw a rock the size of a fist by the man's head. She knew she should follow her previous instinct to run like the wind and call the police, but she was drawn in with the force of a magnet. She bent over slowly, peering at the rock. On the face of the rock, in what was likely the red nail polish, was written *Jerk*.

Andie Rose got a bad feeling in her gut. Something was terribly wrong. She looked up at the turkey vultures still circling, now directly above her. She sniffed. The smell that surrounded her was not that of a homeless man. This man was dead!

13

I was backing my car out of the parking space when I saw Andie Rose running toward me wildly waving her arms to get my attention in my rear-view mirror. I pulled back into the parking lot and took off at a jog toward her as she continued waving until I reached her. Turkey vultures circled overhead, and I shuddered. There was something about birds, but there was *really* something about birds when they were as big as me.

"What's wrong?" I asked, keeping my eyes on the vultures. I wrinkled my nose. "Looks like those things are about to have breakfast." My stomach lurched, and I thought I might throw up.

"Yeah, on that!" she said as she pointed behind her. She grabbed my arm and pulled me with her.

"You okay?" For being a runner, she hadn't gotten very far before getting breathless. When she finally stopped pulling me, I looked at what she was pointing at and stifled a scream. If I had taken one step further with my eyes on the vultures, I would have tripped over their object of interest. There at my feet lay a man dressed like I'd seen for the last time two mornings ago in front of the gym. The lurker. He lay sprawled, face down in the weeds, one leg across the path. I was sure it was the same man. The same black hoodie, denim pants, and black tennis shoes. And I hadn't seen him this morning. Or yesterday. Could the two deaths be related? They had to be!

"I thought he was sleeping at first," Andie Rose said. "Passed out or something. But then I saw blood on the rock." She shivered. "At first, I thought maybe he's the one who murdered Maggie Thompson. I panicked and was going to get the heck out of here. That's when I saw the rock. It says *Jerk* in what looks like red nail polish. What do you suppose that means?"

"I'm assuming you called 911." I squatted down, my rear resting on my heels, as I looked closer.

"Not yet. They always look at the one who found the body. And I don't want to be tied to another death."

I frowned at her and put a hand out, palm up. "So not calling 911 isn't going to make you look even more guilty?"

Her face reddened. "It's not like I'm firing on all cylinders right now. At least I thought about it. I just didn't do it."

"Well, I'd suggest calling them immediately." I looked at the body again. "I wish I could turn him over. Or at least take off his hood."

Andie Rose shook her head vigorously as she plucked her phone from her pocket. "Uh-uh. The last thing you need is for your prints to be anywhere at this crime scene. You're making me nervous just being as close as you are. You already took that key card without letting Detective Walker know. What are you going to do with it, anyway?"

"I'm going to clear myself, that's what." I carefully surveyed everything around the body. "Andie Rose, look at that." I pointed to the man's hand that was furthest from the rock.

Andie Rose squinted and looked closely. "It looks like another key card. Remind me, where's the one from that you found?"

"The Rest Awhile Motel. Same as this one."

"There's got to be a connection."

"That'd be my guess."

"We don't know that the key card in the locker room belonged to Maggie, though. There's a lot of people that come and go there."

I pondered what she said, then shook my head. "I'd bet it was Maggie's since she's from out of town. And I'm not much for coincidence. And why haven't you called 911 yet?"

"Because you distracted me. And the way this is going, one of us is bound to get arrested before the week is over." We both shook our heads slowly. "I'm calling," she said. "If you want to leave and pretend you weren't here, I wouldn't blame you at all."

"No. I'll stay with you."

"Hey, could you do me a favor? While I call 911, could you call Babs and make sure she got my text to let Aspen outside? He's not used to being away from me this long."

"On it," I said. "And quit stalling." I felt like a jerk with my tone, but delaying the phone call would do nothing but get us both in deeper and hotter water. "I need to bust out of here as soon as the police get here. I have to race home, shower, and get to work. I have a client at nine."

"Yeah, yeah, that's perfectly fine. As I said, you can go now if—" She turned her attention away from me and back to the phone when the 911 operator answered.

***

Within five minutes of Andie Rose hanging up, Detective Walker and another squad car came zipping around the corner and to the edge of the field. An ambulance followed.

"A little late for that," I said as I nodded toward it. "Did you tell him the guy is dead?"

"Yep. Not sure he quite trusts me yet."

As if on cue, the coroner's van pulled up next to the ambulance. "Guess they're ready for anything and everything," I said.

Walker shook his head when he reached us. "Why am I not surprised?"

I shrugged. "We didn't have anything to do with it. I had just hung up from Levi when I noticed Andie Rose running toward me, flagging me down."

"Ms. Kaczmarek?" he said, "What were you doing out here?"

"Jogging home to my cousin's. Since my workout was cut short this morning, I thought I'd make up for it. Besides, I wanted to run off some pent-up energy."

"The two of you are double trouble. You know that, right?"

She and I looked at each other. "We do have an odd way of bonding," she said.

I snickered, which got us a scowl from Detective Walker.

"I have to go," I said.

"Not so fast."

"Seriously?" I raised my eyebrows. "Am I being looked at for this one too? I know what they say about the one who supposedly finds the body, but I didn't find this one." The minute the words were out, I looked at Andie Rose and mouthed, "Sorry!"

"She can go, can't she?" Andie Rose asked him. "The only reason she came over here is because I flagged her down. She didn't see or hear anything."

"I need you both to write me a quick statement first, and then you can go," he said. "You both might want to consider having an attorney on standby. And stay inside your houses for a few days," he muttered. "Or better yet, take a vacation somewhere far from Birch Haven."

"I'll tell Levi you'll cover for him while he leaves town for a vacation," I said.

He scowled at me before handing us a statement form and a pen. "Here. Fill this out and be on your way."

Both Andie Rose and I grabbed the paper and pen and scribbled furiously. I wasn't sure what I needed to get away from more, the smell out here or the darn vultures that insisted on circling, though the circle had lifted a bit higher in the sky.

***

When I walked into my house, it was tempting to follow Detective Walker's advice and stay home for a spell. Some time away from what had become my life the past couple of days and time to rest and catch up on sleep was very alluring. So much so that I didn't dare sit down. Instead, I stripped out of my workout clothes and tossed them in the laundry basket despite not exercising in them. I wanted the memory washed out of them. The fact that they were exposed to death was enough to call them dirty in my book.

By the time I showered and dressed, it was eight-thirty. I had time to whip my hair up in a ponytail and apply some mascara and lip gloss before heading back into town. I decided I wouldn't miss not going to the gym and only hoped Claire understood. Once she heard about this second body — well, she might encourage me to stay home. I was looking forward to getting my life back to somewhat normal. And I sure as heck was looking forward to a girls' night. I crossed my fingers that everyone could make it.

We were far overdue. Too much time and energy had been going into this getting healthy stuff.

Claire's car was already in the parking lot when I got to the salon. A near-first, for sure. I was almost always here an hour early, and she typically trailed in just before we opened. Rubie was there already, too.

"Honey, I'm home," I called as soon as I walked in the door. Though faint in the morning hours, the familiar smells of hair color, hair spray, other hair care products, and acrylic nails greeted me. It smelled like heaven.

"Hey!" Rubie called in her chipper voice. "Glad you could make it."

"Smart alec," I said, smiling.

Claire came out from the back and into the salon area. "I was wondering when you were getting here. Why didn't you call me back? I left a few messages."

After calling Babs about Aspen, everything else had swallowed up my attention, and I'd forgotten all about my own messages. "Sorry."

"How was your morning?" she asked.

Oh, you know, another body. Just the typical, average morning. "You wouldn't believe it if I told you."

She stopped and stared at me. "Try me?" It was more of a hesitant question.

I filled them in on what we found in the locker room, including the likely murder weapon and the writing on the pen. I pulled out my phone and showed them the picture, zooming in on the writing. "And then when Andie Rose went for a run, she stumbled upon a body." I tried to drop it into the conversation as casually as one could possibly drop in a comment about a dead body.

As I expected, Claire nearly choked.

"What?" Rubie shrieked. "You'd think I'd be used to this with you by now. Why am I surprised?"

I caught a whiff of her Loves Baby Soft. "I'm not the one that found it," I said, a tad defensively.

"Yes, but you were in the area. Again," Claire stressed. "Why are you always in the area?"

Babs came through the door, looked at me, and silently shook her head before walking past to deposit her things in the office.

I lifted my hands, palms up. "What?" I exclaimed. "I didn't do anything."

"You and my cousin have got to stop *bonding*. It's not healthy for the town folk," Babs called out from the office.

"I curse the day Claire and I were in the office the day I wished for more spontaneity in my life."

"You and me both, sister," Claire said. "If you only knew how many times I've had that thought over the last couple of years. And let me guess, you're going to do your little investigative work to find out who the killer is on this one, too. Or should I say killers? As in plural."

I turned toward my station to set it up for the day—combs and brushes out of the Barbicide, shears ready, and curling irons turned on. I crossed the floor to the desk and checked the appointment book. "Thought I had an appointment at nine, but it looks like we have a few minutes of breathing room at opening—" I looked at my watch— "which is now, but then we're going to be slammed."

"I'll take that as a yes," Claire said.

Apparently, I hadn't done a good enough job of distracting her.

Babs was setting up her nail station, getting it ready for her first client, and Rubie was primping in front of her mirror, neither looking at me nor talking. I watched Claire's reflection in my mirror as she moved around the front desk. Claire was typically the happiest, most genuinely joy-filled person I'd ever known. Today wasn't par, however. I could tell something was off.

"Hey, Claire?" I said. "Want to have a girls' evening at my house tonight."

She looked at me, an eyebrow arched. "I'm not sure that's a healthy thing for me to do."

"Please?" I asked. She continued with her busy work by the front desk. "Instead of working out," I added. "I don't want to go back there."

She stopped what she was doing and turned to look at me. I grew concerned at her hesitation. Was she mad at me? Finally, she said, "Yeah."

Relief swept through me. We just needed some girl time. That's all it was, I told myself. "Rubie and Babs? Can you guys come?"

"Andie Rose and I have plans," Babs said. "But thanks anyway. Besides, you and my cousin need to stay away from each other. Raincheck for after she leaves?"

"You bet. Rubie?"

"Count me in," she said. "It's been way too long since we've had one of those. And you have some explaining to do. You calling Jack?"

"Right now," I said as I picked up my phone from the top of my stylist station. I walked toward the office. "Hey, has anyone heard from Connie?"

"Nope."

"Not me."

"Not yet." They all said in unison.

"What time is her first client?" I asked Claire, who was still by the desk.

"Ten," she said.

I shrugged and punched in the speed dial number for Jack, waiting until I got his voicemail. "Hey, Jack, it's Mel. Can you give me a call when you get this? We're having a get-together at my house after work this evening. Just me, Claire, and Rubie, and we wanted to know if you could make it. Talk to you soon. Miss you and love you."

Jack was a designer of Jack's Originals, a clothing and jewelry line. He displayed his merchandise in salons all over the Minneapolis area and beyond, reaching all the way up to mine and Claire's salon. The three of us have been best friends for years. We'd gone through a lot together, including some relationship hardships, but we grew even stronger through the trials. Claire, Jack, and Nana were my lifeline before all these other people showed up. Levi. Max. Daisy.

I thought about Levi. I hadn't told him about the body Andie Rose found yet. I'm not sure why I was holding back, just that I didn't want to talk about it. Denial was a wonderful thing. But I was sure Detective Walker had spoken with him by now.

As if on cue, my cell phone rang. I looked at the caller ID and groaned. Levi.

14

"Anything you want to tell me?" Levi asked before I could even say hello.

"Not particularly," I said.

"Good God, Melanie."

"Yep."

"I don't even know what to say."

"Me either. So how about we don't say anything?"

"That's how you're going to play it?" he asked in disbelief. "Pretend all is well and nothing happened?"

"Yeah, pretty much." He was quiet, so I plowed on. "It's been a rough couple of days. I'm tired from not sleeping well, as you know. I even cried last night, for gosh sakes. When is the last time you know that I've cried?" Now tears began to well up again. I swallowed them back.

"I'm sorry, babe. I don't mean to be a jerk."

His voice was soft, and it made the waterworks threaten to reappear. "It's all good," I said, my voice hoarse.

"I have some news that should make you very happy."

"Yeah?" I took a breath and sat down in my desk chair. It squeaked the familiar sound as I leaned back.

"The time of death for the woman doesn't fit with the time on her fitness tracker. The autopsy showed the time of death to be much earlier."

"I don't understand," I said, sitting forward again and resting my elbows on the desk.

"She'd been in there for a while. You just happened to be the first one to go to that particular nook."

"But the time on the fitness tracker…"

"Someone set it up to throw off the police. Walker said he was going to call you, so don't let on that I told you."

A tear escaped and rolled down my cheek. I wiped it away and smiled. "You have a lot of faith in my acting abilities."

"I have faith in you in all things."

My heart swelled. Why in the world was I hesitating in setting a date to marry this man? He was beyond perfect. I held my left hand in front of me and stared at the beautiful ring he'd picked out for me all by himself. It was the perfect ring; he knew me well enough to know exactly what I would love.

"I have to go get ready for my first client," I said.

"Go. And have a day as beautiful as you are."

"Hey, Levi? Tomorrow let's set that date." Given the silence that followed, I wasn't sure which of us was more surprised by the suggestion.

He finally cleared his throat and said, "Let's do that."

After we hung up, I sat alone for a few moments, listening to the ladies laughing and talking out in the salon. An unfamiliar voice laughed loudly. Babs' client? I thought of the glorious news Levi had just given me. I wanted to shout it from the rooftops or in the salon at the very least, but I knew I couldn't. I had to keep silent so Levi didn't get in trouble for telling me. I hoped Detective Walker would call me rather than stop by. I could pull off the surprised act much easier if he weren't here to gauge my reaction.

The bell above the door jingled out in the salon.

"Melanie," Rubie called. "You have a visitor."

My heart sank momentarily. Detective Walker? Hesitating for a second longer, I pushed my chair back from the desk and stood. No time like the present. I took a deep breath, let it out slowly, and walked toward the door. It was showtime.

I turned the corner to see Connie had arrived sometime in the hustle, and I hadn't even noticed. She didn't come into the office but instead hung her jacket on the client coat rack. Weird. I scanned the rest of the salon. Jack stood partially hidden behind the front counter. I ran across the salon, giving him the biggest hug ever. "You all are terrible," I said to the ladies. "And what are you doing here?" I asked, playfully punching Jack in the arm. His designer jeans were pressed and creased, as usual, his gray tweed jacket opened, revealing a gray button-up shirt, also pressed. It didn't look like he'd just driven two hours. "When did you get gray at the temples?" I asked him.

"Geez, kid! I was just here a few weeks ago, not years."

"It seems a lot longer than that. Besides, you have to admit it's usually not this long between visits." I pulled back, still holding his upper arms. I turned my head slightly to the side and raised an eyebrow. "Wait a minute, Jack Dancy. Are you seeing someone? Please tell me you didn't give in to Bryce."

Jack rolled his eyes and chuckled. "No and no. And when did you become so dramatic?"

"Why didn't you answer the phone when I called a little bit ago?"

"I wanted to surprise you. Besides, Minnesota is a hands-free state," he teased.

"We're having a get-together at my place after work today. Can you stay?"

"I'll have to check my impossibly busy schedule," he said, trying hard as he could to keep from smiling.

"You are such a brat," I said, swatting his arm.

The door opened, and in walked my first appointment, followed by Claire's. It was time to get this day officially underway, and I couldn't be more thrilled. Besides, it promised to keep me too busy to be tempted to tell Claire and Rubie the good news that I was no longer the key suspect. Or to tell Jack anything about it at all.

"What are you going to do while I'm slaving myself to the bone?" I asked him.

"If you slaved yourself to the bone, as you stated, you'd have no time for trouble. Looks like working too hard isn't a problem for you."

"Jerk," I muttered, then snickered. "So, what are you going to do while I'm *working*?"

"Got some errands to run. Then I think I'll head out to your house and do some paperwork on my computer before you get there."

I hugged him and kissed him on the cheek. "Okay. See you at home."

As I was blow drying my client's hair, I saw the screen on my phone light up. It was an unknown number but the same prefix as Levi's work phone. Assuming it was Detective Walker, I let it roll into voicemail. It wasn't exactly a conversation I could have in front of a client. I would have to call him back after this one left and before the next one came in. But when I finally listened to the voicemail, a return call wasn't needed after all.

"Hey, Melanie, this is Detective Walker. I'll spare us both the time in explaining since I'm not stupid and know Levi has already called you." I heard a slight chuckle. "Just so you know, though, you're not a hundred percent out of the woods, just ninety-nine. I'll be in touch."

I hung up. *I'm sure you will, Detective Walker. I'm sure you will.*

I went out into the salon to Claire's station. "Hey, Claire, can I borrow you for just a second?" I looked at her client, who was facing the mirror. "Sorry, Mrs. Norton. I promise it won't be more than a minute."

Claire rested her hand on Mrs. Norton's shoulder and said, "I'll be right back."

"You betcha. You go right on ahead, dear," Mrs. Norton said. "I'm in no hurry. The faster I get home, the faster I have to get to the housework, dontcha know."

Claire laughed and followed me back to the office. "What's up?" she asked. "You okay?" Her brows furrowed with concern.

"I'm better than okay. Detective Walker just called. I'm ninety-nine percent off the hook for the woman's murder at the gym."

"Woo hoo!" Claire squealed, wrapping me in a hug.

"Hey!" I said, laughing. "Watch those shears, or there'll be a murder right here."

"Sorry," she said, laying them on the desk.

"Hey! What's going on back there?" Rubie asked. In a matter of seconds, Babs and Connie poked their heads around the corner too. "What are we missing out on?" Rubie said.

"I've been cleared from the woman's murder at the gym," I said quietly so the rest of the salon patrons didn't decide to join in. "Ninety-nine percent, anyway."

Connie breathed an audible sigh of relief, Babs high-fived me, and Rubie hugged me, suffocating me in her perfume and glitter. I sneezed. Man, that girl was as girly-girl as I wasn't.

"Well, now we have a good reason to celebrate this evening," Claire said.

"I'm bringing a bottle of champagne," Rubie said.

"Ugh," I said, making a face. I've never been a champagne kinda girl, and now, for reasons unknown, it sounded even worse.

"Wine?" she asked, tipping her head slightly. When I didn't answer, she said, "Wine it is. If no one else wants it, I'll drink it by myself, and ya'll can have something less adultish."

"I'll drink wine," I said.

Claire laughed. "Me too. Now come on, let's get back out there before our clients file complaints."

After they left the office, I stayed put for a moment longer, reveling in the relief of my freedom. Ninety-nine percent, anyway.

***

The rest of the day flew by in a flurry of laughter, the buzz of conversation—some of which one simply couldn't make up and left me shaking my head—and a haze of hair spray and chemicals. It soothed my soul almost as much as Nana's homemade chicken noodle soup. At the thought of Nana's soup, my heart warmed. Oh, how I couldn't wait to tell her the good news!

As we closed up, each of us cleaning our respective stations, making them ready for the next day, I said, "Connie and Babs, you're both still welcome to join us this evening in case anything has changed."

"I need to spend some time with my cousin," Babs said. "And keep her away from you. She won't be here much longer. And once she starts running the inn, she won't be able to get away too often, I'm sure."

"I can't either," Connie said. "But thanks for the invite."

I watched her from the corner of my eye. Something was wrong with her and had been for the past week. She and I had never been terribly close, but lately, she was pulling away even more. I'd bet that within a few months, she would move on, and I wondered if I should mentally prepare myself for her inevitable notice. Other than the nail tech position and one other stylist, our turnover had been zero since we'd opened. I only wish I knew what had transpired to cause this change in Connie.

After Connie and Babs left, Rubie said, "I'm going to run home and change quick. I'll be out to your house in about an hour." She slipped her arms into the sleeves of her jacket and swept her hair out from under the collar.

"I'm going to throw in a load of towels and fold the ones in the dryer before I leave," Claire said.

"Perfect," I said. "I'll get a bit of paperwork done while you're doing that."

Since Claire had moved out by me a couple of years ago, she and I had gotten into a routine of leaving at the same time and following each other home whenever we could. If we went to the gym after work, we'd follow one another home from there as well. It was the perfect arrangement for both of us unless I swung by Nana's before going home.

When we had each finished, we grabbed our jackets we'd tossed earlier on the chair in the corner of the office.

"Do you think Connie's okay?" I asked Claire.

"She's been a little off this week," Claire answered. "I'm not sure what to think about it. I've just been giving her time, figuring she'll open up when she's ready. She's even more of an introvert than you are."

"I think I'm going to talk to her tomorrow."

"Maybe I'll bring her in some Rice Krispie treats. She loves those."

I turned off the lights behind me in the office, and Claire flipped the switch to the ones in the salon. We'd just reached the door when Detective Walker's cruiser pulled up.

15

Claire and I waited inside the front door until Detective Walker strode up. I opened the door.

"I wasn't supposed to call you back, was I?"

"No."

"Am I in trouble again?" I asked, confused. I hadn't even had time to do anything wrong. Not that it takes me a long time to do that.

"Is Connie here?" he asked.

"No. She left about forty-five minutes ago. Why?"

"The bottle of nail polish found at the scene this morning came from your salon."

"But Connie doesn't handle nails. And how do you know that, anyway? About ninety percent of the salons in town probably use the same brand. It's hardly a stranger in the professional industry."

"I can't elaborate on how we know. It's an active investigation."

"Yeah, but—"

"Melanie, please," he said. "You know I can't tell you."

"Wait!" I said, my eyes widening. "You found prints on it. And if you're looking for Connie, that means it's her prints."

Detective Walker tilted his head back and pinched the bridge of his nose, taking a large inhale, followed by a slow exhale. "I'll go to Ms. Jensen's home." He looked from me to Claire and back to me. Pointedly. "I would appreciate it if you don't call and tip her off. Or call anyone, for that matter."

"Not even my grandmother? I wanted to tell her the good news that I've been cleared. Ninety-nine percent cleared."

Claire slapped my arm. "Stop being obnoxious," she said.

"Well, he —"

"Stop," she said. It was more of a command. She shook her head. "You're too much, Mel."

Detective Walker nodded his agreement, and I shrugged.

"I was just getting things straight."

"No, you weren't," she said. Then as if remembering why he was here, she grew solemn. "We won't be able to give you her address, Detective. Not without a warrant. Confidentiality purposes."

I jerked my head in Claire's direction. That wasn't like her at all. She was turning into me, poor thing.

"I wouldn't ask you to do that," he said. "I have my methods. You ladies have a nice evening."

"Thank you, sir. You too," Claire said.

"Detective?" I said as he opened the door. He stopped and turned toward me. "If it is Connie's prints —"

"Melanie —" he started.

"Hypothetically speaking," I said. "If Connie's prints are on the bottle—which would be unlikely since Babs is the nail tech and the rest of us only do nails for requesting clientele—you would have to have her prints on file already to know that. Am I right? Hypothetically speaking," I repeated.

"Hypothetically speaking," he parroted, "yes."

"Can you tell me—"

"No," he said and turned toward the door.

"I was just going to ask what color the nail polish was. I know it was a shade of red since I saw the bottle, and that's the color of the polish that spelled the word on the rock. But what was the name of it?"

"Russian Red My Mind." He rolled his eyes. "What kind of cuckoo comes up with these names? How many bottles do you have on hand?"

"We have a shelf of polishes over here," Claire said, leading the way to the wall with a four-shelf case that held the polishes. "We keep one of each color here. The client chooses which color she wants. When that bottle is empty, we replace it."

"Russian Red My Mind," I mumbled as I looked for the color, picking up the reds and looking at the name on the bottom of each bottle. I came across a spot where a bottle was missing and froze. "Umm...I assume this is probably the color in question. Or *was*, anyway. It's gone."

"Is it a popular color?" Detective Walker asked.

Claire and I looked at each other and then shrugged.

"We wouldn't know," I said. "Like I said, we don't do nails very often. Babs does them."

"With Christmas and Valentine's Day in the recent past," Claire said, "red was probably pretty popular."

"This particular shade? Looks like there's a lot of red bottles on that shelf," he said.

I shrugged again. "We would have no idea. But regardless, if the bottle was empty, she would have replaced it with one from the back and—wait! Let me check the order list. We keep an extra of each color in the supply cabinet. Once that one is gone, I order a new one." I went into the office and rifled through the file in the cabinet until I reached what I was looking for. I scanned the list. "Nope. The last time I ordered this color was several months ago." I took out my phone, opened the search engine, and typed in *Russian Red My Mind Infusion Nail Polish*. I stretched the image for a closer look using my thumb and forefinger. Claire stood behind me, looking over my shoulder.

"That's a very distinct red," I said. "It looked a little different on the rock."

"I thought you saw the bottle," Detective Walker said.

"Not closely. Just that it was there, but everything had a layer of frost. It's not unusual, though, for the colors to appear darker when applied and dried than inside the bottle. So there is that."

He nodded. "Thank you, ladies. Again, I would appreciate it if you didn't call Connie the minute I leave here to alert her to anything."

"Detective," I said as he reached the door, "can I ask one more question?"

"No," he said, and then he was gone.

Claire and I looked at each other, neither knowing what to say.

Finally, I said, "What do you suppose that was about?"

"I wouldn't even want to venture a guess."

"Maybe there's more to Connie's odd behavior this week than either of us could have imagined," I mused. "What I want to know is what her prints are on file for."

"I have no idea," Claire said. "And that's assuming that's what it was." She stared out the window, toward the taillights of Detective Walker's cruiser pulling out of the parking lot and onto the street.

"Dang, Claire, we need to start doing backgrounds on people who want to rent booth space."

She turned toward me. "Are you listening to yourself? If someone did a background on you, you'd be plumb out of luck."

I thought about that, then finally said, "True story." I shrugged. "Come on. Rubie has probably beat us home by now. Do you need to run home to check on Syd first? Make sure Tyler's folks aren't loading her up on sugar or anything of that sort?"

Claire laughed. "No. Since there's no school tomorrow, they've taken her to a movie tonight."

"Lucky girl."

Between Claire's folks and Tyler's folks, all who live out of state, both sets of grandparents went out of their way to visit Sydney as often as possible. Sydney frequently stayed with them on school vacations, including a good portion of the summer. The girl wasn't short for attention between her grandparents, Claire, and me.

We locked the door behind us and walked to our cars. "I need to take Daisy to a movie one of these days," I said. "Maybe all four of us could go."

"Speaking of Daisy," she said, "How's Max's business doing?"

Max purchased the only drug store in town from Harvey, one of the town's folks who'd lived here forever; Harvey had retired after owning it for fifty years. The timing was perfect for Max since he'd gotten an inheritance from our good-for-nothing father, who'd just died in January.

"He loves it. Well, as much as he shows any emotion, anyway. I have a hard time reading him most of the time. He's putting some money into it. Upgrading a bit."

"That's great. And for you, too," she said. "That means he's pretty much locked into staying around for good."

"I suppose."

We'd reached our cars, where we stopped and stood still. I kept my gaze on my car but could feel her looking at me. "What's that mean?"

I shrugged. "It means I suppose."

"Stop being a brat."

I looked up at her. "Do people do that?" I asked. "Stay around for good?"

"Yes, Mel, they do," she said quietly.

Since Claire had lost her husband, she had every reason to feel this way, yet didn't. I felt a little ashamed. I thought about the people in my life who had stayed—the ones who mattered—Nana, Claire, Jack, Levi. And I realized how badly I hoped Max would be one of them. Having had no family for my entire life except Nana and Granddad, and then Nana when Granddad died, having a brother was pretty cool—especially having a niece. I loved that little girl. And if Max stayed, that meant Daisy stayed.

I opened my car door as she went to hers and opened it. We stood in silence. "All right then," I finally said and nodded as I looked at the street and then at Claire. "I'm happy he's staying."

Claire just grinned and got in her car. "See you at your house in fifteen," she said before shutting her door.

***

Unable to wait until I saw her, I called my grandmother on the way home and filled her in on the good news that I was removed from the suspect list. "Ninety-nine percent," I'd told her, grinning. Ninety-nine percent was good enough for me. And apparently for my grandmother, too.

"Don't cry, Nana," I had told her. "This is a good thing."

"Why, yes, it is. These are tears of joy, dontcha know," she'd said.

We had talked until I reached my driveway. Before we hung up, she said, "Celebration dinner soon. And when we do, bring that man of yours. And Claire and Sydney and Max and Daisy. And Jacky and perky Rubie. Bring them. This is a celebration! I haven't seen nearly enough of those kids lately."

"Join the club. I haven't either," I told her. "Even Claire these days, except at work. Between her time spent with Cole and mine with Levi, our time together is limited. That's why I'm excited about this evening."

This summer, I was going to see to it that we kept up our time lazing in the boat on the lake. My log home with lakeshore property was a perfect fit for me. It was cozy, peaceful, and incredibly beautiful. I had a small fishing boat that I kept tied to a small dock in the water. The times that Claire and I had spent out in the boat, sometimes with a fishing line or two to cast over the side, and sometimes just lying in the boat chatting it up with sun tea and a book, sometimes laughing so hard one of us would have to use the pee bucket, were some of my favorite memories.

I parked in the garage and crossed the front yard. Jack's car was parked off to the side, Rubie's car next to his. Claire pulled in next to Rubie's. My heart swelled as I looked at all three vehicles. I was one lucky lady.

I waited for Claire before I climbed the steps. Jack opened the door. "Welcome to my home," he said.

"You wish," I said, laughing.

"Not really." He put an arm around my shoulders and kissed my cheek. "As much as I love coming here, I'm more of a city guy."

"Yes, you are. There's no arguing that. You just like to come here to see me," I teased him, giving him a once over. His jacket and shoes were still on. As much as I have tried to get him to loosen up out here, it was a slow process. "For gosh sakes, take off your jacket, Jack." I reached up and mussed his hair. "There. Now we're making progress."

"You're a pain in my backside, Hogan," he said as he smoothed his moussed jet-black hair. The hard side part was new, as was the absent black-framed glasses.

"What's with the new 'do?" I asked. "And where are your glasses?"

"Just wearing my contacts."

"Since when do you have contacts?" I asked, narrowing my eyes. "You *are* seeing someone, aren't you?"

"No, I'm not. I'm very happy being single, thank you very much. And I've had contacts for a long time. I just don't wear them very much."

"Like never," I said. "At least never when you're here."

"I understand you've gone and gotten yourself in a hot mess again."

I glared at Rubie.

"What?" she exclaimed. "I thought you'd already told him."

She looked cute as could be in a pair of jeans with shredded knees and a scoop-neck long-sleeved pink tee. Her feet were bare, her toenails painted – what else? – pink.

"She *should* have told me," Jack said, mirroring the glare that I had just a second ago given Rubie.

"I tried calling you this morning. You didn't answer."

"It happened yesterday morning," he said, cutting me no slack at all. "And, again, this morning? What is it with you?"

"You tell me," I said. "And I had absolutely nothing to do with the body this morning. Andie Rose found it. But the good news is that I'm cleared from yesterday's murder. Almost."

"What do you mean *almost*?" he asked. He held up a hand, closed his eyes, and shook his head slowly. "It's disturbing that you have to distinctly say *which* body you're referring to."

I couldn't even begin to argue with him on that or formulate any kind of defense that made sense. "Walker said — that's the detective — "

"Yes, we're all getting to know Detective Walker a little too well," Jack mumbled.

"Well," I said, choosing to ignore Jack's comment, "he said that since I found the body, it means there's still a little room for me to be a suspect. But you'll never believe what happened before we left the salon."

"After I left?" Rubie asked, eyebrows raised. "That was less than an hour after me. Can you not be left alone for a hot minute?"

"Nope," Jack answered dryly, but not without a hint of a smirk.

"Let me run upstairs and change quick. I'll be right back down. Claire, you still have a pair of yoga pants and a t-shirt here if you want to change."

"I do," she said. "It feels like I have little hair slivers poking through my clothes."

"They're in the dresser in the guest room."

"That's not the guest room, that's my room," Jack said, smiling.

"You ladies change, and I'll pour the wine," Rubie said.

"None for me," I said. "I'll just have seltzer water with orange."

"You said you were drinking wine with me," Rubie accused.

"Yeah, well, I need to be on my game in the morning in case there's — "

Jack scowled and held out his hand. "Don't even say it." I shrugged and headed for the loft. "You have any decent beer?" he called after me. "Something that's not carbonated water?"

"Only if you left some here last time," I called down from the top of the stairs.

My bedroom was in the loft, and I loved it up here. Large windows looking over the lake lined the stairs up to my room. At one time, they had been without window coverings. But after an incident where some pervert was outside my house looking at a friend and me through the windows, it creeped me out enough to have them fitted for blinds. I closed them every evening as I climbed the stairs to my room. My favorite part, though, was the skylight in the ceiling right above my bed. I loved looking at the stars on clear nights and the moon when it's positioned just right. On stormy nights, I watched as lightning cut through the sky, lulled to sleep by the sound of the raindrops splashing on the thick glass.

Levi and I hadn't talked yet about where we would live when we finally got married, and at times the anxiety it gave me was suffocating. I'd purposely avoided the subject for fear of the outcome. While I could understand Jackson, his son, might want to stay in the apartment Levi lives in now, I couldn't get myself to part with my slice of paradise out here. I'd thought of selling points to add to the eventual discussion, such as a house is more practical than an apartment, despite being small; Jackson and Sydney could be closer to each other; there's more room here; and resale value. Like I'd ever sell. I couldn't leave Claire out here by herself. Jackson lived with Levi part-time and with his mother part-time. Thinking about it now churned my stomach with anxiety. I knew it was a critical conversation that couldn't be avoided and probably should have been discussed by now. Not unlike the child conversation. Thankfully, since I can't have kids, the housing conversation would be the only one we needed to have.

I slipped into a pair of gray sweatpants, a navy hoodie, and slippers, cracked open a window for some fresh air, and headed back downstairs.

Claire had already changed and had a glass of wine in hand. Jack was tipping back a bottle of Guinness. "Where'd you find that?" I asked him, pointing to the bottle.

"Behind a loaf of bread that looks like you should have thrown it out weeks ago."

Rubie wrinkled her nose. "Gross, Melanie."

"What can I say? I don't eat a lot of bread."

"Apparently," he said. "I took care of it for you. It's in the trash."

I opened the fridge and opted for a can of grapefruit-flavored seltzer water instead of my typical orange. "Did anyone order pizza yet?"

"Done," Jack said. "It'll be here in an hour."

I smiled, completely content. This is precisely what all of us needed. We all fell into place like cogs in a wheel.

16

When all settled in our usual places—me on one end of the sofa, throw pillow lying loosely on my lap, one leg tucked underneath me, Claire the same on the other side of the couch, Jack sitting too properly on the chair caddy-corner from me, and Rubie on the matching chair, but both feet pulled up. Her arms were wrapped around her legs, her wine glass in one hand. Creatures of habit, we were.

"Tell us what happened before you left the salon," Rubie said.

"Yes, do tell," Jack said.

"First, can I say—" I looked at Claire, "that I think I'm going to quit the gym? I just can't get myself to want to go anymore. Think I'll get some equipment here and put it in the basement. We could still work out, just do it here."

"Heck yeah!" she exclaimed. "That works better anyway because Syd could come here instead of Mrs. Carter staying with her. It's much more convenient. I'll chip in for some equipment."

"Deal," I said. "When Claire and I were leaving the salon, Detective Walker showed up. That's why we're as late as we were. Get this—" I stopped and looked at Rubie. "Do you think Connie has been a little off lately? Like she's just not herself?"

"Yeah. She said it was because of her husband, though."

"She told you what's going on?" Claire and I both asked.

Rubie shrugged. "Yeah, why?"

"How come she didn't tell me?" I asked.

"Did you ask?" Rubie said.

"No. I was giving her space."

"Me too," Claire said.

"If you didn't ask, why would she have told you?" Rubie said matter of fact.

"I didn't want to pry," I said. "I just figured that—"

"What, that she would just spill her personal life without you asking her about it?" Rubie said. "Remember, she has your personality type on steroids."

"What's going on with her husband?" Claire asked.

"She thinks he's cheating on her."

My heart sank for Connie. I knew what that felt like since that's what my ex, Cain, did to me. "Rat bas—"

"Hey, hey," Jack said, putting his hand up, palm facing me.

"What? I was going to say rat basket."

Jack scowled, suppressing a grin. "Sure you were."

"Geez, Jack! You think I have a potty mouth, or what?"

"What did Detective Walker say?" Rubie asked.

"He was there looking for Connie," Claire said. "The nail polish bottle found at the crime scene was from our place."

"How can they know that?" Rubie asked. "Almost every salon in town uses the same brand we do. Heck, probably the entire state."

"Exactly," Claire said, taking a sip of wine.

"The fact that he was looking for Connie and knew the bottle came from our salon tells me that Connie's prints were on it," I said.

"Does she do nails?" Jack asked.

"We all do, but maybe once in a blue moon," I said. "That's Babs' specialty. Rubie, do you believe Connie was telling you the truth about her husband?"

"Why would she lie?" she said, taking a sip of wine. "Connie's not exactly the type who craves attention by spewing lies."

"It's just odd, is all," I said.

Jack sat forward on his chair. "How would they know Connie's prints were on the bottle unless they were already in the database?"

"Right?" I said. "That's what I asked Detective Walker, but he couldn't answer because it's an active investigation."

Claire shivered. "No one stays alone with Connie until we find out what's going on."

"Do any of you think she's capable of murder?" Jack asked, looking at each of us.

"I don't think so," Claire said.

"Who knows," I added.

"I don't think so, either," Rubie said. "She seemed legitimately genuine when she told me about her husband."

We all fell silent for a few moments. "Well," I finally said, "I agree with Claire. Until we know what's going on, no one stays alone with her at the salon."

"What about Babs?" Rubie asked. "Do we tell her?"

"No," I said. "Claire and I weren't supposed to tell anyone."

"So, what, we just leave Babs in the dark and put her at risk?" Rubie asked. "That's kind of messed up." She took a sip of wine, eyes leveled on me over the rim of the glass.

"No," Claire said. "One of us will always have to be sure Babs isn't alone. Might be tricky to do without her wondering why we're stalking her."

Jack removed his shoes and sat back in his chair again. "Careful, there, Jacky," I said. "We wouldn't want you getting too comfortable."

"Zip it, Hogan," he said, and I laughed. "What about the body this morning?" He shook his head and muttered, "And, again, how pathetic that I have to clarify which body I'm referring to."

"What about it?" I asked.

"You're not a suspect in that one, are you?"

"No. I already told you, Andie Rose found that one. They're connected, though. They have to be."

"How do you know?" Jack asked.

"Two bodies found within two days, both within close proximity, both had key cards for the same motel. Coincidence? I don't think so," I answered before anyone else had the opportunity.

"Um...what key cards?" Rubie asked.

Crap! Too late now. I briefly closed my eyes and took a breath before filling them in. "We have no proof that it belongs to the crime scene," I said, trying to justify my behavior. "There was a lot of stuff that didn't belong to it."

"Yeah, and that's why you took it," Rubie said. "Because you thought it would be cool to have one." She rolled her eyes.

After a grumbling from Jack, followed by "I don't even know why I'm surprised," we moved on.

"Let's brainstorm this," Claire said, lifting her other leg and sitting cross-legged with the pillow still in her lap, leaning slightly forward. She held her wineglass in her right hand, her left picking absently at the pillow.

"Since when have you wanted to get involved in a murder if I haven't asked, begged, and pleaded?" I asked.

"I'm not getting involved in it," she said to me. "We're at your house and not out hunting a killer."

Rubie stood and fetched the wine bottle, filled her glass, and then Claire's. "You planning on spending the night, Rubie?" I asked. "Claire's within walking distance, but you, not so much."

"Nah," Rubie said, plopping back down into her chair. "If we're going to be solving this crime, we'll all be here a while. I'll be good by the time I leave."

"It's a school night for the three of you," Jack said. "You might want to go easy."

"True story," I said.

"Are you thinking it's the same killer?" Jack asked.

"I don't know yet. But I know they're connected." I got up and walked to the kitchen. I cut open two brown paper grocery sacks and taped them on the knotty pine wall. Next, I took out a black Sharpie from a drawer. "Here's what we have," I said. Across the top, I wrote, *Maggie*. Next to her name, I wrote *Dead Man*.

"Dead man?" Rubie balked. "Can't we at least give him a made-up name? Dead man sounds—well, it just sounds—"

"He's dead," I said, looking at her. "I don't think he cares what we call him." Next to *Dead Man*, I wrote Connie's name, followed by Andie Rose.

"Andie Rose?" Claire asked, surprised. "I thought you liked her. You think she could be guilty of murder?"

"We can't rule anyone out yet," I said.

"Why not?" Rubie asked. "We've ruled you out."

I narrowed my eyes at her and wrote my name next to Andie Rose's.

"For gosh sakes, I was just teasing," she scoffed.

"No, it's all good, Rubie. This way, we can get concrete ways to clear me a hundred percent instead of a mere ninety-nine."

"There is that," Jack said, shaking his head. "And, again, the fact that we have to clear you, *again*," he stressed, "is becoming routine. I'm going to move you down to Minneapolis so that I can keep an eye on you."

"She's not going anywhere," Claire said, glaring at Jack.

I think Claire was born with a smile on her face. And if she's not happy, I worry about her. Why she loves my sarcastic behind is beyond me. We're as opposite as two people could be. She wears brightly colored signature hair scarves to tame her wild dark curls, and my hair is highlighted blond, fine with natural waves, typically worn down or in a ponytail; Claire wears her makeup to perfection on her gorgeous hazelnut skin, and I wear little makeup except for mascara, a touch of blush, and tinted lip gloss; she wears maxi dresses or miniskirts in bright colors, and I wear jeans and lots and lots of black; she's tall with an athletic build, and I'm a mere five-two with a thinner, almost boyish, build; where she's open, a tad flighty, and loves everyone, I'm much more reserved, not so trusting, but loyal to a fault. Once I let someone in, they're in, by golly. Whatever differences there could be, we were on opposite ends of the spectrum. And yet you'd never find two people who complemented each other more.

I smiled at Claire warmly. "No, Claire, I'm not going anywhere." I thought again about the living situation when Levi and I finally tied the knot and vowed it would have to be here.

"I'm not sure I could handle you full-time anyway," Jack said. "I've already got a full-time job."

Claire, Rubie, and I all laughed loudly.

"I am not a *job!*" I finally exclaimed.

"Maybe a nut job," Rubie mumbled.

I gasped, then laughed. "Now getting back to business," I said. "There's a connection between the two deaths. If they're looking at Connie in connection to one of them, does that mean she had something to do with the other?"

"Wait!" Rubie exclaimed, sitting on the edge of her chair. "Has anyone ever seen Connie's husband?"

"She used to have a picture of him at her station tucked in the corner of her mirror," I said. "I guess I've never looked closely, though. In fact..." I tried to see her station in my mind, "I don't think it's been there for a couple of months or so." My eyes popped open wide. "Are you thinking what I'm thinking?"

"Was the dead man Connie's husband?" Jack said.

"When she told me about him and their problems, it sounded like it was something pretty serious," Rubie said gravely.

"Cheating is," I said dryly and shook my head, forcing away fresh anger. "He was lying face down with a hood over his head, so I didn't see what he looked like," I said. "I honestly couldn't tell you if he resembled Connie's husband or not."

Claire frowned. "This could be worse than we thought."

"But it means Babs isn't in any danger by us not telling her."

"Why not?" Jack asked incredulously. "If Connie's the one who killed him, I'd say you all have every reason to worry about your safety."

"Wait, why aren't we telling Babs again?" Claire asked. "Jack's right. And it seems deceptive to keep this from her."

"I like Andie Rose and think she would be fun to hang out with, not to mention she's great at this crime-solving stuff, but like it or not, she's still a suspect on the list. I would hate for Babs to get caught in the middle by knowing something she shouldn't."

Claire shrugged and said grudgingly, "I suppose you have a point."

"What makes me think it wasn't Connie's husband is the motel key card. And both the dead woman and the dead man had the same one. *If* it's even hers," I added. "It's just a strong suspicion I have." I paced back and forth for a moment and then jotted down the similarities on the taped-up brown paper bag under their respective headings.

"If the dead man is Connie's husband, and both victims had the same motel key, that could mean he and the dead woman were hooking up," Jack said, taking a swig of his beer. He unbuttoned his jacket and leaned forward, elbows on his knees, hands cupped around his beer bottle.

"Which makes things look even worse for Connie," I said.

Rubie groaned. "Oh, man, I wish she hadn't told me about her husband."

"But we don't know for a fact that the key card in the locker room belonged to the dead woman," Claire said. "What proof do you have other than your gut?"

"It was found on the floor, right below where we found the murder weapon. I can just feel it, Claire. I can't explain it."

"But that leads me to think it probably belonged to the murderer more so than the victim," Jack said.

I pointed at him absently. "You have an excellent point. And that lets Connie off the hook, too. What would she be doing with a motel key card?"

"What was her husband doing with a motel key card?" Rubie said.

"If it was her husband," I said, exhaling loudly. "There are far too many unknowns at this point."

Jack groaned. "Which means you're going to make sure you know more."

I shrugged a shoulder and smiled at Jack sheepishly.

17

"If Connie is the killer, those of us working with her need to know. And if her husband was cheating and she killed him, kudos to her." When three sets of eyes grew huge and jaws dropped, I held out my hand, palm forward. "Not that I would, but just sayin'. And if she's not the killer, then those of us working with her have a responsibility to clear her."

Claire inhaled sharply. "I just thought of something. If word gets around that she's a suspect, think of what that could do to the salon business."

I nodded. "Another reason why we need to help clear her. I don't want to think Connie is capable of murder. Even if she does—did?—have a cheating husband."

"Me either," both Claire and Rubie agreed.

"She's been at the salon with us almost from the beginning, Mel," Claire said. "She's going to need us now."

"Ladies," Jack said, "don't you think you might be getting ahead of yourselves? You don't know for sure that it was Connie's fingerprints that they found. Detective Walker wasn't definitive about that, was he?" I shook my head. "And you don't know for sure if the key card you found in the locker room had anything to do with this whole situation."

I scribbled some more items on the spread-out grocery bags, then stood back for a full view. I drew a line from the nail polish to Connie and another to the dead man. I drew a line from the motel key card to the dead man and a dotted line from the motel key card to Maggie Thompson and another to the question mark that signified an unknown potential killer in case it wasn't Connie at all.

After tossing around a few more ideas and scenarios, one of which was the person the question mark symbolized killing both of them and having nothing to do with anything at all that we'd discussed, Rubie stood and stretched.

"I need to hit the road. Scott's coming by after his shift." Scott was Rubie's significant other. Despite spending all their spare time together, it had taken Rubie and Scott a while to admit they were a couple. Scott had some demons in his life he had to work out first and didn't want to drag Rubie down while he worked on himself. Rubie would never have stuck it out with anyone else she'd ever dated. Which there were a lot.

Claire stood too. "Yeah, I need to head out as well. It's getting late. Syd will already be in bed, but if I know my bug, she'll be lying awake waiting for me to tuck her in like a little burrito. Thank goodness it's a Friday night, and she doesn't have school tomorrow."

"Hug my girl for me," I said as I hugged Claire, then Rubie. "Rubie, you drive careful. Are you sure you're good to drive?"

"For gosh sakes, Melanie, I didn't even finish my second glass of wine. I'm good."

The two slipped into their jackets, and I walked out onto the porch and stood watching as they talked between themselves a moment in the front yard, then got into their respective vehicles. I stood on the porch after their taillights faded out of the driveway. They both turned the same way onto the road, except Claire turned into her driveway a mere couple of yards down, and Rubie zoomed on toward town. Heck, Claire could have just driven across the field between our houses if the trees hadn't been there.

I watched her headlights turn into her driveway, then sat on the top step, wrapping my arms around my legs. Bright shining stars splattered across the sky, the half-moon hung, suspended in midair as if it might come crashing down at any moment. I marveled at the wonder of the universe and the God who made it all. The One who, despite the hardships of my mother leaving me, Cain leaving me, my birth father leaving me, and my inability to have children, had blessed me so abundantly. Nana, my friends, Levi, and now Max and Daisy, my salon, my home. I had so much to be thankful for.

I heard the front door open behind me, and Jack sat next to me.

"Isn't it beautiful out tonight, Jack?" I said, still in wonder.

"It's quiet," he said.

"You can take a man out of the city, but you can't take the city out of the man," I teased, bumping his shoulder with my own.

"What are you thinking about? Or do I even want to ask?"

"That the biggest problems I've had in my life for as long as I can remember are no longer looming over me like a Goliath. What I do have is far bigger and much more important."

He lay an arm around my shoulders. "That, girlfriend, is huge for you to admit."

"My mom—or lack thereof—and Cain being a jerk," I looked at him then straight ahead again, "even not being able to have kids…it's just all part of who I am."

"You've come a long way in the last few years."

I looked at him from the corner of my eye. He looked different without his glasses and with the new hair. "Are you lying to me about not seeing someone new?"

He chuckled softly. "Not lying. I'm good on my own. I'm comfortable being by myself. I've come to like it."

"Yeah?" I asked. I wanted more for him than that.

As if reading my mind, he said, "Not everyone wants to share their life with a partner. You, of all people, should be able to understand that. I'm happy for you and Levi. It's good for the two of you. It works. But I don't want the same thing. And, no, not because I'm bitter. Because I'm truly happy and content."

"For now, or forever?" I asked.

"For today. Tomorrow isn't here yet. Quit planning my life for me." He squeezed my shoulder and took his arm back.

"I just want you to be happy."

"I am," he said softly. It was the most genuine two words I'd ever heard from him. "Come on. Let's go inside." He stood and held out a hand to me. "I've had enough outdoors for tonight."

I laughed. "You're getting better at this country stuff, Jack, but you have a long way to go."

***

I woke early and lay in bed for a minute, enjoying the quiet, the stillness, and the warmth of my bed. I lay looking through the skylight. The moonlight revealed clouds gathering in the sky. A late spring snowstorm was in the forecast for tonight, and it looked like we just might get it. It would be a good night to be tucked in my house, snowed in with Levi. Or maybe it would be a good night to have Daisy spend the night. We could have some girl time, just the two of us.

I lay there pondering the possibilities, grateful I'd decided not to hit the gym anymore. Not to mention the evenings when Claire and I had met there after work. I could reclaim my mornings for having coffee on the deck overlooking the lake. I longed for summer to sit out there in my Adirondack chair, my feet propped up on the black wrought iron railing, admiring the water's surface, smooth as glass. And the orange sailboat that lazily drifted by every summer morning. I missed the birds singing and the squirrels playing. Until the weather was warm enough to do that, having the extra time at home let me sit in my reading chair with coffee and my devotional, followed by reading the St. Cloud Times on my iPad.

Yes, I'd made the right decision. I would start looking for a treadmill and an elliptical today to put in my basement. I could set them up in front of the large picture window and look at the lake while I'm exercising. Since it wasn't a New Year's resolution, I might stand a chance of succeeding and not sell the equipment in a yard sale in six months which, more often than not, was the norm for people who purchased equipment. I mused at all of the yard sales I'd seen over the years with treadmills, ellipticals, rowers, you name it, that looked brand new. Between all of it, however, the thought of bodies kept interrupting. I couldn't get away from them anywhere.

After one last stretch, I swung my legs over the side of the bed, stood, and slipped into my robe. All was quiet downstairs. Jack wouldn't be awake for at least another hour. I whipped my hair into a ponytail and padded downstairs, opening the blinds along the stairs as I went. The sky was beginning to lighten ever so slightly, lending a grayish cast in the air. I wasn't a fan of spring storms from fear of breaking branches on trees that leafed early and smashing my already-struggling tulips and daffodils along the front of the house.

I'd forgotten to program my coffee maker last night. After I got it up and going, the machine gurgling and choking to life—sounds letting me know I needed a new one immediately—I picked up my iPad from the kitchen table and hunkered down in my chair. I tucked my legs underneath me and covered up with a gray sherpa throw blanket, cutting the damp morning chill. I logged onto my iPad and into the St. Cloud Times, the front-page headline waking me up quickly. *Police Have Lead in Murder Investigation.*

My breath caught in my throat, and I sat up straight. Had they talked with Connie last night? The article went on to read, *Police caught a break in the murder of a Spirit Lake woman and a Birch Haven man in the vicinity of the Northern Health & Fitness Club. The Public Information Officer couldn't elaborate on what that break might be, claiming it's an open investigation. Stay tuned as Jeremy Turner continues to investigate.*

After scanning it a few more times, I sat back, staring off into nothingness as my mind took a journey of its own, twisting and turning through all the possibilities. When it finally landed again, I shook my head, trying to rid myself of the lingering images of dead bodies that kept popping up faster than I could push them away.

I'd finally snapped myself out of it to realize the coffee pot had stopped. I wrapped the sherpa around my shoulders as I walked to the kitchen. I patted the coffee maker gently, relieved it worked at least today until I could get a new one when I was in town. I poured a mug full and settled in again before going back to the newspaper. I looked at the weather, which claimed the storm should be hitting Birch Haven around five o'clock. Great. Just in time for the drive home. And when Birch Haven got snow, Claire and I usually got hit harder out in the country. I was grateful for the Jeep I'd bought a year and a half ago. The car I had before my Jeep, a snappy little Nissan 370Z, had an unfortunate accident in one of my crime-solving escapades. While I loved that car, it wasn't exactly practical for brutal Minnesota winters. Or even Minnesota springtime, for that matter.

I scanned through the rest, briefly considered doing the crossword puzzle, but I passed. Unless every answer was *dead* or *body*, or anything related, I'd get even the simplest ones wrong today.

I took a sip of coffee. I wanted to call Connie, but it was still too early. If I remembered correctly, she wasn't exactly an early riser. Then another thought occurred to me, and my heart picked up its pace. Maybe she wasn't even home! Was she in jail?

I typed in *Maggie Thompson, Spirit Lake, Minnesota*, and up popped pages of results. The number one hit, though, was about her death. *Margaret Thompson, reporter for Lakes News and Reviews, was found dead in Birch Haven, Minnesota on Thursday morning. Police believe they have a new lead in the case. Ms. Thompson was actively investigating the controversial story of a company accused of polluting several area lakes.* The article went on, but my mind blurred as I began replaying the past couple of days. Something about the name of the publication Maggie worked for—what was it? The writing on the suspected murder weapon flashed through my mind—the writing under the blood. I went upstairs to grab my phone from the charger and pulled up the photos I'd taken at the crime scene.

I zoomed in on the pen and looked closely at the words. Sure enough. Now that I looked at it more closely, I could make out the words *Lakes News and Reviews.* Someone used that specific pen by choice. I was sure of it. Suddenly I believed more than ever that Connie was innocent. I believed this murder went much deeper than a woman's suspicions of her husband cheating. But if the dead man was Connie's husband, were the deaths not related at all? And if that were the case, would two murders a day apart in a small town make sense? Why did he have a key card to the same motel as Maggie or the murderer? Or didn't it belong to either one?

Next, I zoomed in on the photo I took of the open notebook page. With my face an inch away from the screen and stretching the picture as large as possible, I struggled to make out a barely-there imprint from a pen or pencil next to the writing.

My phone rang, and I jumped, stifling a scream. So much for a relaxing morning before heading into work. I looked at the display. Levi.

"Morning, babe," I said.

"Hey. Are you sitting down?"

My mouth felt dry, and I fought a wave of nausea. "I am now. Why do I think I'm not going to like what you have to say?" I held my breath.

"Connie has disappeared."

18

"What do you mean Connie has disappeared?" Trying to keep my voice down so I didn't wake Jack, I vigorously paced the floor.

"Exactly what I said. Detective Walker went to her house to talk with her about something he found, and—"

"He found her fingerprints on a bottle of nail polish at one of the crime scenes, didn't he?"

"How did you know that?" Levi was clearly confused.

"It wasn't hard. I detected it," I said flippantly. I shook my head, clearing the jumbled thoughts. "What did Detective Walker find? Was Connie's husband there?"

"No one was," Levi said.

"Then how do you know she disappeared? Maybe she was sleeping or just didn't answer the door. Maybe she left early to go somewhere. Walker didn't bust it down, did he? That seems like a bit of overkill. Pardon the expression." Possible explanations tumbled out.

"No, he didn't kick it in. This isn't a cop show." I could hear the amusement in his voice. He knew I hardly ever watched TV. "When she didn't answer the door, he spoke with the neighbors who were outside by their car. They said they hadn't seen Connie's husband for a few days. Said they saw Connie leave late last night with two large suitcases."

I sat back down and sighed. *Oh, Connie. What have you gone and gotten yourself into?* "I'll try to call her."

"Walker did. No answer."

"I don't suppose she would answer his call," I said. "But maybe she'll answer mine."

"Let me know."

"I see how you police-type work. You want us to give you information, but you don't like to share with us."

He chuckled. "I share everything with you. Speaking of, what are you doing tonight?"

"Getting snowed in at my house with you?" *Sorry, Daisy.*

"Hmm…" he said. I could hear the mischief in his tone. "I like how my fiancé thinks."

"Yeah?" I grinned. "Me too."

"I'll stop and pick up dinner."

"Don't trust me yet after all this time?"

"I'm not the one with the trust issues," he said.

Touché. "Yowzers! Painful but true. I'm getting better, though. Admit it." I just hoped improving my trust issues didn't take as long as getting better at cooking had.

"You're a work in progress," he said. "But no matter, I love you just the way you are."

"Well, isn't that special," I said, giggling. I thought about Connie and grew serious again. "I have to go so I can call Connie."

"If she shows up at the salon today, I want you to call me immediately, okay?"

"Like she's just going to roll into the salon with her suitcases?"

"Promise me," he insisted.

"Promise. See you this evening."

***

When we hung up, I thought about the request to call him. Not Walker, but *him*. That meant I had to have graduated from a mere ninety-nine percent not-a-suspect to one hundred, or he wouldn't be able to be on the case. I breathed a sigh of relief and smiled.

I hesitated before dialing Connie's number, preparing myself for everything she could potentially tell me, if she answered at all. I finally inhaled deeply, punched in her number, and waited. When it rolled into voicemail, I realized I'd been holding my breath.

"Hey, Connie, this is Mel," I said after the beep. "You probably know why I'm calling. I just wanted to check on you. You know, make sure you're okay. See you at work."

Yeah, right. There was a higher chance of the snowstorm missing us than Connie showing up at work today. My business mind took over. What would we do with her clients? The rest of us had tight schedules the way it was. And Babs was solely a nail tech. No hair cutting or coloring going on there. I'd better get my butt moving and into the salon. I'd been slacking off a bit, distracted with murders and all, and I was eager to get back to a routine. And I needed to check Connie's lineup and reschedule where I could.

I took the steps two at a time, my thigh muscles still rebelling a bit from my halfway workout the other day. By the time I reached my bedroom, I heard Jack in the kitchen.

"Hey, Jack!" I yelled downstairs. "I have to take a shower and head in early. Help yourself to coffee and breakfast." When he didn't answer, I stayed rooted on the top step and yelled, "Jack?"

"Go!" he called back. "I'm going to follow you in. I need to check my inventory at your salon and then head back home before the storm hits."

I had just gotten into the shower when my phone rang, the ring tone telling me it was Nana. She probably wanted me to stay there tonight instead of driving home after work in the snow. I felt a pang of guilt. In my pre-Levi life, I would have stayed with her. And now... well, now things had changed. I didn't see her as much as I used to, and while I knew she was disappointed about that, I also knew she was crazy about Levi and over the moon that I had someone serious in my life. Just maybe, though, she was relieved someone else was putting up with me, so she didn't have to as much. *Nah!* Feeling caught between the two of them, splitting my time, caused me anxiety. Not to mention knowing I should be—and wanted to—spend more time getting to know my brother and niece. And then there was Claire. But I wasn't too worried about her since Sydney and Cole sucked up so much of *her* time. I just missed her.

I rushed through my shower, so much so that I wasn't even sure I'd rinsed out all the shampoo. As I reached for the phone to call my grandmother, it rang, and I startled. I looked at the display to decide whether I wanted to answer or not before calling Nana. I sucked in a breath when I saw the caller ID.

"Connie? Where are you?"

"I won't be in today, Melanie."

"I figured as much." I haphazardly wrapped my hair with a towel and slipped into my robe. "Where are you?" I repeated.

"You're going to hear some things," she said, sounding weirdly flat. "But I'm asking you not to believe them."

"What am I going to hear?" I asked, wondering if she would tell me.

"I didn't kill him, Melanie. I swear, I didn't."

"Is the dead man your husband?"

"Yes. But I didn't do it," she said, a hitch in her voice followed by a slight hiccup.

I frowned. Had she been crying or drinking? "Connie, if you didn't do it, then you need to stay here. Running only makes you look guilty." She sniffled but didn't say anything. "You didn't, did you? Do anything?"

"No."

179

But doesn't everyone say they didn't do it? "Then why are you running?"

Ignoring my question, she hiccupped again. "You can't honestly believe that I would kill him," she finally said in disbelief.

"Of course not," I said, perhaps a little too quickly. "But you need to stay here so the police believe you didn't do it."

"Are you crazy? They're not going to believe me. The spouse is always the first one they look at."

"I'll support you, Connie. I'll tell Levi. He can talk to Detective Walker."

"Did you know he was having an affair? At least I think he was." *Hiccup*. "He was acting suspicious, and I found a motel key card in his pocket."

"When?"

"I don't know when. I've been tailing him for a while on his odd-hour *meetings*." She sniffled again.

"I mean, when did you find the key card?"

"Night before he went missing. He was getting ready to go to one of his *meetings*." She chuckled bitterly. "Yeah, right, a *meeting*. How dumb was I?"

"So, Thursday night?"

"No." Her voice trailed off. "He was gone for a couple of days. I thought he was with *her* the whole time. Now I don't know. Maybe he was out there in the forest. Alone." She started to cry quietly.

"Was the key card for the Rest Awhile Motel?"

The crying stopped, and she gasped, followed by another hiccup. "How did you know that?"

"Connie, have you been drinking?"

"Maybe a little."

"Come back so we can talk." I looked at the clock on my nightstand. "I could meet you at the salon in half an hour. Or I could come to you," I added quickly. The last thing she needed was a DUI. Or worse yet, a crash, injuring herself or someone else.

"Are you kidding? The fact that I suspect he was cheating makes me look all the more guilty. The police will be watching the salon to see if I show up. I'm not stupid."

"I can't help you if you're not here," I pleaded.

"You can't help me no matter where I am, Melanie. Besides, I didn't call for help. I only wanted you to know I wouldn't be into work."

"For how long? How long do you plan to run?"

"However long it takes."

"Did you do a manicure on anyone recently?" I asked.

"One. Last Saturday."

"On who?"

"I don't remember who it was. It was a walk-in, and Babs was booked solid."

"I'll look on the appointment book."

"It wouldn't be on there. I don't always write down walk-ins."

I frowned and shook my head. "But you have to have made some kind of note somewhere. We document *all* of our clients. We require it."

"I didn't see any need to on this one. All she wanted was a polish, and she paid in cash. I was able to fit her in while I had a hair color processing."

I squeezed my eyes shut and pinched the bridge of my nose while I made a mental note to check the bank deposit slip for that day. My towel threatened to fall, and I grasped it tightly, my knuckles turning white. "Do you remember anything about her at all? Anything!"

"Not really."

"Not really?"

"No one I'd seen before. That's all I know."

Andie Rose? But why wouldn't she have Babs do her nails? Or why wouldn't she do her own, for that matter? Especially if it was just a polish. So many questions to which I needed answers.

"Connie, have you met Babs' cousin, Andie Rose?"

"A long time ago. I think I saw them out shopping once. Why? What does that have to do with any of this?" Another hiccup.

"No more drinking, okay? Promise me that."

"The bottle's gone anyway."

"The bottle or the liquor in it?" I asked with a shake of my head.

"Both."

I sighed. She was going to bury herself right along with her husband. Joined together in life and death. "Could Andie Rose be the one who came in? The one whose nails you polished last Saturday?"

She was quiet for a moment, making me wonder if she'd hung up. "No. No, I don't think so."

"Was Babs at the salon at the time?"

"Yes. I already told you that. She was booked, remember? But it wasn't her, Melanie. I'm telling you. This woman looked nothing like what I remember Andie Rose looking like. I have to go."

Yeah, I remembered all right, but I had to make sure, given her current mental state. If Babs had been in the salon, she and Andie would have talked, and it would have gotten my attention. I, too, was now convinced it wasn't her. But who was it? Despite claiming she had to go, she still hadn't hung up, and I fretted over what I could say or do to keep her here.

"What did she look like? Can you describe her to me?"

My heart felt heavy as I listened carefully to a noise in the background. What was that? People were talking, but there was a squeal, a screech, then a voice over what sounded like an intercom saying, "The bus to Santa Fe will be leaving in ten minutes. Please report to your gate."

"Are you going to Santa Fe, Connie?"

"My sister lives there."

"What about your husband?"

183

"Paul wanted to be cremated when he died. I've made the arrangements to have that take place, and I'll have a memorial for him later."

"There's nothing I can say to convince you to stay?"

"No. Goodbye, Melanie."

"Wait!" I said, but it was too late. "What color was the polish?" I muttered to the dead phone line, feeling dejected. I stood still, staring at the phone in my hand. Her goodbye sounded sad.

"Hey!" Jack called upstairs. "Let's get a move on! I thought you wanted to be early."

I poked my head around the corner and down the stairs. "You go on ahead. You have the key. I'll meet you there."

"Your call," he said. "See you there." I wanted to tell Jack about the phone call, but with my hair still wrapped in a towel and the rest of me nearly naked—well, it wasn't exactly the time. I didn't want to put the poor guy through that. And he was in a hurry to get a jump start on the weather. I'd fill him in at the salon if he had time.

I heard the door close downstairs. I listened for the key to turn in the lock. When I heard it click into place, I rushed through the motions of drying my hair, applying light makeup, and getting dressed, all the while replaying Connie's phone call over and over. If she was innocent, as she claimed, what was her rush in getting out of town? And why wouldn't she stick around to see to Paul's cremation? Innocent or not, it all seemed a bit suspect. It wasn't like Connie to just up and leave her job. Heck, nothing about this was anything like the Connie I knew. I'd realized I'd forgotten to ask if she contacted any of her clients. I punched the last number called. An automated recording said, "You have reached a number that has been changed, disconnected, or is no longer in service. If you feel you have reached this recording in error, please hang up and try again." So I did. I got the same message.

"Oh, Connie," I said and exhaled slowly. "I'm afraid this doesn't look good for you."

I took a deep breath, looked at the clock, and high-tailed it downstairs. After pouring a cup of coffee in a travel mug—from the coffee pot that had gurgled its last dying breath—and slipping into a pair of high-heeled black boots, I grabbed my jacket and purse off the chair and headed to the salon.

19

As I crossed the front yard to my garage, I looked off in the distance to the north. The clouds were gathering, and a slight northeast wind chilled me to the bone. At least, I think it was the wind. I closed my car door and started the engine, staying put a moment while I examined every angle of my conversation with Connie. Initially, I'd been certain that she wasn't the killer, but people can snap under these circumstances. Had Connie? Had we all been working at the salon with a murderer? Given my history with dead bodies and suspicion swirling around me with a couple of them, she probably worried about the same thing. But deep in my heart, I refused to believe Connie could be capable of murder. I had to find something that cleared her. And to do that, I couldn't tell Levi yet until I'd had some time. Whether she decided to come back to Birch Haven or even to A Cut Above, I had to do this not only for her but for my own peace of mind.

I cruised the back road that led to the highway, trying to recall even the smallest detail that could clear her. It sure would have been easier had she not abruptly up and left, something a guilty person would do. "Think, Melanie. Think!" I grumbled. Andie Rose had found Paul's body, and though I was no expert, it looked to me like he wasn't murdered just that morning, but that he'd been there for a while. By the smell, if nothing else. A couple of days prior? A light layer of frost blanketed his body as well as the rock, but not enough to conceal the red nail polish spelling the word *Jerk* written on it. Also, no visible fingerprints had melted the frost on the rock for it to have happened this morning. Without touching the body, I could tell he was stiff. I'd once heard rigor mortis could remain for up to thirty-six hours—disturbing, at the least, that I remembered that fact—and Connie said her husband had been gone for a couple of days. He could have potentially been lying out there, dead, while someone else killed Maggie.

Relief that it wasn't Andie Rose, and shame that I had even considered her to begin with, mixed together like salt and warm water. But at this point, I was eyeballing everyone in the vicinity of the victims when they were killed. Unfortunately, Connie had the biggest motive, especially if Paul was having an affair. Even more so if it was with Maggie Thompson. But Connie wouldn't be at the gym. Unless it was a middle-of-the-night thing? But how could she have gotten in without a membership card?

From the corner of my eye, I saw quick movement, and I swerved to miss hitting a deer, nearly sideswiping a car that was passing me. What I didn't miss was the one-finger salute the driver flipped my way. *Sheesh!* "Keep your mind on the road, Hogan," I scolded myself.

I pulled over briefly to recompose myself and remained there a moment while I tried to put myself back at the crime scene in the locker room. I mentally retraced my steps. There were drops of coffee by Maggie's body. The kid working at the gym's front desk had a cup of coffee on the counter in front of him. I saw no one else had coffee, nor could I imagine anyone bringing coffee to a gym. Coffee wasn't your typical workout beverage. Maybe before heading to the gym, a little caffeine for an added energy kick, but not during a workout. He had to have been one of the only people, if not *the* only one, with coffee the morning in question. Hmm. Maybe I would go to the gym again after all, even if it wasn't to work out. I'd seen that particular kid there on several occasions. It wouldn't be out of the question to find him if I ran by this morning on my way to the salon.

When I got into town, I turned toward the gym. The parking lot was packed. Apparently, this was the prime time for people to get in their daily exercise on a Saturday. I had to park in *Timbuktu*, as my grandmother used to say. When I neared the door, I looked through the window at the front desk. Luck was on my side. The same kid was sitting on the counter, hunch-backed, his back to the gym, as he talked with a teenage girl. I strode up to them, and the boy jumped off the counter and turned toward me, pointing at the scanner for my card, stopping short when he recognized me.

"I'm not here to work out," I said. "I just have a question."

"Want a pamphlet?" said the girl. She reached toward the back counter.

"No," said the kid, "she's been here before."

For the life of me, I couldn't remember his name. I was a little distracted by a dead body, not his name, and the badge on his shirt wasn't visible. "I'm sorry, what's your name again?"

"Sean."

"Yeah, that's right." I looked at the girl. "I already have a membership."

"This is the lady who found the dead body. The one the cops are looking at."

The girl's eyebrows shot up, and her hand jetted beneath the counter.

I immediately thrust my hand forward before she could hit the assumed panic button. "No, they're not." I glared at Sean. "I have a solid alibi. What about you?"

His hands came up, palms facing me, as he turned his head slightly, still looking at me. "I didn't do nothin'. I was right here—"

"Busy, I know." I rolled my eyes. "I noticed you were drinking coffee that morning, and—"

"Me?" he said, his thumb pointed at his chest. "I don't drink coffee. I can't stand the stuff."

"But there was a coffee cup on the counter. Right here." I pointed to the spot in which I remembered seeing it.

"Nah, wasn't mine. Someone else had it when they came in. They musta left it here on their way through."

"Do you know who it was?"

He shrugged. "No. I wasn't paying that much attention because I was—"

"Busy," I interrupted. "Yeah, I know."

His eyes opened in relief that I would understand his pain, and the wall he built between us vanished. He leaned over the desk, forearms resting on the counter. "I thought it was kind of weird, though. I mean, who brings coffee to the gym?"

"My thoughts exactly," I murmured. *So much for being too busy to notice.* I had a hunch this kid knew more than he was letting on. "Did the police take the cup?"

"No. Why would they?"

"No reason."

"I dumped it. Coffee and all."

Disappointment nipped at me. I'm not sure why. What else would I have expected? That he kept the cup as a souvenir? I tapped my knuckles on the countertop and said, "Hey, thanks for your help. Sean," I added with a smile, covering my bases. I may need to ask more questions and would have more luck with the invisible wall down than up.

"Sure." He turned toward the girl again.

When I reached the door, I pivoted and went back to the desk. "Just one more question. How often does your garbage get emptied here?"

"We take it out every day," said the girl. "Sometimes twice, depending on how busy it is."

"I meant, how often does the garbage truck come to get the trash from the dumpster out back?" I remembered seeing a gigantic green dumpster in an enclosure behind the enormous building.

"Every Monday morning. Why?"

"No reason," I said with another smile. "You guys have a good day."

While walking to my car, I formulated a plan. Now just to see if I could bribe anyone into coming with me.

***

When I got to the salon, Jack was just finishing up. "What took you so long?" he asked. "It's not like you're a primper."

I stopped and stared at him for a second, cocking my head to the side. "I'm not sure how to take that."

He rolled his eyes and let out a breath. "Don't read into it, Hogan. It's just that you don't usually take a long time getting ready. I thought you'd have been here a long time ago."

"I made a detour on my way in."

"Do I want to ask where?"

"The gym."

He frowned. "You went to work out? I thought you didn't want to go there anymore."

"Not to work out. And I hadn't planned to stop this morning, either. Until I had a thought and decided to visit Sean, the front desk kid."

He eyed me suspiciously. "Melanie?" he said slowly.

"I have to go through their trash tonight. The dumpster is behind their building and in an enclosure, so no one will see me. Especially if it's snowing. No one will be out. Want to come with me?"

Now he looked at me as if I'd lost my mind completely. "Oh, yes, because digging through a dumpster in the middle of a snowstorm sounds like the time of my life. No!" he said a bit too forcefully.

"That's a hard no, then, or is there wiggle room?" I asked.

"A hard, loud, resounding no. And you're crazy if you do."

"They close earlier on Saturdays, so I can swing by on my way home from work."

"I thought they were open twenty-four-seven," Jack said.

"Not the staff; they have set hours. And if there's a snowstorm tonight, they'll either close entirely or no one will be working out anyway."

"What are you looking for?" he asked, still looking as if he was planning to call and have me committed to the loony bin at any moment.

"I think the killer may have tried to set up Sean, the front desk kid. There were a few drops of spilled coffee at the crime scene and a cup of coffee sitting on the front desk when I left. No one brings coffee to a gym for working out. The kid at the desk said he doesn't drink coffee and that someone left it there."

"And you're going to believe him? What's gotten into you?"

"Jack, if this isn't Levi's case and the police missed that, how can we count on them to clear Connie? We can't." I went on to tell him about the conversation I had with Connie just that morning when she called. When I finished, he stared at me slack-jawed.

"Melanie, Connie is burying herself too deep for you to rescue. You cannot save everyone."

"She's scared, Jack. I just know that's all it is. I know Connie."

"Do you?" he asked incredulously. "Listen to yourself. It sounds to me like you're willing to do everything to help someone who's doing nothing to help herself. How does that make sense?"

I'm not sure I'd ever seen Jack so upset with me. It stung. "Jack—"

"What's going on?" Claire asked. I hadn't even heard her come in.

"Melanie is up to one of her idiotic schemes. This time she's gone over the top."

Claire was taken aback. "Melanie?" she asked hesitantly. "What have you done?"

"Nothing yet." I filled her in on my plans after work. "I want to help Connie, Claire. And I completely believe the two murders are connected."

"Which could be good or bad for Connie," Jack said. "If her husband was having an affair like she suspected, and the dead woman is the *other* woman, then Connie's in a vat of hot water."

"Unless I can prove someone else killed Maggie. Keeping the innocent kid at the front desk from taking the blame is added incentive."

"Stop being the savior, Melanie. You know what Levi would tell you, don't you? You know he'd not only say no but hell no."

"I'll go with you," Claire blurted, stunning both Jack and me into silence.

20

I thought I was going to fall over. My eyes grew huge. "You'll what?" I finally said. I totally hadn't expected her to volunteer for this job. Jack's silence and the look he gave Claire told me he hadn't either.

"No," Jack said. "Neither one of you is thinking clearly."

"Oh, Jacky," I said, "You know what happens when someone tells me no." I gave him a coy look.

"Ladies, please. Get some common sense here. Going through garbage?" he squawked. "How low can you go?"

"If it helps clear Connie, it's worth it," I said.

"That's why I agreed to help," Claire said. "I can't believe that the woman we've worked side by side with for years is capable of murder."

"In all fairness, Claire," Jack said, "and I don't mean this negatively, but you wouldn't believe *anyone* is capable of murder, even if they've been tried and convicted."

"This is different," Claire said. "It's Connie."

"And for goodness sakes, Jack, it's not like we're going to be dining on the garbage. I just need to find the bag with the coffee cup in it. Easy-peasy. He said he dumped the coffee in the bag along with the cup. The bags are clear. I checked when I was there this morning." I looked at Claire.

"I need to be home before seven because Levi's coming over. If we can't find it quick-like, we can leave."

"Okay," she said. "Tyler's folks are still here, so I'm in no rush."

I finished filling Claire in on Connie's phone call. "I know I don't know Connie super well, even after all the years she's worked for us," I said, "but other than being completely trashed, she sounded kind of off. Like not herself at all. I'm not sure if she's spooked about something, devastated at the loss of her husband—I mean, come on." I put my hands out, palms in the air. "Even if he was having an affair, the guy is dead—someone she loved. Or loves," I said. "I can't imagine what she must be going through."

"I can," Claire said so quietly I almost didn't hear her.

"Oh, man, Claire, I'm so sorry," I said.

"Tyler didn't have an affair, but his death still affects me to this day."

"I know." I put an arm around her and squeezed. I looked at Jack, who silently took in the exchange between Claire and me. I could tell he was softening a bit, though.

I walked behind the desk and looked at the appointment calendar. "I don't know how we're going to take care of Connie's clients if she didn't contact them. We're booked all day."

Claire looked over my shoulder at the schedule. "I wouldn't be surprised if some cancel later in the day because of the weather, but that doesn't help us for the morning and early afternoon.

I tapped the appointment book in two places. "I can squeeze in these two. They're during chemicals I've got going on. I'm already doing a haircut during the processing time of each one, but I can try to squeeze in one more. There may be someone who has to wait a bit, but..."

"Just make sure it's not a chemical client left waiting," Claire said. We both groaned at the memory. One of our prior stylists left bleach too long on a client's hair while she went outside to have a cigarette, where the stylist then saw the cute delivery guy and got to talking. We were all too busy to notice what one another was doing. The client left with an exceptionally short haircut and sugar-white hair.

Claire studied the schedule and pointed to a couple of them. "I can get these two." She tapped one of the names. "I think this one's a kid. A standard little boy's cut. It'll go quick."

"I wish Babs had her hair license," I said, still studying the book. "Maybe Rubie can squeeze in one or two. The problem is we won't know who, or if, Connie called until they come in or not." I looked at my phone in case Connie had called and left me a message. No luck.

"Here comes Rubie," Jack said.

He'd been so quiet I almost forgot he was still there.

"Hey ya'll," Rubie called as she opened the door. "Geez! Why so grim? Who died?" She quickly added, "Ew! Bad question to ask around here." She looked from me to

Claire to Jack. She wasn't wearing pink today, a rare occurrence. She had on a pair of red jeans with red boots and a waist-length soft white sweater. She carried an umbrella at her side. She must have seen me look at it. "In case it's snowing when we leave," she said, holding the umbrella up then dropping it back down by her side. "Why all the serious faces?"

I filled her in on Connie's phone call. "So, we were trying to figure out who we can fit into our already packed schedules and who we will need to reschedule. I don't see that any of us can fit in her two hair color clients or her perm."

Rubie scrunched up her face. "Or if we reschedule them. After today, I mean. From what I understand, we don't know when, or even if, she's coming back."

"Precisely," I said, tapping a pencil on the appointment book as I studied it again.

"I curse the fact that she put us in this position at all," Rubie grumbled, her high mood plummeting. "I like Connie, and I empathize with her, but this was irresponsible."

I sighed. I couldn't agree with her more.

"Well, I say instead of getting into a tizzy about it yet," Claire said, "let's wait and see if these people show up or not. She may have called them, and it won't be a problem at all."

"Just wait and see?" I almost shivered. That went against everything I was. I was a planner to the core. *Waiting to see* wasn't something I could do easily.

"You can go ahead and plan all you want, Melanie, but you might be wasting a whole lot of time." She patted my back. "You can do it. Live dangerously."

"You're patronizing me." I narrowed my eyes at her. "My planning has saved our butts more than a few times."

"And *waiting to see* has served us well a time or two as well, if I remember correctly."

"I'm with Claire on this one," Jack said.

His silence was throwing me off. "Jack?"

"Melanie?" he said, meeting my eyes.

"You're mad at me, aren't you?"

"Why is he mad at you?" Rubie asked.

"I'm not mad," he said with a sigh. "Just frustrated. Oh, so frustrated." He rubbed the back of his neck, his other hand tucked in the front pocket of his perfectly pressed jeans.

"Is anyone going to tell me what's going on?" Rubie asked, looking from me to Jack.

"Here comes Babs," Claire said.

Saved! I didn't want Rubie any more involved than she already was.

"Are we letting her know about Connie?" Claire asked me.

I shook my head. "I don't think so. Connie's not here anyway, so in the worst-case scenario, Bab's isn't in any danger. And I think spreading it beyond these walls isn't a good idea. I don't want to put Babs in the position of keeping something from Andie Rose."

"Why would she have to?" Claire asked.

We watched in silence as Babs stopped to hug someone. She laughed, listened to something the person said, laughed again, and once more started toward the door.

"What are we going to say?" Rubie asked.

Claire and I looked at each other as Babs pulled the door open.

"Hey, Babs," Claire said. "Connie won't be in today."

Today? I shot Claire a look.

"Okay," Babs said as she headed toward the back room to drop off her jacket. "Is everything okay?"

"I'm not sure," I said. Which wasn't a lie. I *wasn't* sure. "I hope so." Again, not a lie. I *did* hope so.

When Babs was out of the room, I looked at Claire and whispered, "Connie won't be in *today*? How are you going to explain tomorrow, the next day, and the day after that?"

She smiled and gave me a side hug. "A day at a time, my friend."

***

Jack was eerily silent the rest of the time he was there and left shortly after the whole exchange about Connie. He hugged Claire, then Rubie, and finally me, kissing the top of my head.

"Love ya, kiddo. I'm just pretty ticked with you right now."

"I know," I said. "And I'm sorry. But I hope you can try to understand."

"Yeah." He shook his head and waved over his shoulder. "I'll work on that."

Once clients began coming in, work was back to usual. The flurry of activity occupied our minds, the salon humming with chatting, laughing, blow dryers, stationary dryers, and water running. We'd discovered Connie hadn't called her clients, so Claire, Rubie, and I fit those in who we could, rescheduling those we couldn't, letting them know we weren't a hundred percent sure when Connie was able to return. *It's a personal matter I'm not at liberty to discuss. Yes, I sure will give her your best. Thank you, she will appreciate your prayers.* And on and on.

At twelve-thirty, I turned to see Andie Rose through the haze of hairspray. With her was one of the trio we'd met in the locker room at the gym the morning of our investigation. I racked my brain, trying to remember her name. *Natalie!*

"Hey!" I called to them, smiling. "What brings you guys in here?"

"We heard A Cut Above is the happenin' place of Birch Haven," Andie Rose said, grinning.

"Yeah?" Rubie said. "Well, whoever said that knows what they're talking about."

I spun my client around in the chair to face them. "Judy, this is Andie Rose, Babs' cousin. And Natalie."

"Hi, girls," Judy said.

It was a happy, joyous time, and our woes about Connie were all but forgotten for the moment. Until it wasn't.

"Where's Connie?" Natalie said.

"You know Connie?" I asked, surprised.

"Natalie and I were at the gym at the same time again this morning," Andie Rose said. "We started talking and decided to go to lunch today since we're both women of leisure for another week or so."

"Andie Rose filled me in about that guy," Natalie said, shivering. "Two in two days? Horrible!" She shuddered again, then said, "Sorry. But blood, death—" She grimaced. "I'm not sure I can go back there after today."

I shook my head. "That's what I decided too."

"What happened?" Judy asked over the buzz of the blow dryer.

"Long story," I said, turning her chair to the side. I looked at Natalie and discreetly shook my head.

"Are you referring to the murders?" Judy's voice rose above the buzz. "Why, we've nicknamed them the Birch Haven Murders and are waiting for one of those true-crime TV shows to pick it up."

"We? Who's we?" I asked, turning off the blow dryer momentarily and turning her toward me.

"Good heavens, dear, the whole town knows about those. This is Birch Haven, after all. We look after one another here. I must say," she added in a quieter tone as if she were telling me a secret, "none of us are surprised that you're right in the middle of it, dontcha know." My cheeks felt on fire, and I froze in place.

She reached for the hand holding the blow dryer. "Goodness sakes, I'm afraid I've said too much." Her eyes softened. "No one is blaming you, it's just that...well, you do seem to find yourself in some, shall we say, *egregious* situations."

The salon was silent, all attention on us. Finally, I stammered, "I—well—I—I don't even know what to say to that."

"Well, I can say you should hold your head high, and the town owes you because you've helped the police find the killer in every one of them," Claire said, winking at me.

Thank God for my bestie. That's all it took to break the proverbial ice before the salon action began again. But I couldn't shake the weight in my chest. I wasn't comfortable in the spotlight. At all. It went against my nature. *The whole town?* I glanced around, not a single person the least bit interested in me, not even Judy, who was talking on her phone—loudly—to someone about dinner that night. I took a deep breath. I needed to end this whole thing—quickly.

Babs looked up from the acrylic nails she was applying and glanced at Andie Rose. "I'll be done in about ten minutes. You guys want to hang around and wait? There are some magazines over there." She pointed toward the waiting room in the corner.

Natalie tucked a strand of hair behind her ear, and I froze for a moment before quickly finishing up Judy's blow-dry, spraying it in place, and whisking off her cape. I turned the chair so she faced the desk, waited for her to stand and stretch out her back, then followed her to the desk. I rang her up and got her jacket for her, helping her into it.

With a brief hug, she said quietly, "Don't you go letting anyone else take you down, honey. You keep on solving these murders so Birch Haven can be safe again." A last squeeze and she was out the door.

It would have made me feel better, but I didn't want to keep solving these murders. I wanted my humdrum life back that I'd had prior to longing for excitement. But I'd never think of it as humdrum ever again.

While my next client looked at some product on the shelves, reading the back of a bottle carefully before picking up another, I took advantage of the extra minute.

I walked over to the waiting area where Andie Rose and Natalie chatted up a storm.

"Natalie, that's a beautiful color of polish on your nails. What's the name of the color?"

She smiled with red lips and held out her hand, studying her nails. "Hm. You know? I'm not sure. I remember it had a weird name."

"Russian Red My Mind?" I asked.

She stuck her finger in the air. "Yes! That's what it was. I remember thinking, Geez! Who names these things?" She laughed.

"Did Babs polish them for you?"

"No, no. It was last Saturday, and she was gone or busy. I don't remember which. Heck, I can't remember what I did yesterday. And I'm not even old yet." She shook her head slowly and exhaled. "But that's how I met Connie. She did them for me."

My next client strolled over to the waiting area, the bottle she'd evidently settled on in her hand.

"I would sure like to use that color," I said, "but I can't seem to find it on the shelf." *Like I'd ever wear red. Now, black, on the other hand…*

"Oh!" Natalie said. "That's probably because Connie loved the color so much, she decided to take it home and do her own. She said she would bring it back in when she was done. Said it was one of the perks of the job."

21

Natalie's revelation about Connie taking the nail polish replayed in my mind over and over. But somehow, I still couldn't get my head around the fact that she would be capable of murder.

Our last clients across the board had canceled earlier in the day in anticipation of the incoming weather, except for Rubie's. She had a five o'clock who kept her appointment because she was getting married that evening—a private ceremony with only a few friends at her house. Most women loved a big wedding, but I thought it sounded perfect when Rubie described her client's plans.

Babs volunteered to stay with her until she finished. None of us particularly liked staying alone after dark. And while it wasn't dark by five o'clock at this time of the year, Babs still insisted on staying. Given the fact that Connie was a suspect in a murder, and we weren't positive she'd left town at all or just wanted us to believe she did, neither Claire nor I argued. And Rubie, having the same knowledge we did, certainly didn't object. We hadn't disclosed why we were leaving early, and no one asked, probably assuming it was weather-related. It was unusual that Claire and I went before everyone else. In fact, I'm not sure it ever had happened. It was possible, I supposed, that they didn't ask because they didn't want the answer.

Especially when I grabbed the folding step stool from the closet on our way out the door.

I'd called the gym earlier to get a handle on their plans for the day with the incoming storm.

"Looks like we're going to get hit, so we're closing early," the person had said.

"How early?" I'd asked.

"Four."

"Well, darn," I'd said, not wanting to make him suspicious. "Will I still be able to get in with my card?"

"You won't want to be traveling in this, miss. It's supposed to be bad."

"But I can, if I wanted to, right?"

The kid probably thought I was a few cards short of a full deck.

"No. We're shutting everything up tight. Staff has to stay to clean and pick up, but we'll be gone by five at the latest." He cleared his throat. "If you're that desperate to use the facility, you'll wanna be here no later than two-thirty. And since it's already two twenty-five, you might want to skip it today."

Smart alec. "Gotcha. Thanks, anyway."

We figured taking one car was best. We took my car, not wanting Claire's vehicle caught on any security cams should this plan go awry. I was already involved, whether I liked it or not.

"What's the plan?" Claire asked.

"I'll look through the trash while you stand guard," I said.

"Even on the top step of that stool, you'll never be able to see in there, much less go through the bags. How about I do that part?"

I looked at her legs. "Yeah, right. You have a mini skirt on."

She stuck out a leg. "With leggings and boots. Besides, it's not like anyone else will be out there. If they were, we wouldn't be doing this."

"So, you're just going to let your tush hang out there? You'll freeze."

She laughed. "It's not that cold yet. I think everyone is overreacting. I don't know how it will snow when the temps are above freezing. We'll probably just get rain."

"Still," I said, "I think I should be the one to do the dirty work. I've got jeans on."

"When *don't* you have jeans on?" she said.

"Hey, now. Be nice."

"I'm just saying, would wearing a dress now and then kill you?"

"You wear enough for both of us."

***

We turned the corner into the gym to find two cars left in the whole parking lot—a black sporty-looking thing and an old beater with a cracked windshield that looked like it probably didn't even run. They were both parked at the back of the lot. I drove in front of the doors. All the lights were off, and it looked empty.

"Doesn't look like they're from the gym," I said. "It's closed up." I turned on my wipers as it began drizzling. "Sure you want to do this?" I asked her. "I wouldn't blame you if you wanted to wait in the car. You could keep watch from there."

"And what, blow the horn if someone's coming?" She snickered. "I told you I would do this with you, and I'm doing it."

I squinted at her. "I know. Which is still confusing me. You hate to join in on my murder-solving escapades. And Jack," I exclaimed, rolling my eyes. "I've never seen him so outraged."

"It's Jack," Claire said. "I don't know why you're so surprised." She chuckled. "Frankly, I don't know why *he* was surprised." She shrugged. "It might be as simple as he doesn't like to be dirty, so the thought of us digging in garbage made him break out in hives."

I looked at her and narrowed an eye. "Who are you, and what have you done with my best friend?"

She laughed. "What are you talking about?"

I shook my head. "Another time. Let's get this going so we can get out of here." I pulled around back and tucked my Jeep between a corner of the building and behind the dumpster. "This spot was made just for this," I said.

"Yeah, but so much for a quick getaway if we get caught."

I looked up, scanning for security cameras. "There's a camera up there," I said, pointing, "but who knows if it even works. Levi said it's frustrating to them when they're trying to get footage. Most businesses' cameras don't work. Besides, no one will be looking at them if we don't give them a reason to." I glanced around. "No one can see my car, and it's not like someone's going to say, 'Hey, let's go hang out at the dumpster.'"

"Except for us," she said.

I slipped on a pair of rubber gloves and handed her a pair. "Here."

"Man, you came prepared. Not that I'm complaining," she added quickly.

I opened my door. "Here goes nothin'."

Claire and I hoisted up the cover from one side of the dumpster. It slipped from our hands and slammed loud against the back, echoing in the otherwise silence. Something scurried out from underneath, brushing against my leg, and apparently Claire's too. We both screamed, then cringed and stood deathly still as if that would prevent someone from hearing. A cat stood rooted in place as if too spooked to move. "What are you looking at," I said to it in a harsh whisper. "You're the one who gave us a heart attack. Shoo!" I waved my hand at it, and finally, it skittered over toward my Jeep.

"Poor thing!" Claire crooned. "What if it doesn't have anywhere to go and gets stuck in this weather?"

"Claire, I love your soft heart, but can you put it on hold until later? Please."

When we were sure no one heard all the commotion, I set up the step stool. Claire put her foot on the bottom step.

I placed my hand on her arm. "No, I can't let you do that. I'll do the dirty work. You stand guard."

I climbed the step stool and swung one leg over the edge of the dumpster. Even though I had sunk so low as to dumpster dive, I was grateful the gym didn't share a can with a restaurant. The smell wasn't unbearable. Bad enough, but not intolerable. Leaning over into it, I started picking up bags, shining the flashlight on my phone to better see through the plastic. I held up each bag, tossing aside the ones I was sure didn't contain the evidence in question. When I couldn't reach the bags anymore, I swung the other leg over, my bottom resting on the edge.

"What are you doing?" Claire said in a harsh whisper.

"What I never in my life thought I'd do." I shuddered, then hopped down.

"How are you going to get back out?" she whispered, peering over the top.

"Hm." I looked around me then up at her. "Hadn't thought that far ahead." Unusual for me, for sure. I looked around me, then got down to business so I could get the heck out of there.

"Melanie!" Claire's tone alerted me to something I was sure I didn't want to hear. "Someone's coming!"

I stood utterly still and heard two voices in the distance getting closer. "Claire! Help me out of here!" I said in a hushed tone, hoping she could hear me.

"Too late," she said. "Hide."

Hide?! Where does one hide in a dumpster? Claire tapped on the back of the metal, letting me know she was still there. At least I hoped that it was Claire.

"What the heck is the dumpster doing open?" It was Sean.

Another kid said, the voice I recognized from the earlier phone call, "Someone probably dumped something in here and left it open." A bag came hurtling over the edge, followed by a piece of chewed gum that missed my hair by a breath. I shuddered.

"Good thing I brought the booze to stay late," Sean said. "If this woulda stayed open all night, we'd a been in so much trouble, dude."

Like drinking on the premises when you're all of maybe eighteen wouldn't? They needed to hurry and leave. If I had to stay under the bags one more second, I thought I might puke. Thank the good Lord I'd felt better today. Earlier, anyway.

The top slammed closed, and I gasped. *No!* Panic began to rise in my throat, my chest felt heavy, and I was sure I would be in a full-blown panic attack at any moment. I listened as their voices retreated, the blood pulsing in my ears as I struggled to remain calm. *Think of Nana, think of Levi.*

Finally, after what felt like hours, the top opened back up, and I heard Claire's voice. I burst through the bags and to the top, taking in a big gulp of air. "Get me out! Get me out!" I cried. "Ew! Ew! Ew!" I tossed one of the bags out of the dumpster, then piled bags on top of one another, swung one leg over the edge, then the other. I jumped down and shuddered.

"Melanie, I'm so sorry," Claire said, picking something out of my hair.

I shuddered again. "I curse the breath I used to voice this stupid idea."

Claire pointed to the bag on the ground. "Why did you throw that one out? Did you find something?"

"I had the flashlight on from my phone app. That's the bag in question. I'm sure of it." I grabbed hold of it and began toward my car. "Can you grab the step stool?"

She scrambled to fold it up and was by my side. "Where are you taking the bag?"

"I'll look through it at home."

"But what if it's not the one?"

"I am not getting back in there," I said, pointing to the dumpster as if it was alive. "Man, I can't wait to take a shower." I held my hand out, palm toward the sky, and turned my face up. "Maybe I'll stand here in the drizzle for a while."

"You'll catch your death," she scolded as if I was Sydney. "It's more like sleet now. Come on. Let's go to the salon to get my car. But will you be okay to drive home from there? I can give you a ride if you need me to, and we can come back in tomorrow to get your car."

"No, I'm good. I'll just never be able to get near a dumpster again without having a panic attack."

She picked at my hair some more. "Come on."

***

I called Nana on my way home. Her voice calmed my frayed nerves. I pictured her in my mind, a long silver braid hanging down her back, blue eyes crinkled at the corners, the slightest hint of pink in her cheeks, and a small smile on her lips. I imagined the smell of her kitchen, the perpetual smell of bread baking in the oven. Through the years, she'd baked so many loaves it was as if the scent permeated the walls and furniture.

The sleet mixed with soft flakes, each shape mesmerizing me before it melted and squiggled its way down my windshield. But by the time I was halfway home, the beautiful flakes gave way to all sleet, and the roads were beginning to freeze over. Blue and amber lights blinked on snowplows spreading sand on the streets. I'd hoped we were done with the snow for the season. I had summer fever something horrible. But having lived in Minnesota all my life, I'd learned always to expect the last gasp of winter.

The lights glowed through the kitchen window when I pulled into my driveway. Levi was already there. I pulled into my garage next to his car and took a moment to brace myself for the questions I knew would come when he saw me carrying a bag of garbage. And when he saw the state I was in. *Slow inhale, slow exhale. Slow inhale, slow exhale.*

As soon as I opened the front door, he looked up from where he sat at the kitchen table, a file of paperwork open in front of him. At first, he didn't say anything, he just looked at me, taking all of me in, and finally, he looked at the bag in my hand. He frowned.

"Do I even want to ask?"

"I thought it might be a fine night to do some dumpster diving." I held up the bag. "Dinner?"

22

I was plumb exhausted *before* I started into the story of what had all transpired that evening, and even more so by the time I finished. Levi simply stared at me, apparently not knowing what to say—or maybe trying to decide if he *should* say what he wanted to say.

Finally, he spoke. "I think this was the craziest thing you've done yet." He looked half amused. He'd gotten so used to these escapades of mine that he wasn't even surprised anymore. "I don't even know what to say, except maybe a shower is a good idea." He pinched his nose with his thumb and forefinger.

I held up the garbage bag. "You don't want dinner first?"

"How about we eat what I brought instead."

I shrugged. "If you insist. But we might be missing out."

He shook his head. "Somehow, I doubt that."

"All right then. I'll go take a shower and be back down in a minute."

"Take a few minutes. One might not be enough."

"Good thing I love you," I called over my shoulder.

"Ditto!"

My legs were so heavy I had all I could do to make it up the stairs to the loft. I was dying to lie down for just two minutes but didn't want any part of my clothes to touch anything in my room.

I stripped out of the stinking clothes and put them in a plastic bag I'd snagged from my pantry. Ironically, these clothes were going back in the garbage, not in my washing machine. I stepped into the shower, letting the steaming hot water relax every inch of my body. I washed my hair, lathered lavender-scented body wash on a loofah, and scrubbed off all memories of getting shut in the dumpster. When I finally felt human again, I toweled off and slipped into a pair of yoga pants and a long-sleeved T. I looked at my bed. It was calling my name, beckoning me. And I couldn't resist. *For just one minute*, I thought. I sprawled across the bed on my stomach and slipped my forearm under my cheek, and it was lights out.

The next thing I remember was Levi's soft voice in my ear, his hand caressing my cheek.

"Hey, blondie."

I opened one eye and looked at him through a sleepy fog. He began covering me with a soft sherpa blanket. I rolled over onto my back, and he lay beside me, his head next to mine. We looked up through the skylight, thick flakes floating down, coming to rest on the glass. It felt like we were in a snow globe, and it was the most beautiful, peaceful feeling I'd had in a long time. My heart swelled, and I felt emotions at the back of my throat. I'd never thought I'd feel this again with a man. Levi's breathing was slow and easy next to me.

"What time is it?" I asked, my voice an insult to the silence of the room.

"Eight-thirty." His voice was little more than a whisper.

I looked over at him. "Did you eat?"

"No. I wanted to wait for you. When I realized it was too quiet up here, I came to check on you."

I smiled at him and touched his face gently. "Because I'm usually not quiet?"

He lifted himself on one elbow and looked down at me. "I'm worried about you. I think you should go see a doctor."

"Because I was quiet?" I raised an eyebrow.

"I'm serious. You've been tired for a while now. When was your last physical?"

I looked back up through the skylight and tried to remember. "Hm. I'm not sure. About six years ago, maybe?"

"Six *years*?" he said in disbelief.

I'd been putting off going to the doctor for reasons I hadn't shared with anyone, not even Claire. Violet had been gone from my life and Nana's for so long that neither of us really knew her entire medical history. She could have developed anything, for all I knew. And I knew nothing at all of my birth father's history. I didn't know what kind of hereditary medical monsters might get me. I pushed it from my mind.

"I've been eating terribly lately. Not to mention burning the candle at both ends. It's no wonder I'm tired. And tonight, I got closed in a dumpster." I shuddered. "That would wear anyone out." Levi leaned over and kissed my forehead. "Looks like the snow is lightening up for now." I watched it fall softly, the flakes smaller. I looked at him and smiled. "I'm hungry. Let's go eat."

"Food's cold by now. Give me ten minutes to heat it up," he said.

"How about I heat it up?" I grinned. "Surely you can't be afraid of me heating something." It's no secret that I used to be a terrible cook. Not awful so much as that I just didn't know how. I was pretty much clueless in the kitchen. After a lot of Nana's time and a world of patience, she'd taught me enough to know my way around the kitchen pretty well. One of our favorite things to do together was cook.

Levi's phone rang, and he looked at the display, then held his phone up briefly. "Walker. I better take this."

"I'll go heat up dinner." I brushed my lips against his. "Give him my best." With a chuckle, I headed out the door and down the stairs.

I had just finished setting the table when Levi came into the kitchen. "Walker has a lead on Connie." I didn't say anything, only continued to move about the kitchen. "Did you hear what I said?" he asked.

"Uh-huh."

"Something you want to tell me?"

"No."

"Melanie?" he asked. When I didn't say anything, he cleared his throat. "You know where she is, don't you?"

"Maybe," I said quietly, looking at him out of the corner of my eye.

"Were you going to tell me?"

"You didn't ask."

"Uh-uh. That innocent act isn't going to work, my love."

"What do you mean?" I asked, looking at him full on now, my eyes wide.

"You know exactly what I mean."

I shrugged and went back to putting the food on the table.

"How long have you known?" he asked.

"Since she left," I mumbled.

"You could have saved Walker time by telling him that."

"Probably. But I needed to buy me time to help clear her." I stopped and looked at him. "She's innocent, Levi. I know it."

"She has a poor way of showing it."

"She knew how bad it looked," I argued.

"And she made it look even worse. She's not helping herself here."

I sighed and sat down on a kitchen stool, my elbow on the counter, my chin in my hand. "I know." I looked at the trash bag next to the door. "Want to look through that with me? I have a feeling the answer to at least one of the murders lies inside that bag."

"Have you heard of tampering with evidence? Oh, wait!" he said before I could say anything. "Yes, you have. Because you do it frequently."

I turned one side of my mouth up in a half-smile. "Come on. It's garbage. It's not like it was inside the building or on private property."

"Dinner first. I don't want to lose my appetite."

"For a big, strong man, you're so sensitive," I teased. He snickered and shook his head slowly. "Let's eat," I said. "What do you want to drink, a beer or water?"

"Water. I'll get it. You sit down."

"Detective Wescott, why are you being so good to me?"

"Because I'm hoping you'll finally agree to set a date to make it official."

"It?" I laughed.

"Us," he said, planting a kiss on top of my head before sitting down caddy-corner from me.

"Natalie said—"

"Who's Natalie? And we're still not setting a date?"

I couldn't say what the hesitation was because I wanted to marry him. Badly. "Can we wait until this whole Connie mess is over and done with?"

A heavy pause fell between us. Finally, he said, "What does one thing have to do with the other, Melanie? You're making excuses again."

"Why are you in such a hurry?" I asked gently. "Things are so good right now. And I love being engaged."

"You think sharing our lives together wouldn't be even better?" he asked.

"We are sharing our lives. What do you think we're doing now?" He didn't say anything. Disappointment was ripe in his eyes. I lay my hand on top of his. "I'm sorry, Levi. I want to marry you more than anything in the world," I insisted. "But what if I screw it up? Screw *us* up?" I looked down, then back up at him. "I'm afraid of losing you."

"That's not going to happen."

"No?" I challenged him. "Can you promise that?"

He picked up my hand and put it up to his lips, kissing it gently. "Yes, I can. I thought we'd been through all of this. Many times."

My phone rang, saving me from the gnawing in the pit of my stomach. I looked at the display. *Unknown.* I briefly contemplated letting it go to voicemail but then decided to answer. What if it was Connie?

"Hello?"

"Hi, Melanie. It's Andie Rose."

"Andie Rose," I said, a bit surprised. "What's up?"

"Babs and I were talking about Maggie Thompson's death. I thought I'd drive up to Spirit Lake tomorrow and ask around at the magazine she worked for. Want to go with?"

"Yes," I blurted. "The roads, though—" I saw Levi watching me closely.

"They're not bad at all. We only got a fraction of the snow they predicted. I know it's still early, but they're not bad here in town. According to the websites I've checked, toward Spirit Lake, they've gotten even less."

"Perfect! What time?"

"It's a two-hour drive, so how about nine? We could meet at Babs' apartment. Or I could even come out and pick you up."

"No, no. I'll come into town. Babs' place at nine. Got it." I looked at Levi as he shook his head slowly. I had to give the guy credit, though; he didn't try to talk me out of it.

"I'll drive," she said. "I'm bringing Aspen with me. I hope you're okay with dogs."

"If he's okay with me, I'm okay with him. Is Babs coming?"

"No. She and Nate are hanging out."

"See you tomorrow then. Hey, Andie?" I said quickly before she hung up.

"Yeah?"

"Did you call to see if the magazine is open tomorrow? It's Sunday. They might be closed."

"Melanie Hogan," she said, amusement in her tone, "what kind of detective do you take me for? Of course, I called."

"A good one," I said, smiling. "See you tomorrow."

I hadn't even set my phone down when Levi asked, "Where are you going tomorrow?"

"Andie Rose asked me to go with her to the magazine that Maggie worked at. In Spirit Lake."

"Why?"

"She likes my company," I said with a grin.

"How well do you know her?"

"Well enough to know that I'm sorry she's not staying in Birch Haven. Or that we hadn't met a long time ago. I think we would have gotten along fabulously."

"Well, I, for one, am glad circumstances are as they are. I'm not so sure it would have been good for the Birch Haven Police Department if you ladies spent more time together."

"We would have given you all something to do. You know, job security."

"You do that just fine on your own."

"Ouch," I said, laughing.

***

To my relief, as soon as we finished eating, he agreed to go through the garbage bag with me. I spread out a large sheet of plastic on the floor and grabbed a pair of latex gloves I kept under the sink for when I cleaned.

The inside of the bag collected a foggy mist making it so we couldn't see clearly through the plastic. We'd have to get down and dirty. *Yuk*!

After a few minutes of sifting through what seemed like thousands of gross, sweat-dried paper towels, some still damp—*eww*! —on the bottom of the bag lay the Styrofoam coffee cup in question. I held it up with two fingers. Levi nabbed a plastic bag, and I dropped it in. He zipped up the baggie.

"I'll take it into the lab in the morning."

"How are you going to explain it?" I asked him. "It's Walker's case. Won't he ask what you're doing meddling in his investigation? Or do you people only ask me that?"

"Yeah, pretty much," he said, winking at me.

"That's rude. Maybe I should bring it into him and tell him you know nothing about it."

"Like he's going to believe that," he scoffed.

"But what are you going to say?" I insisted. I'd gotten him into a few pickles while we've been together and didn't want to get him into another.

"One word is all it will take, and they'll understand." I looked at him expectantly and blinked. "Melanie."

I scowled. "That doesn't even warrant a response. But I guess it's true," I added under my breath.

I stood and began closing the bag, eager to set it outside on the porch until morning when I would drop it in my garbage can. For tonight, just getting it out of the house would be good enough.

Before securing the top of the bag, I shook it a bit, rifling the paper towels one more time when through the now sheer-again plastic, I noticed something I hadn't earlier. Rather than the wheat-colored paper towels, this was lighter with coffee stains that made it blend a bit and a torn edge. Paper from a notebook? It was lying on the bottom, against the side. I carefully reached in and pulled out the wrinkled paper between my thumb and forefinger. Still clutching it between two fingers, I turned it every which way before flattening it on the floor and smoothing it with both hands. I read the words as best I could, guessing at the words that were smeared too badly to read. I looked at Levi.

"Looks like we found something much more valuable than the coffee cup," I said.

"What is it?"

"Notes from, I'm assuming, Maggie. It's hard to read because the coffee and condensation smeared a lot of it. Still, it appears to be something about Grand Pharmaceuticals, a big pharmaceutical company in Minneapolis, polluting the lakes. According to this, it looks like they're discarding their medications carelessly by flushing them down the drains, and it's polluting the freshwater lakes, streams, and ponds. It says that it's killing the fish and altering the algae, causing them to produce toxins." Levi frowned as he listened to me read.

"It goes on to say how it's harmful to humans and how someone needs to stop this company." I held the paper up in the air. "Levi, Maggie was a reporter for *Lakes News and Reviews* based in Spirit Lake. The morning she was killed, a notebook was left lying open on the locker room floor. A page had been torn out, but—"

"How could you tell?"

"Because it was a spiral-bound notebook with a company logo, and the edge of the paper was left in the spiral rings." I picked up my phone and found the photo I had taken. I zoomed in close and held it out for Levi to see. "The bulleted lists and scribbles make a lot more sense after seeing this." I pointed to the paper on the floor. "Stuff about big pharma and doodles of fish, a fishing boat, and the name of the magazine. The CSI would have collected the notebook, so it has to be in evidence." We locked eyes.

"Melanie," he said grimly, "we knew Maggie had been working on a controversial story about lake pollution, but I think this is bigger and runs a whole lot deeper than any of us thought."

23

I pulled into Babs' apartment parking lot at nine sharp. Andie Rose opened the door before I even got to the top step. She looked stunning with her red curls pulled back into a ponytail. She wore blue jeans, brown boots, and a tan sweater. A gorgeous red-gold retriever trotted by her side, appearing pleased at the prospect of a car ride. I smiled. So this was Aspen. Andie Rose held his leash loosely in her hand.

"Let's hit the road," she said, pulling the door closed behind her. "I've got a feeling we're going to get some answers today."

I wasn't used to someone else taking the reins, which threw me off my game for a minute. I was always the one trying to coax someone into helping me. I had called Claire on my way into town and let her know what I was up to.

"I wish I could go with you guys," she'd said, "but Tyler's folks are leaving tomorrow, so I better hang out here with them. Plus, my little bug wants mama home today."

We'd hung up with the promise that I'd tell her whatever we found *when* we found it.

"Wait until I tell you what Levi and I discovered last night," I said to Andie Rose.

She opened the back car door, sprawled a blanket out across the seat, and moved to the side. Aspen obediently hopped in, curled up, and lay down, his big brown eyes looking at me in an accusatory manner.

"I take it he usually sits in the front," I said.

Andie Rose laughed. "Oh, yeah. You'll probably get the treatment for a bit, but he'll get over it. Just give him some lovin', and he'll be in the palm of your hand."

After I got in and shut the door, I turned my attention toward Aspen. I reached between the seats and rubbed his nose and the top of his head. "Sorry, buddy." As I stroked him, his eyes softened, and he lay his head on his front paws. "If only people were this easy," I said.

"Right?" Andie Rose exclaimed. "Aspen has taught me a lot about people and life in general."

"You mentioned the other day that he goes with you everywhere?"

"Yep. He's a service dog. Kind of."

I glanced over at her. She looked perfectly normal. "Oh," I murmured. "I'm sorry."

"No need to be sorry." She reached back and gave Aspen a gentle pat on the head. "I have a seizure disorder. Not bad. I've only had three in my whole life. Aspen knows to alert when a seizure is approaching. It gives me peace of mind."

"I can imagine! I didn't know golden retrievers are service dogs."

She started the car and clicked her seatbelt. "Yeah. They're excellent for that: intelligent, easy to train, and trustworthy."

"Did you train him?"

She laughed. "No, are you kidding? I wouldn't know the first thing to do. Specially trained people do that. I don't qualify for one of those dogs, though, because my seizures are so few. Since I started seizure meds a little more than three years ago, I haven't had another one. Certain dogs have the ability to sense a seizure coming on, which isn't something that can be trained. And Aspen is one of them. Mostly he and I just hang out. We're sidekicks."

"You don't need him at the gym?"

"Like I said, my seizures are pretty much under control with my meds. But I take him almost everywhere else. Including to work. Which will work nicely when I'm running the inn in Spirit Lake." I was pondering everything Andie Rose had told me when she said, "Hey, you said something about what you and Levi discovered last night. Provided it's G rated, I'd love to hear."

This time it was me who laughed. "Totally G rated!" I paused, wondering how to tell her without revealing the whole story behind *how* I found it and *why*. Finally, I decided just to tell her. She trusted me enough to ask me to go on this excursion to Spirit Lake. I took a deep breath. It was a long story, but it wasn't like we didn't have time. We were beginning a two-hour road trip.

"You know Connie, right?"

"Yes."

"Well, the dead man was her husband. She suspected him of cheating on her."

Andie Rose's mouth formed an *o*. She finally said, "Oh boy. Babs said something about that. But I don't think she knows it was Connie's husband that was murdered. That's horrible!"

I looked at her sharply. "She knew he was cheating on Connie?"

Andie Rose nodded. "Uh-huh. Connie had mentioned it to her last week."

"Well, the police are zeroing in on Connie, who has since disappeared."

Now it was Andie Rose who gave me a sharp look. "So Babs was right."

"Right?"

"Babs wasn't convinced that Connie was gone from the salon 'for the day' as you all told her. She had this weird feeling, a premonition. She tried calling Connie, but her number was disconnected. That's when she really knew something was up. She told Nate and me that she had a feeling you knew something more."

Guilt punched me squarely. "Why didn't she say something?" I asked.

"She figured you didn't want her to know, or you would have told her. Either that or she was wrong, and you didn't know about it. And if that was the case, she didn't think it was her business to say anything."

I rested my head against the seat and looked straight ahead. There was a fresh layer of white powder covering the earth, and it was stunning. "I should have told her what we knew. But I didn't want her to be more involved than she had to be."

Andie Rose shrugged. "It's no matter. She figured there was a reason. She's more forgiving than I am. Or maybe she's just not as nosy. Like you and I are." She smiled and briefly glanced at me. "Go on. What did you find?"

I finished telling her the entire story, including what we knew from the page from the notebook accusing the pharmaceutical company of pollution. But it wasn't until I reached the part about getting shut in the dumpster that she said anything.

"Oh, man! That must have been terrible!" she cried.

"You have no idea." I shivered. "That'll be the last time I dumpster dive. I'm pretty sure I'll have PTSD for years to come. Maybe I should look into getting a service animal too." I told her about the cat when Claire and I began our adventure, and she laughed loudly.

Aspen lifted his head and cocked it to the side as he watched her. She reached behind her with her right hand and stroked his nose. "Sorry, buddy. Didn't mean to scare you."

"Does Spirit Lake have a pharmacy?" I asked.

"Yeah. It's on the main drag through town."

"Hm. I wonder if it's in any way connected to the Grand Pharmaceutical fiasco we're discovering," I said. "Do you know the owner there? Of the drugstore, I mean."

"Other than picking up a few prescriptions for my grandparents over the years, no. Seems I heard the owner's kid is running it now, though. Never met him."

"Huh."

After a second of pondering the thought, we talked non-stop for the next hour before stopping at a convenience store to get coffee.

Andie Rose opened the back door, and Aspen stepped down from the seat. She slipped a service dog harness on him and clicked his leash to it. "I'm kind of a coffee shop snob," Andie Rose said as we walked into the store. "I love me a good coffee shop—the coffee, the atmosphere, everything about them. But this will have to do for now. They've got two amazing coffee shops in Spirit Lake alone."

"The big chains?"

"Nope," she grinned. "No big-name coffee shops there. Only small, privately owned, with the best of everything. We have one at the inn, too."

Aspen stayed patiently by Andie's side as we each poured ourselves a coffee, Andie Rose dark-roast and black; I doctored mine with syrups and creamers. She grabbed a protein bar on the way to the counter, and Aspen stayed close. If I didn't know better, I'd think he was territorial and making sure I didn't invade his turf;

Andie Rose was his. I snickered. We paid and headed back to the car, a ten-minute stop from beginning to end.

When we pulled back onto the road, she said, "Hey, Melanie? That blue Mazda has been following us since we left Birch Haven."

"Yeah, I've noticed that too," I said.

"I didn't think much of it until they pulled into the same gas station we did and then got back on the road behind us."

"I was hoping it was just my over-active imagination."

"I don't think so." She slowed down, and the Mazda slowed as well, staying a consistent distance behind us. The tinted windows were too dark to see anything, much less who it was.

"There's no license plate on the front," Andie Rose said.

"There's gotta be a temp tag in the back," I said, looking into my rearview mirror. "Let's turn off somewhere and try to lose them. I don't want to lead them to where we're going."

"There's a small town about twenty miles before we reach Spirit Lake. If they're still following, I'll pull off and take a detour."

"I have a feeling this person knows what we're up to." I kept my eyes on the car. "The only person I told was Levi. And we were at my house. Unless someone bugged my house, which isn't totally out of the question given my past. Who did you all tell?" I asked, ripping my gaze from the rearview mirror to her.

"Just Babs. But we were in a public place." She looked at me and scrunched up her face. "That means pretty much anyone could have heard. It didn't occur to me that someone creepy would be listening. And if they were, they had to be following me to begin with." She shuddered, and Aspen alerted. Andie Rose reached back with her right arm and patted him. "I'm okay, boy."

"Did you recognize anyone? From the gym? Or anywhere, for that matter."

She appeared to try to recall her conversation with Babs. Finally, she shook her head. "No. But I didn't look at people either. I was pretty careless, now that I think about it." One side of her mouth curved downward. "Gee, sorry, Melanie."

"Don't be silly. We shouldn't have to be so careful." I looked in my rearview mirror again and saw precisely what I expected. The blue Mazda still followed at a safe distance, close enough not to lose us, far enough that we couldn't see anything distinguishable about the driver. "Unfortunately, it looks like we do have to be careful, though. Someone seems concerned that we're going to Spirit Lake." I thought of Levi's words last night. *I think this is bigger and runs a whole lot deeper than any of us thought.* If that was the case, it could be a lot more dangerous than we'd thought.

"What?" Andie Rose said.

I startled, not realizing I'd spoken out loud. "This could be a lot more dangerous than we thought. If you want to turn around and go back to Birch Haven, I'm okay with that."

"Is that what you want to do?" she asked, looking at me with an arched eyebrow, then in her rearview mirror.

"Heck no," I said. "I'm just saying that if you—"

"No," she said. "I don't want to go back. I'm not about to let someone intimidate me."

I grinned. "You're going to be great at running that inn," I said.

"I sure hope so. I want to make Gramps proud."

"I've no doubt he is already," I said, smiling. "Grandparents are the best, aren't they?"

Andie Rose smiled, the love softening the lines in her face. "We have a lot in common, you know that?"

"We do. Too bad you're moving in a few days."

"Meh. Spirit Lake isn't too far. But potentially, I could be moving further later."

I looked at her inquisitively and said, "Do tell."

"If my parents offer me the inn in Colorado, it might be an offer I can't refuse. But I'm a Minnesota girl at heart, and I'm glad I'll be running this one. For now." She looked at me and smiled. "But one never knows. I like having options."

Before we knew it, we reached the turnoff for the town before Spirit Lake. Glancing in our rearview mirrors again, Andie Rose veered onto the off-ramp. We pulled up to the stoplight and looked in our rearview. Just as we'd expected, the Mazda pulled off as well, slowing down, maintaining a safe distance behind us.

"The guy thinks we're idiots," she said. "Like we're not going to notice him?"

The light turned green, and we took a left. Andie slowed to a crawl, hoping the Mazda would get stuck at a red light. But, instead, it sped up to make the green light too, bringing him closer to our tail. Still, we couldn't see who it was.

We turned right, then the first left, another right, and another left down an alley. The car was no longer behind us. We'd finally shaken him. Andie Rose drove around the neighborhood streets for a few minutes, staying away from the main road. Eventually, after about ten minutes, we cruised to Main Street, back to the ramp onto the highway, and began our last leg to Spirit Lake. Aspen laid in the back seat, calm as could be. I think he'd even forgiven me for taking the front seat. I reached back buried my fingers in his fur, finding comfort.

When we'd reached the sign reading *Welcome to Spirit Lake, Home of the Friendly Ghosts*, my jaw dropped. I looked at Andie Rose. "They take this ghost stuff seriously, don't they?"

She laughed. "Oh, you have no idea. And don't even think about pooh-pooing it around the locals."

I looked behind us and said, "Um, Andie Rose? I think we've got bigger problems than friendly ghosts." The blue Mazda was back.

24

"Let's go to Spirit Brew Coffee House and see if this person follows us there. We can go in and grab a table, go over our plan, and see if this person comes in," Andie Rose said.

"I don't think that's going to happen. If they wanted us to see them, they would have let us already."

"Then we've got nothing to lose," she said. She drove up and down streets like an expert.

"You're pretty familiar with this town, huh?"

"I used to visit a lot. And I drove my grandparents around when I was here."

"What's the story with you and Babs? Why did you get the inn and not her?" I startled and narrowed my eyes. "Wait a minute—is she leaving the salon and taking the inn in Colorado?"

Andie Rose ignored my question as she pulled into a parking space right in front of the bay of windows in the front of the coffee house and took a deep breath. My heart already felt a loss it didn't want to feel at the thought of Babs leaving.

We each looked around us, but the Mazda was nowhere to be seen. *Had we been suspicious for nothing?* I got out and looked in all directions. Nothing.

Andie Rose snapped Aspen's leash on the harness he still wore. She walked him around the side of the building into a grassy area. He walked a bit, sniffed, checking it all out thoroughly, then lifted his leg on a bush that was just beginning to get tiny buds for leaves. I marveled that they didn't have any snow here. We walked back toward the door, both of us still looking for the mystery car. Nothing. When I pulled the door open, Andie nudged my shoulder.

"Hey," she said, then nodded her head. "Over there." Across the street, the blue Mazda was parked in front of the town drugstore Andie Rose mentioned earlier. "Here," she said. "Can you hold onto Aspen for a minute?"

Before I could answer, she'd looped the leash around my hand. Aspen gave me an accusatory look as Andie Rose left. "Listen, buddy, I didn't ask her to desert you." He hung his head as if he understood what I'd said. I reached down and rubbed his neck. "If you'd give me a chance, maybe you'd like me, too," I said.

I kept one hand on Aspen, leash wrapped around my fingers, and held my phone at the ready in my free hand. Andie Rose looked both ways before she crossed the street, and when she was halfway across, the door to the Mazda opened. Andie Rose paused a moment then continued when the man got out of the car. I crossed over with Aspen in tow, jogging to catch up.

"Excuse me," Andie Rose said. "Why have you been following us?"

The man looked confused. "Following you?"

"We're not stupid," I said. "We've been watching you follow us since we left Birch Haven."

He shook his head and squinted. "I have no idea what you're talking about. I live here in Spirit Lake. Some woman just asked me if I could park her car because she doesn't know how to parallel park."

Andie Rose and I looked at each other. "Where is this woman?" I asked him.

"She said she had to run an errand and to just leave the keys with the pharmacist in there." He jerked his thumb toward the drugstore.

Andie narrowed her eyes at him. "Do people always just trust you like that? I mean, who gives their keys to a stranger, asks him to park her car, and then doesn't even stick around to be sure she gets the keys back?"

"Look, I didn't say she was smart, and she's lucky I'm a trustworthy guy, but I'm just telling you why I was in this car. But I can assure you, I did not follow you from Birch Haven."

His look of amusement was disconcerting. I couldn't get a read on whether he was telling the truth or not. And given what Levi and I found out last night about Grand Pharmaceuticals, was it a coincidence that this was happening in front of the drugstore? My suspicion that it involved the drug store owner's kid somehow grew bigger. Aspen began wagging his tail and nudged the man's hand. That seemed to be all it took for Andie Rose to decide she believed this man's story.

"You say you're from here?" she asked him.

"Born and raised." He smiled and stuck out a hand. "I'm Wes Wilson."

"Andie Rose," she said. "I'm the new owner of the Spirit Lake Inn. Almost."

His eyes lit up, and he smiled a smile that transformed his entire face. "You're old man Kaczmarek's granddaughter!"

"That would be me. One of them anyway."

I hung back and watched the exchange, amused with what was going on here. After Wes left, I looked at Andie Rose. "That was interesting."

"What?"

"What?" I said, chuckling. "There was kind of a connection going on there."

"I have a boyfriend," she said.

"Which, from what Babs has said, isn't an ideal match for you."

She shrugged, then said, "Is there such a thing as a perfect match for people, Melanie? Brad is good to me."

A pang of pity gnawed at me. I wanted more for her than settling for someone because he was good to her. As important as that was, I had discovered when I found Levi that there can be so much more to a relationship. I would rather be alone than *settle* for someone.

"Come on," I said, "let's go get a coffee and sit by a window. Eventually, the owner of this car will come back for it. At least we now know it's a woman."

I walked behind the car, snapped a photo of the temp tag on the rear window, and followed Andie Rose into the Spirit Brew Coffee House.

We placed our orders, one at a time, so one of us could keep a lookout on the car across the street. When both of us were finally at the table, I said, "You never did tell me the story of you and Babs. And is she leaving the salon?"

Aspen lay down on the floor next to her, his nose resting on his crossed paws. "No, I guess I didn't," she said. "And no, she's not leaving." She tilted her head and raised a brow. "Not that I know of, anyway." After a brief pause, she continued. "It's nothing. Her dad—my uncle— and my grandpa had a falling out. Her dad refused to have anything to do with Gramps since then. Didn't even patch things up before Gramps died. They're both stubborn if you ask me. Babs and I kept hope alive that they'd both get over it, but neither did. And now," she said, her eyes looking similar to Aspen's when he didn't get the front seat, "it's too late. For a long time, Gramps wasn't in the mental state to forgive, and then Babs' dad kicked the bucket." She took a sip of her coffee, then added, "The thing is, it was all kept hush-hush, so no one but them knew what happened. Not the whole story, anyway. Not even Babs' mom or Gran. If they did, they kept mum about it." She took another sip. "And honestly? I'm not sure either Babs' dad or Gramps would have been able to tell you the details of what happened."

"Hard-hearted," I murmured. As close as I'd been to Granddad when he was alive and still am with Nana, the story broke my heart. "If you don't mind my asking, why aren't your parents running the inn?"

"Their life is in Costa Rica now. They come back to visit but had no desire to live here again."

Both of us quickly turned toward the window as if we'd momentarily gotten caught up and forgotten to keep watch. Aspen stirred and sat up. Seeing that nothing changed, we continued visiting while watching through the window, and Aspen lay back down again after a scratch on his head from Andie Rose.

"So, you got the inn," I said. "Did that create hard feelings between you and Babs?"

"Not at all. Gramps had it set up to transfer to my mom and dad when he died. They're transferring the Spirit Lake location ownership to me and keeping the Colorado location. They'll find someone to run that one for them. I told Babs I would put the one here in both of our names; we could each own fifty percent. But she didn't want me to do that."

"Why not?"

"She said she didn't have any interest in running an inn or moving to Spirit Lake."

"But what about the investment part of it?" I asked.

Andie Rose shrugged. "I asked her that too, but she said no, that she didn't want it. I told her if she ever changes her mind to let me know."

"That's very kind of you."

"Not really. We're family. It's what family does."

I looked out the window toward the drugstore and thought of Max. He didn't have to find me and let me know he was my brother, that we shared a father, therefore sharing the sizeable inheritance said father left us after someone murdered him; and yet Max did it anyway. He didn't particularly want to have a sister, yet he worked to find me. New appreciation for him surfaced. "Yeah," I murmured. "Family is pretty special."

The door to the drugstore opened, and I sat straight up in my chair. Andie Rose did the same, and once again, Aspen sat at attention. Andie Rose rested a hand on his head. We stared a hole through the glass in front of us as we waited for the person lingering in the doorway to turn and show themselves. Finally, just as the door opened a little wider and we thought we would get a look at the person following us, the door closed again. Only to open again, and out walked a woman holding a child's hand with her right hand, a bag with medicine in the other. The little girl coughed and coughed, the woman leaned over and said something to her, and then they walked past the blue Mazda to a silver SUV up the street.

I exhaled the breath I'd been holding. "This is nerve-wracking!" I exclaimed.

Andie nabbed a dog treat from her purse and lowered her palm to Aspen. "What's our plan?" she asked. "We had the entire trip here to talk about it and didn't. Guess we both assumed we'd just know."

I hadn't told her yet, but I did have a plan. I always had a plan. I just didn't talk it through out loud. "I think we should go to the magazine and ask if we can talk to whoever Maggie's supervisor is."

"The magazine is open but running on a skeletal staff with it being Sunday and all. I'd be shocked if her supervisor was working today."

"The fact that they're open at all on Sunday is shameful," I said. "I mean, it's good for us, but not for the people who have to work."

"Welcome to business," she said. "I feel the same way as you, don't get me wrong, but the business world doesn't care what day of the week it is."

"You'll be working Sundays too, won't you? It's not like an inn closes for a day or two, I suppose."

"It'll be different for me. It will be like working from home. I'll be able to spend my days in the kitchen, meeting new people..."

She had a dreamy look on her face when she trailed off. It was clear this was going to be the perfect job for her.

"Will you be able to work at the mortuary here as well, or will you be too busy running the inn?"

"It's not like they have a ton of people dying here—I wouldn't imagine so anyway—but no, I'm not going back to that. I'm moving on."

"I better not come visit you," I muttered.

"Why?" She looked away from the window and faced me instead.

I shook my head. "Let's just say I seem to be a magnet for dead bodies. I've been keeping the Birch Haven Police on their toes."

"Is that how you met Levi?"

I chuckled softly as I recalled meeting him. "Yeah, as a matter of fact, it is. We met when a client died in my chair. But when he spilled coffee on me—well, since then, my heart has been captured."

She laughed. "Odd thing to have captured your heart."

I grinned. "So, it hasn't been all bad," she said.

I pictured him this morning before I left when he kissed me goodbye and smiled. "No, no, I don't suppose it has been all bad. If he were smart, he would have run like heck in the opposite direction."

She smiled at me again. "Nah. I have a feeling he's pretty smart and knows exactly what he's doing."

"Well, let's hope Detective Walker is just as smart so this whole nightmare can be over."

Andie grinned. "Speaking of Detective Walker, if he's as smart as he is cute, we have nothing to worry about."

I laughed. "Should I tell Levi?"

She put her hand out, palm facing me. "No! I said I have a boyfriend. I'm not looking for anything else."

The door to the drugstore opened again, and both Andie Rose and I sat up and inhaled, then relaxed again with an exhale. Another false alarm. This time, Aspen

251

decided it wasn't worth noticing. He lay snoozing by Andie Rose's feet. An elderly man with a cane walked to the business next door.

"This must be what it's like for Levi when he does surveillance." I glanced from the window, back to her. "Back to our plan. We could ask for her supervisor; if he or she is in, great. We can ask all the questions we want and hope we get the answers we're looking for. If they aren't in, we can tell the receptionist—assuming there is a receptionist—that I'm Maggie's sister and there to collect her things from her office."

"Don't you think the police will have done that already?"

"If she says they've been there—well, do you trust me?"

"Sure. That's why I asked you to come with me."

"Okay. When we get there, just go with me and follow my lead."

"No!" she said, standing up.

Aspen sat up from his peaceful slumber, and I jumped, startled. I hadn't expected that response. It was just a simple request, for goodness' sake. And then I saw. In the briefest of moments, while neither of us watched the car, someone had slipped in and was now pulling away from the curb.

25

"She must have slipped in on the passenger's side," I said, picking up my phone. "I'm going to send the photo of the temp tag to Levi." I typed in my message: *This car followed us all the way from BH. Even stopped at same gas station. Think we r being watched. This is the temp tag.* I attached the picture and hit send.

"Well," she said, draining the last of her coffee, "let's get moving. I want to get there before lunch."

"Unless Maggie's boss isn't in today. Then lunchtime would be a perfect time. We could snoop around with no one there."

She pointed a finger at me and smiled. "I like how you think. Unless they lock up for the lunch hour."

The magazine was only two blocks down, so we decided to walk. Aspen didn't argue. I thought it was probably because he didn't want to stoop to having to sit in the back seat. Regardless, we had become fast friends.

We reached a red brick building with a sign over the entire front that read *Lakes News and Reviews*. Someone exited when I opened the door—one less person to worry about. I glanced at my watch. Eleven fifty-five. I strode up to the empty front desk and tapped the bell. A girl, who couldn't have been older than eighteen, appeared from around a corner. She spotted Aspen immediately and broke into a huge grin. "Oh! I love him! Can I pet him?"

She came around the desk without waiting for a reply from Andie Rose. *Aspen, my friend, I think you're a bigger asset than I could have ever hoped for.* The girl knelt on one knee beside Aspen and stroked his neck and back.

"Can I give him a biscuit?" she asked, looking at Andie Rose with eyes that mirrored Aspen's. "We're a very dog-friendly town, you know. I think every business here has biscuits of some sort for these little angels." She looked at Andie Rose. "They bake them at the inn, you know. Specially for dogs." By the look on Andie's face, she didn't know but appeared pleased, nonetheless. The girl looked at Aspen again, hugged his neck, and said in a child-like voice, "Oh! He is the sweetest thing ever." Finally, she stood up and smoothed her shirt. "What can I do for you ladies?"

"We're wondering if the owner or the manager is in today," I said.

She laughed and waved a hand. "Are you kidding? He never works on Sundays. I'm his daughter."

Andie Rose and I exchanged a look. "Did you know Maggie Thompson?" I asked.

The girl's entire expression changed, and I thought she might cry. Guilt stirred. But not enough to make me stop.

"It's absolutely horrible what happened to her," she said. She stuck out her hand. "I'm Jill."

I shook her hand then Andie Rose did. "I'm Andie Rose." She nodded toward me. "This is Melanie."

"I'm Maggie's sister," I said. "I was wondering if I could—"

"Maggie had a sister?" Jill said, brows furrowed. "I thought she didn't have any family. But then she was a super private person," she added almost to herself.

"Half-sister," Andie Rose said. "She's Maggie's half-sister."

"And she doesn't have any family in the area," I said. "Maybe that's why you're confused."

She tipped her head to the side and studied me a moment, then said, "Huh. I suppose you might be right." She touched my arm. "Well, I am so sorry for your loss."

I swear I managed to bring a tear to my eye and looked directly at her. "Thank you. I was wondering if I might collect her things from her office."

"The police came and went through her things already. Didn't they tell you that?" she said in a tone that screamed how sorry she was for me.

"Yes, but they didn't take everything, did they? From what I understood, they only took things pertinent to the investigation."

"I believe you're right. I was here, and it didn't look like they removed a lot. But they're keeping Maggie's door closed, so I haven't seen inside."

Wow! She was good. I wouldn't have been able to help myself to even the tiniest little peek.

"Do you know what the police took?" Andie Rose asked.

Jill shook her head. "No. And even if I did know, I wouldn't be able to tell you anyway. Isn't there something about being an open investigation or something like that?"

What was she, a Girl Scout? Andie Rose and I didn't stand a chance of getting inside that office.

Andie Rose gave it one more shot. "You wouldn't mind if we looked in there for just a minute, would you? Maggie has something very sentimental to Melanie that belonged to their mother. We wouldn't be asking you if it wasn't important."

Jill shook her head. "I'm sorry, ladies, but I can't. Tell you what, though. If you tell me what it is, I'll look for it as soon as we're allowed to go in there." She looked at me. "Leave me your number, and I'll call you if I find it." She handed me a slip of paper and a pen.

"Well, okay then," I said as I jotted down my number and handed it to her. "Here you go." Andie Rose and I looked at each other, and she started for the door, Aspen close by her side.

"You didn't tell me what it is you're looking for," Jill called out behind me.

I turned around. "Oh. It's a silver locket. You'll know it if you see it." I started for the door again and turned back. "Perhaps I could use your restroom before we leave? It's a long ride back to Birch Haven."

"You're from Birch Haven?" Jill asked, eyebrows raised. "But that's where Maggie was when she was—you know," she said, drawing a line across her neck with her finger.

"Well, yeah," Andie Rose said. "She was visiting Melanie."

"Duh!" Jill sang. "Yes," she said to me, "you may use the restroom." She pointed down a narrow hallway. "It's right down there. Last door on the left. It should be open with everyone out to lunch. Well, all two and a half of us, anyway." She put her hand to the side of her mouth and said, "Bill only counts as half. He's a piece."

I wanted to ask 'a piece of what?' but given she felt the need to whisper, I could pretty much figure it out.

"Aspen and I will wait here for you," Andie Rose said.

I began down the hallway, looking at the gold-plated signs on the doors announcing whose office each was. When I was almost to the restroom, I found Maggie's. Making the extra five steps, I turned on the bathroom light, closed the door, and turned back to Maggie's office. I looked toward the front. Jill was out of view, likely kneeling beside Aspen. I hoped the furry guy would entertain Jill so she would lose track of time and not wonder what was taking me so long.

Turning the handle to Maggie's office as quietly as I could, I opened the door and closed it behind me without a sound. The blinds were closed, but enough light shined through for me to see where I was walking. I looked around the small office and took my phone out, shining it on Maggie's desk using the flashlight app. I glanced at her desk calendar. She'd had a meeting with Grand Pharmaceuticals two days before her murder. I went to snap a picture of it and dropped my phone. It clattered loudly against the desk and onto the floor. *Shoot!* I cringed and held my breath.

"Everything okay back there?" Jill called out.

"Yup! Sorry about that!" I called back. "Dropped my phone on the floor." It wasn't a lie, I tried to rationalize. Specifying *which* floor wasn't necessary. The fact that one was carpeted and the other not...well, I'd come up with something if Jill put it together.

I rifled through some papers and glanced at photos on her desk, none that meant anything to me, but I snapped a picture of them anyway. Her laptop was missing. No doubt the police had confiscated it. Darn it! Not that I had a password, nor did I have time to try and figure it out. And it's not like I could have stuck it down the front of my pants and gotten away with it.

A manila folder with the label Grand Pharmaceuticals caught my attention. I set my phone down and opened it up. Inside were several papers with handwritten notes, numbers, and what looked like chemical configurations I couldn't begin to decipher, but all of it promising a potential far-reaching scandal. How had the police missed this folder? Someone placing it here after the police had already come and gone didn't make any sense, but that was the only explanation. Maybe someone had inside info that the police were planning to return to the office? But even then, what was the purpose for planting it here? The office was still off-limits after all. What I did know was that if someone *did* plant the folder, it definitely wouldn't have been the Girl Scout out front. She doesn't break *any* rules. I snagged the papers out of the folder, stuck them in my jeans' waistband in the back, and yanked my jacket down.

I panicked when voices came down the hallway. "Hey, Jake," Jill called. "Someone's in the bathroom, so don't go in there. She should be out in a minute."

"Who else is here?" he complained. "I thought it was just us and Bill, and he's at the Cantina."

"A visitor. Maggie's sister."

My stomach sunk. *Oh no*!

"Maggie doesn't have a sister," he said. He was right in front of Maggie's office door. I hoped he didn't decide to come in. The door handle moved, and I leaped around the desk and dove underneath, hitting my head on the drawer. *Ouch*! I rubbed my head with the heel of my hand. I panicked when I realized I'd left my phone on top of the desk. *Please don't ring! Please don't ring!* My heart thumped viciously.

The door opened. "Someone in here?" the man asked.

"Jake, if you want to keep your job, get out of there!" Jill called.

"Thought I heard something," he said. "Maggie's ghost," he said quietly with a chuckle. There was a pause before the door closed.

I took a deep breath and crawled out from under the desk. I snatched my phone from the desk and cracked the door open, looking into the hallway. Empty. As quickly as I could, I closed the door behind me, opened the bathroom door, and closed it again. I flushed the toilet, ran the water in the sink, ripped a paper towel from the dispenser, and opened the door.

When I got back to the front, Jill said, "I was just about to come and check on you. Are you okay?"

"Sorry about that. Must have been something I ate." I rubbed my stomach. "Ready, Andie Rose?"

When we turned to leave, Jill gave Aspen one last pat. He turned, and his tail knocked a photo frame down from the edge of a small table beside Jill's desk.

"Oops! Sorry about that," I said, setting the photo upright again, looking at it as I did. My breath caught.

"What a beautiful picture," I said to Jill. "Boyfriend?"

She grinned. "Yes. Hopefully soon to be fiancé if I get what I want for my birthday." She held out her left hand and wiggled her fingers.

I squinted. "How old are you?"

"Twenty-four."

Holy moly! I was wrong on that one! I studied her a moment until she squirmed. "Does he live around here?" I looked at Andie Rose then back at Jill.

"No. Not yet," she said. "He travels a lot, so we don't get to see each other too much."

"Yeah?" I said. "What does he do?"

"Private investigator," she said, clearly impressed.

"Well, good luck to the two of you," I said and pushed against Andie Rose's back. "Go," I whispered.

As soon as I was sure the door closed behind me, I grabbed Andie Rose's arm and said, "We just found out who Connie's husband was having an affair with."

26

Aspen walked between us on the way back to the car, pulling Andie Rose off to the first patch of grass. I yanked the papers from my waistband.

"What are those?" Andie Rose asked, nodding toward the papers clutched in my hand.

"I found them in Maggie's office." I shoved them in my handbag with a brief explanation. "I'll get them to Levi."

When Aspen decided he was done, we continued on. He was clearly calling the shots here. Both Andie Rose and I busily processed in our own way what we'd just learned; Andie Rose talked a blue streak while I silently tried to figure it all out in my head while listening.

"I need to find out for certain who that motel key card belongs to," I said. "I have a strong hunch it holds some answers."

We were nearly back to the car when Andie Rose asked, "Have you seen the blue Mazda again?" We both looked around.

"Nope."

"Has Levi texted you back yet?"

I looked at my phone. "Nope." Just as I tucked my phone into the pocket of my jacket, it chimed with an incoming text. I looked at the display. "Speak of the devil."

Car registered to Marco Vega.

Did u look him up? I texted back.

Clean record. From BH, came the reply.

K. Thanks. Running by Spirit Lake Inn on our way back.

Be careful. Xoxo

Always, I texted back with a kiss emoji.

I tucked my phone away and looked at Andie Rose as I climbed into the front seat. She opened the back door for Aspen, and he appeared a bit more forgiving this time.

"The Mazda belongs to a Marco Vega. Does that name mean anything? What's that?" I pointed to a small card between her thumb and the forefinger of her right hand as she closed her door with her left.

"Maggie's business card." She tapped it against the palm of her hand. "Someone tucked it under my windshield wiper blade."

"When?"

"While we were inside."

"How much you want to bet that someone drives a blue Mazda."

"Yeah, but why? What purpose would it serve? Just to throw it in our faces that he knows what we're up to?"

"That'd be my guess."

"Levi said the car belongs to a Marco Vega?" she asked as if she just remembered what I'd said.

"Yeah. Do you know who that is?" I asked.

She shook her head. "No. Do you?"

"The name sounds familiar, but I can't place it. Vega is a pretty common name, so I could have heard it anywhere. But I can't say I know any Marcos."

"Did Levi run his name in the database?"

I gave her a sideways look. "Yeah. No criminal history. And how do you know about the database?"

"I will never tell."

It sounded like she was teasing. But was she? Maybe there was more to Andie Rose Kaczmarek than I'd thought.

"We haven't even been able to tell if the driver was a man or a woman," I said. "Just because it's registered to a man doesn't mean a man was driving it. Your buddy, Wes, earlier said a woman gave him the keys to park the car."

She chuckled. "Yeah, my buddy."

I chewed on my bottom lip as I thought about where I'd heard the name Marco Vega before. Andie Rose started the car and pointed it in what I assumed was the direction of the inn. We drove in silence for the five blocks or so to get there. When we pulled up in front of the inn, we sat in the car, Andie with a big smile on her face, me in admiration. With its brick and log exterior and windows along the entire wall that appeared to be perhaps a dining area, I think this was the cutest place I'd ever seen.

Finally, Andie Rose opened her door, stood, then opened the back door for Aspen. She reached in a bag on the floor in the back seat and pulled out a second bag. She unzipped it and pulled out a covered bowl. Removing the cover, she set it on the ground in front of Aspen, who sniffed then began to take a bite delicately. Andie laughed as she looked at me. "Yeah, he eats pretty daintily for a big dog."

"I'd say," I said. "I eat faster than that. Speaking of eating, I'm starving. What have they got for food around here?"

"I could make us something to eat here at the inn or stop somewhere else. Do you have a preference?"

I looked at the building in front of me. "This place is haunted, you say?"

"That's what *other* people say," she said, her eyes lighting up. "As creepy as it seems, I'm not afraid. Actually, the opposite. And I've never seen anything all the times I've been here."

I shrugged, then took a deep breath, resting my hands on my hips. "Okay. Let's eat here."

As soon as Aspen finished his food, which I was getting ready to help him with if he didn't hurry up, we closed the car doors, not bothering to lock them, and walked up the sidewalk to the entrance.

"Andie Rose," a woman said as she met us at the door, enveloping Andie in a hug. "Welcome to your new home. Are you here for good?"

"Melanie, this is Rita. Rita, this is my friend, Melanie."

I extended my hand toward Rita. "Nice to meet you."

Andie Rose rested her hand on Rita's arm and looked at me. "Rita was a caretaker for Gramps. She took over here when Gramps couldn't do it anymore and has agreed to stay on for a while." She looked at Rita. "No, I'll be here in another week. The paperwork isn't final until then."

"Pshaw," she said with a wave of her hand. "Paperwork doesn't mean anything at this point. It went to your folks when your grandpa died; you know that. So they officially own it until the paperwork transferring to you goes through. I can't imagine they would care."

"Thanks, Rita. I know they wouldn't care. I just don't want to push you out before you're ready."

"You want to be here, you move in today. I'm staying in the little cottage out back anyway."

Andie Rose appeared to consider that, then she said, "I suppose I could come earlier. But not today. I don't have anything with me. My stuff is packed and ready, it's just not *here* today."

"Well, anytime works for me. I'm ready to get a move on. I'm going to live with my son and help take care of his kids. Nothing more special than grandchildren, you know."

"Except grandparents," I added. I liked Ms. Rita.

"You know, I used to help Gramps and Gran when I stayed here, but I'm sure I'll need more training if you wouldn't mind."

"Not at all. I expected you would. Like ridin' a bike, though. You'll catch right on."

When Rita heard we wanted to catch a bite to eat there, she ushered us in. "I'll make you ladies something."

"No, I won't hear of it," Andie Rose said. "You go do whatever it is you were doing when we got here. I'll make it. I do remember the kitchen."

"Andie Rose Kaczmarek," Rita scolded, "if you don't sit your butt down on that chair right there, I'll whoop it." Andie Rose's eyes grew huge, and we broke out in laughter. "I'm not kidding. Since I don't have your grandfather to care for anymore, I'm going crazy. Don't know what to do with myself."

"Okay, Rita. We would love for you to make us lunch. But please don't go to a lot of trouble. I'll show Melanie around the place while we wait."

"You go on ahead. Give me fifteen minutes," Rita said.

As we toured the place, I couldn't help but be impressed. The cuteness factor of the outside extended well within. We were on our way back downstairs when I stopped suddenly and turned around. Andie Rose nearly ran into me.

"I know where I've heard that name before. Vega!" I exclaimed. "I know where I've heard it. When we were in the locker room the morning after the murder and the three ladies came in. Natalie introduced her sister as Sonia Vega."

"Hmm," Andie Rose said as she appeared to remember. "Yes, she did. But we also said that it's a common name."

"It is, but in Birch Haven? The car followed us from there, and Levi said its registered owner, Marco, is from

Birch Haven." I took out my phone and looked in the White Pages for Birch Haven. Four of them were listed: Pat Vega, Sonia Vega, Manuel Vega, and Juanita Vega-Juarez. I read them to Andie Rose. "No Marco. Sonia's name is listed. Maybe she's married to Marco? Or he could even be her ex."

"Maybe she has nothing to do with Marco at all. If she's married, maybe her husband's name just isn't listed with hers."

"Yeah, but what are the chances of that? A woman we happened to have met with the last name of Vega, the car following us to Spirit Lake registered to a Vega. With Connie's husband having an affair with the girl working for the magazine—a magazine who was writing a story threatening to spill the beans on big pharma, mind you— the reporter who was spilling said beans killed in Birch Haven at a gym Sonia Vega frequents...well, it's all too much to be a—and I can't believe I'm even saying this word—*coincidence*. It's not a surprise we had two murders in Birch Haven, after all. It wasn't *about* Birch Haven." My breath quickened as I put the puzzle pieces together—or at least pulled them from the same box. "Was she at the gym the other day when you and Natalie came into the salon?"

"Sonia?"

"Yes."

"Yeah. I'll go tomorrow morning and see if she's there. See what I can find out."

"I'd meet you there, but—"

"That would be great!" she said. "Between the two of us, one of us should be able to get something useful."

That wasn't how I anticipated spending my morning tomorrow. Or any morning, for that matter. Once I made up my mind about something, I usually stuck with it. It was the *planner* part of my personality. And I had made up my mind about not going to the gym. But I didn't feel right about leaving Andie Rose to do this on her own.

"Okay," I said reluctantly. "It's a plan."

***

The trip back to Birch Haven was pleasantly uneventful. The blue Mazda apparently decided following us wasn't necessary anymore. Andie Rose and I talked about our grandparents and Aspen in between frequent scans in the mirror to ensure the Mazda hadn't decided to reappear. And I was more sure than ever that had Andie lived in Birch Haven, we would become fast friends.

When we reached the Welcome to Birch Haven sign, Andie Rose said, "Hey, do you have the motel key on you?"

"Yeah."

"Let's swing by the Rest Awhile Motel before going back to Babs' place to drop you off at your car."

"I can stop on my way home," I said.

"Nonsense," she said. "We go right by it. It would be crazy for you to circle out of your way. And this way, I get to see who it is."

I shrugged. "Okay. If you don't mind, that works for me."

"I don't mind," she said. "I'm a lady of leisure for another couple of days."

"Couple of days? You're going to Spirit Lake earlier than expected then?" I looked over at her, then reached back and gave Aspen a little love.

"Yeah. It sounds like Rita would like to get moving on. I don't blame her. Without caring for Gramps anymore, she's free to go help with her own family. Besides, I'm so excited I can hardly stand it." Her smile lit up her entire face.

"I know exactly how you feel," I said. "That's how I am with the salon."

"It will be fun to get reacquainted with the staff. Two of them are still around from when I visited there as a kid every summer and school break."

"How many people work there? Other than Rita."

"The chef, a sous chef—who's really just a fill-in for the chef's days off—the maintenance guy, the gardener, and two people for the front. I think the gardener, one of the front desk staff, and the sous chef are all new. Or at least since I've been there last."

"Will your boyfriend be moving to Spirit Lake?"

271

She let out a soft laugh. "We haven't talked about it yet. If I had to venture a guess, though, I'd say no. He enjoys his life in the city. And with all the traveling he does...well, I just don't see it happening."

"That doesn't leave much hope of a future for the two of you, does it?"

"We're both content with the way things are," she said. Her eyes took on a distant look.

"Are you happy with that, Andie Rose? Being content? I mean, I'd rather be alone than just be *content* with someone. I think." Then I added more to myself than to her, "But I've done alone too well for years."

She looked at me and smiled. "I could think of much worse things to be than content."

"Hmm," I murmured. At one time, I might have been okay with that too. But then Levi Wescott came into my life, and there was no going back. Ever. I glanced at the ring sparkling on my finger and felt giddy.

She turned into the Rest Awhile Motel and pulled into a parking spot near the front entrance. We both got out and looked at the place before starting for the door. It was a cute, quaint little place, red doors against dark blue-gray walls, painted since I'd last seen it.

"You have the key card?"

I held it up between my thumb and forefinger. "Right here."

She pulled the door to the main office open, holding it for me. I took a moment and looked around the small room. Dark gray carpet with red flecks covered the floor. There was a gas fireplace in the corner with two wingback chairs in front of it, a small table between them. A man in a jogging suit sat in one of the chairs and looked over at us. Andie Rose smiled at him. A smile the man assumed meant more than it did.

"Careful there, slugger," I said under my breath. "Looks like he thinks you're offering him a good time."

"All I did was smile," she said. "Besides, I don't think this is that kind of motel," she said, frowning.

"That we know of."

We turned toward the front desk. The man behind the counter watched us over the top of his wire-rimmed glasses.

"Help you ladies?"

He had a severe comb-over, partially covering a still-obvious bald spot. He buttoned his tan cardigan over a white collared shirt. I glanced at the gold-plated name tag pinned to his cardigan.

"Hello, Stew," I said as I walked toward him. Andie Rose stood beside me. "I found a key card belonging to your hotel, and —"

"Where?"

"Excuse me?" I said.

"Where did you find it?"

"At the Northern Health & Fitness Club. But I was wondering if you could tell me who it belongs to."

He shook his head while holding out his hand, palm up. "Can't divulge customer information. That's confidential." He pushed up his glasses with a knuckle.

"Even if the person is deceased?"

He gasped. "Is that a fact?" He narrowed one eye. "How do you know the key card belongs to someone who's deceased?"

"I found the body, then found the key card."

"Oh, dear." He blew air out through pursed lips. "Do you know the name of the deceased?"

"Tell you what," Andie Rose chirped up. "You tell us the name of the person to who the card belongs, and we'll let you know if it's the deceased or not."

He studied her a moment, then looked at me, obviously weighing what was more important to him—keeping confidential information confidential or getting the information he wanted. "Give me the card," he said, holding his hand out once more.

I smiled and placed it in his palm. He did whatever he had to do on the computer with the card, then tapped the edge of the countertop a couple of times as if weighing once again what to do.

"Marco."

I inhaled sharply. "Vega?"

"That'd be the one," he said.

27

"Tell me," Stew said. "Is he the deceased? Am I going to have to eat the bill on this one?"

Andie Rose's jaw dropped, and I was dumbfounded. Neither of us was sure how to even respond to that.

I cleared my throat. "No, Stew, getting your money won't be a problem."

His face turned pomegranate red. "You must know I didn't mean it like that. I—I—"

"I'm sure you didn't," Andie Rose said.

"The deceased is Maggie Thompson," I said. "Thank you, Stew. You've been a big help."

"With what?" he asked, his skin returning to its pasty color.

"Solving a murder," I said.

"Are you with the police?"

"Kind of but not really," I said. *Kind of but not really the truth.* That pesky word "with" could be taken other ways, and I took advantage of that. After all, I was *with* Levi, and he's the police.

When we turned to leave, the man in the wingback chair was still watching Andie Rose.

"Dang, girl, let's get you out of here," I said under my breath. "I think the guy has you completely nude by now in his mind." He leered at us, creepy as all heck.

Andie Rose sniggered. "I can hold my own. Trust me."

As soon as the door closed behind us, I said, "It's a good thing Stew obviously doesn't read the newspaper or watch the news. We wouldn't have had any leverage over him."

"Small-town newspapers are one thing, but to be honest, on TV, I only saw a brief clip on the news about it. Apparently, unless it's somebody important, death doesn't matter. Big cities don't pay attention to what happens in a 'burb of the actual 'burbs."

Sadly, I knew she was right. "So I could die, and no one would know?" I teased.

She laughed and slapped my upper arm with the back of her hand. "It could be that they're trying to keep it quiet because they know something they don't want to get out."

I tilted my head to the side. "Hm. You have a point."

Aspen sat in the front passenger seat and looked at me through the window. "He's challenging me," I said, laughing.

Andie Rose opened her door. "Aspen, back." He looked at her with eyes like melted chocolate.

"I can sit in the back," I said.

"You will do no such thing," she said. "Aspen, come on, boy."

She reached in and snapped her fingers toward the back. Reluctantly, he turned and stepped into the back seat. But not without a final look at me. How a dog could make me feel so guilty was a mystery.

"I want to know who this Marco guy is. And is he connected to Sonia? If so, how is Sonia involved in all this?"

"I'd wonder if she's the killer, but she seems too young and naive to commit murder. Especially to get away with it," I said. I enjoyed working on this case with Andie Rose, but I missed Claire. Even though she gave me grief about all the shenanigans I'd gotten myself into over the past few years, I knew she enjoyed working them with me. She's the teabag to my hot water. Without her, I'm not nearly as successful. "I need to get home," I said. "Spend some time with my grandmother."

"Of course!" she exclaimed. "Sorry if I kept you too long."

"No, you didn't at all. I'm glad we went. It answered a lot of questions. But raised equally as many." I rolled my eyes. "I'll call Levi and see if he can run a deeper search on Marco Vega. There's got to be something there. In the meantime, with you moving sooner than expected to Spirit Lake, I'll talk to Claire and see if she can keep a lookout for Sonia at the gym and chat it up with her. Claire can get a conversation out of a tree stump," I said, chuckling.

When we pulled into Babs' apartment complex and the spot next to my car, I gave Aspen one last pet on the nose. He licked my hand, so I assumed he had forgiven me for taking his seat.

Andie Rose walked around to my side, hugged me, and said, "Let me know if there's anything you need from me. I'll keep you posted if I find out anything else."

"Perfect." I opened the door to my car, put one foot in, and turned toward her. "Hey, it was great to meet you. I can't believe Babs didn't bring you around before now."

"She and I were both so busy. When we got together, it was a last-minute coffee date or lunch."

I laughed. "Yeah, I know how that is. I hope you have a wonderful move, and the inn is everything you expected."

She grinned. "I have a feeling we'll be seeing each other again, Melanie."

"That would be nice."

I got in, and with a final wave and a light tap of my horn, I headed to my grandmother's.

I had just turned onto her street when my phone rang. I glanced at the display on my car. Levi.

"Hi, babe," I said. "Hang on for a second." After pulling into her driveway and in front of the garage, I said, "Ok, I'm back. I just got to Nana's house."

"Hey, blondie. I have some news for you."

"I have some for you, too. You first."

"It's looking like the dead woman killed the dead man. How's that for a twist?"

"What?" I exclaimed. My jaw dropped. I looked toward the house and saw Nana in the kitchen window looking out at me. I held up my phone, then one finger, letting her know I'd be just a minute. She nodded, smiled, and disappeared.

"Walker said she had debris under her fingernails that matched the rock and vegetation from around the man's body."

"Levi, that guy was there the morning before. How long do they think his body was lying there? It couldn't have been very long, or I'd think someone would have come across it. Not to mention it would have started to smell worse than it did."

"I can't imagine many people cut across that field and onto that trail at this time of the year. They're putting the time of death the same morning as you found Maggie's body."

"Which means she killed him right before *she* was killed," I said, staring at the garage door in front of me without seeing it. I chewed on my lower lip and twirled a strand of hair.

"Yup."

"Do we know for sure what time the woman was killed?"

"Early. About four in the morning."

"Someone went through a lot of work to throw the police off with the whole fitness watch misdirection," I murmured, still processing what I'd just heard.

"They did."

"There couldn't have been very many people in the gym so early," I said. Nana peered out the window again, and I held my finger up once more.

"The people that checked in have all been interviewed. While all are suspects in a sense, none of them are likely."

"Is Walker competent to handle this investigation?"

Levi chuckled. "Very. And there are only two homicide investigators."

"And why can't you investigate it?"

"There are two of us for a reason. I can't do them all. Not that we had many until you voiced a request for a little action in sleepy Birch Haven," he added.

"A statement I've cursed since," I grumbled. "I still don't understand why you can't investigate this one."

"Because Walker already has a bead on it. And, really, it's still a conflict of interest. You're the one who found the body. One of them anyway," he explained patiently as if talking to a child.

In his defense, I *was* behaving like a child, pouting because this investigation wasn't getting handled the way in which I wanted it to. My spoiled self wasn't happy.

"But I'm not a suspect anymore," I said, continuing to argue.

"You found the body, Melanie," he said, still unbelievably patient.

"Huh."

"What's this news you have for me?" he asked.

"I took the key card to the Rest Awhile Motel to see—"

"What key card?"

Oh, shoot! I hadn't told him about the confiscated key card from the floor in the locker room. I desperately struggled to come up with an explanation.

"Melanie? What key card?" His tone held a warning. Gentle, but a warning all the same.

"Um, well, there was, uh—"

"Spit it out."

I took a deep breath. "I found a key card to the Rest Awhile Motel on the floor of the locker room, and—"

"You didn't turn it in?" He groaned. I imagined him running his hand over his bald head in frustration, eyes closed. "Melanie, that's tampering with evidence. Again!"

"What do you mean?" I asked, trying to exude all the innocence I could muster. Innocence I knew he wouldn't buy but was worth a try. "The tech didn't take it as part of the evidence, so how was I supposed to know it had anything to do with the murder?"

"How indeed," he muttered.

"I found a pair of panties too; should I have turned those in?"

Amusement broke through his sigh. "What did you find out about the key card?"

"Well, being the good citizen that I am—" I heard him chuckle. "I went to turn it into the motel and found out it belonged to Marco Vega. That's a little suspect, don't you think? That the car following Andie Rose and me was registered to Marco Vega and so was the motel key card?"

I quickly continued before he could say more about keeping the key card. "The morning after Maggie's murder, when Andie Rose and I were in the locker room—the morning we found the key card—we met three women. One of them, Natalie, is from Spirit Lake and was here visiting her sister. Know what her sister's name is? Sonia Vega."

Levi was silent for a moment, then said, "Vega is a pretty common name."

"Yeah, yeah." I took a breath. "I looked up how many there are in Birch Haven. Surprisingly, not so many. I'm gonna ask Claire if she'll strike up a conversation with Sonia when—or if—she sees her at the gym."

"How about you *don't* ask Claire to do that, and Walker talks to her instead. This is getting too dangerous. Sonia could be connected to the killer."

"Or she could *be* the killer," I said, "which is even more reason to find out sooner rather than later. Maybe Walker doesn't work out in a gym. Even if he does, hopping on a treadmill or an elliptical next to a woman and asking her personal questions may come off as being kind of perverted."

I heard him inhale long and slow. Finally, he said, "I have a feeling you're going to do this regardless of what I say."

"And still you love me," I said, grinning.

28

While I was at Nana's, I called Claire and scheduled a girls' night out at Grizzley's Tap House, our favorite joint. We even had what we like to think of as our booth. They didn't take reservations, but they'd gotten to know us well enough by now that if we called and told them we were coming, most of the time, they'd save it for us unless someone new on the staff answered the phone. Then, if it was occupied when we got there, we'd wait until it opened. It was worth the wait.

Nana and I hung out in her kitchen most of the time, a favorite place for both of us. We sat at the kitchen table, a table that has witnessed a mountain of conversations over the years from the day's events, to broken hearts, to bad days and milestones. You name it, we've talked about it.

"When are you and that man of yours going to get married?" Nana asked me as she scooped rounded spoonfuls of dough onto a cookie sheet.

"When we do," I said, taking a sip of my chamomile tea.

"Melanie Hogan, that is not an answer." Her blue eyes and silver hair made her appear as I imagined angels would look. "How have you been sleeping?" Nana used to be a nurse for most of her life, and she swore that adequate sleep and a healthy diet were the best medicine given to man.

"I have an appointment with Dr. Cannon Tuesday afternoon. I tried to get in tomorrow since the salon is closed, but she's booked solid. She'll call if she has a cancellation." Nana used to work with Dr. Cannon back in the day. She'd been my doctor forever. Or as Nana and Grandad used to say, *forever in a coon's age.* But I knew it was only a matter of time before she retired. "I slept better last night, so I'm feeling rested."

"I can tell," she said, smiling. "You finally have some color back in those cheeks. But it takes more than one night of good sleep, dontcha know. Keep that appointment so that you can get something. If you don't need it, then don't take it, but you'll have it in case you do."

Nana slid the cookie sheets into the oven, and we moved our conversation to the sunny little breakfast nook, now shaded from the late afternoon sun. A bench lined one side of the alcove, two chairs on the other side. I slid onto the bench, my usual spot, and Nana sat on one of the chairs. The birds flitted in and out of the houses and on and off the feeders from shepherd's hooks that surrounded the bay window. Patches of lingering snow spotted the ground.

"Getting a jump start on calling the birds in, huh?" I said as black-capped chickadees swooped in and landed on the feeder nearest me.

"Saw my first robin yesterday." She smiled. Nana loved spring because it meant she would soon spend time tending her gardens. And she had immaculate gardens. They were the envy of the neighborhood.

We talked until it grew dark. Usually, when I was here in the evenings, we cooked dinner together. Nana had always been a spectacular cook and had taught me how to make some pretty darn good Minnesota hotdishes over the years. Tonight, however, since I was leaving to meet Claire and Rubie at Grizzlies, we ate leftovers she'd had in the freezer. Eating leftovers always reminded me of Granddad. He had always preferred leftovers to anything else.

At seven-thirty, after we'd washed dishes and Nana was tucked under her favorite blanket in her favorite chair with a good book and a cup of tea by her side, I let myself out. I locked the door behind me, checked it twice, then headed to Grizzley's. It had been a near-perfect day. After seeing Claire and Rubie, and then Levi, *then* it would be perfect.

***

Grizzley's looked busy for a Sunday evening. I spotted Claire's car, Rubie's close to hers, and I nabbed an empty spot nearby. As soon as I walked in, I zeroed in on our booth. Claire sat on one side, Rubie on the other. Rubie was laughing, her blond curls bouncing. When I reached the table, Claire slid out and hugged me; Rubie following suit.

"Jack's coming too," Claire said as she slid back in, patting the seat beside her for me to sit.

To say I was ecstatic was an understatement. Even though we'd just met at my house a mere two nights ago, this was our special place, and we hadn't been here for a long time. And waiting until my birthday, a short week away, even seemed too long.

"That is the best news ever!" I said, grinning so wide I thought my face would split in two. The server, Gia, was by my side before I took my jacket off.

"What can I get you, Mel?" she said.

I looked at Rubie's sickeningly sweet Tom Collins drink and Claire's glass of white wine. "I'll have seltzer water with orange for now until I decide what adult beverage I might want. Thanks, Gia!"

A basket of chips and salsa sat in the middle of the table. I snagged a chip, dipped it in the salsa, and barely made it to my mouth before salsa dripped on the table. I chewed, swallowed, and fanned my mouth, taking a drink from Claire's water glass. My eyes teared. "Holy Moly! That's some hot salsa!"

"You're just a sissy girl," Rubie said, laughing. As if to prove her point, she grabbed a chip, scooped up a good portion of salsa, and chowed it down. Her eyes watered as she struggled to be tough.

I laughed. "You're such a bully!"

"Hey, hey!" I heard Jack's voice before I saw him. "Name-calling isn't nice," he said, reaching over to hug me, then practically leaning on me to hug Claire. Finally, he hugged Rubie and slid in on the booth beside her.

"Here," I said, sliding the chips and salsa toward him. "Have some salsa. It's delicious!"

Claire giggled.

"Why don't I believe you?" he said, narrowing one eye behind his black-rimmed glasses. No contacts tonight, and I was oddly happy about that. Gia whisked back to our table for Jack's order—a porter beer on draft. He looked at me. "I'm here tonight instead of next week. I can't make it for your birthday. Sorry, kid."

I waved him off. "Don't worry about it. I'd rather you be here tonight. Where are you going next week?"

"Paris."

"Paris?" Rubie exclaimed, nearly drooling. "The city of love." She was swooning, her eyes dreamy. "Take me with."

"Even though Scott has nothing to worry about, I can pretty much guarantee he wouldn't appreciate you going to Paris with another man," Jack said.

"Yeah," I said. "He's a keeper, so be good." I lifted my glass, toasting her relationship with Scott.

"I am," Rubie said, defending her honor. "I would never do anything to jeopardize our relationship."

"Except ask another guy to take you to Paris," I said, laughing.

"Come on, it's Jack!" she said as if that explained it all.

Gia came back to the table to drop off Jack's beer. "Can I get you guys anything else right now?" she asked, looking at each of us.

"No, thank you," Claire said.

"Not right now," Rubie said.

"Got any mild salsa?" I asked, hopeful. "I can't handle this new stuff."

Gia pointed to the bowl on our table. "That *is* the mild one."

Jack scooped some salsa on a chip. I watched as he casually chewed, then swallowed. I waited for him to drain his beer or ask for water. Nothing. I watched his eyes. Nothing there, either.

"Are you dead, or what?" I asked incredulously.

"There's nothing wrong with the salsa, Melanie."

"Rubie thought it was hot too," I said defensively.

"Yeah, but Rubie thinks cinnamon is hot," Claire said, giggling.

Rubie nodded. "It is!"

"What's new with your investigation?" Claire asked. "What'd you and Andie Rose find out in Spirit Lake today?"

"You're still involved in that?" Jack said, brows furrowed. "I'd hoped you'd given that up by now."

"There's a killer out there. And I found one of his—or her—victims. Andie Rose found the other. I'd think you would understand why we want to find the killer."

Jack shook his head slowly. "Hogan, you're killing *me*."

"On the contrary, my friend. I'm saving you by *catching* a killer."

"What have you got so far?" Claire asked.

"Funny you should ask," I said. "Are you going to the gym in the morning?"

Jack gave me a sidelong look. "She didn't ask how she can help you; she asked what you've got so far."

"I know, I know." I harumphed and waved a hand in dismissal at him, then looked at Claire again.

"I haven't decided yet. Depends on what time we get out of here tonight. Why? Want to go? I thought you were swearing it off."

I shook my head. "No. You remembered correctly. It's deadly, remember?"

"Only when you're there," Jack said.

I made a face at him. "Hush!" I looked at Claire. "Andie Rose and I met some women there the day after I found the body. One of them is Sonia Vega. The car that followed Andie Rose and me to Spirit Lake this morning was—"

"Wait," Claire said, grabbing my arm, her eyes wide. "Someone followed you guys?"

"Good to know I'm not the only one in the dark," Jack said.

"Nope," Rubie said. "It would appear all three of us are." She looked at me. "Maybe starting at the beginning would be a good idea?" She snapped up a chip, reached for the salsa, hesitated a moment, then popped the plain chip in her mouth.

I filled them in on the trip to Spirit Lake, including the bit about Aspen's resentment of me taking his spot riding shotgun.

"And you've never seen this car in Birch Haven?" Jack asked.

I shook my head. "No. But I've never looked for it, either. You know how it is when you never see a certain kind or color of car until you have a reason to notice one, then you see it everywhere? I'll probably see blue Mazda's everywhere from now on."

"Okay, now that we know the beginning, continue on about the car following you," Rubie said.

"It's registered to Marco Vega."

"Related to this Sonia from the gym?" Claire asked.

"That's what I want to find out. I thought if I described her to you, you could look for her in the morning and talk to her. She's super chatty, so the two of you should hit it off fabulously."

She sat back and looked at me, then laughed. "What exactly are you saying?"

"That you could get a conversation out of the glass you're drinking from." I smiled at her. "You know I say that with love. The key card I found in the locker room, the one for the Rest Awhile Motel, belongs to Marco Vega too. Andie Rose and I stopped there on our way back from Spirit Lake."

"It sounds like you ladies had a productive day," Jack said dryly.

Despite his less than enthused tone, I knew he meant well. I would say he worried himself needlessly, but with the hot water I'd gotten myself into on more than a few occasions, I had to cut the guy some slack. I reached across the table and put my hand over his, nearly spilling his beer. "I promise I'm being as careful as possible."

He grabbed for his beer just before he ended up wearing it in his lap. "Why am I not confident when you tell me you're careful?" he grumbled.

"What else did you find out?" Rubie asked, saving the mood.

Jack nudged her with his elbow. "Quit encouraging her."

Rubie nudged him back. "She's going to do it anyway. Besides, don't you want the killer caught? Or killers, plural?" She looked at me. "Do you know if it's the same killer for both victims?"

I wondered how much I could reveal without getting anyone into trouble. Looking at each of them, eyes waiting expectantly, including Jack's, though he would never admit to that. "No. Not unless the woman killed herself."

"What do you mean?" Claire asked.

I looked around our booth to see who was sitting within hearing range, then leaned in slightly, speaking as quietly as I could. "Looks like the dead woman killed the dead man. Right before she was killed." Claire and Rubie both gasped. Jack looked at me, his eyes narrowed slightly as he appeared to process the revelation. "That information does not leave this group."

"That goes without saying," Rubie said.

Claire, Rubie, and I all reached in and locked pinkies. I looked at Jack. "Jack Dancy."

"Who am I going to tell, my designing notebook? I don't think my designs care."

"Jack," I warned. I must have sounded threatening enough, or maybe it was the arrows I shot him with my eyes because, after another brief pause, he relented and locked pinkies with us.

29

I filled them in on the photo I saw of the woman at the magazine with Connie's husband. "Her name is Jill. And she looks as different from Connie as two people can be."

"What a sleazeball!" Rubie griped, throwing a wadded-up napkin across the table.

"Speaking of Connie," I said, "has anyone heard from her?"

"Nope," Claire said.

"Not a peep," said Rubie.

"I wonder if Babs has," I wondered aloud. "Probably not," I answered myself. "If she had, she would have told Andie. One of them would have said something to us. You should have seen the guy at the motel checking out Andie Rose," I said. "He wasn't discreet about it at all." I made a face and looked at Jack. "You men."

He shook his head and held up his hand, palm facing me. "Oh no, you don't."

"What?" I asked innocently.

"Don't lump me in with all of the male race."

"The male race?" I said, laughing.

"Hogan," he warned. But his eye twitched, and I knew he was trying not to laugh.

I continued filling Jack in on the dumpster escapade with Claire, and he was hooting with laughter by the time I finished. Being the composed person he is by nature, Jack rarely laughed like he was.

"It wasn't funny at the time," Claire said. "That darn cat freaked me out!" She shuddered.

"No, it wasn't funny, Jack! I was locked in there."

"Because of your own lack of judgment," he said. "And if you'll remember, I told you not to do it. I just wish I could have been there when the cat came out." He laughed again.

I narrowed my eyes at him. "Jack—"

"Don't even pretend to be mad at me, Mel," he said, still laughing. "And you," he said, looking at Claire, "I still can't believe you went along with the whole thing."

"Yeah, but—"

"Yeah, but nothing," he said.

"Levi and I stumbled across a huge breakthrough in that garbage bag," I said. I'd filled Claire in already but not Jack and Rubie. When I finished telling them about Grand Pharmaceuticals and mine and Levi's suspicions, Rubie sat speechless, something that's only happened on a handful of occasions. Jack's brown eyes pierced mine.

"That's unsettling," he finally said. "This thing could be a lot more dangerous than any of us ever imagined."

"Big pharma," Rubie said in a harsh whisper. "They've got nothing to lose if they're in the middle of this, Melanie. You need to stay out of it." She looked around us as if expecting someone to be listening in.

"Finally, someone in this group with some sense besides me," Jack said quietly, not taking his eyes off mine.

"Please tell me Levi said the same thing."

I tilted my head to the side. "What do you think?"

"Hard to tell," he said.

"Like she'd listen, anyway," Rubie said, shaking her head.

Silence fell around our table as the rest of the place seemed to get even louder. Each of us peered around our table once again, making sure no one was listening in. Chills ran up and down my spine. The feeling of being watched was so strong it was palpable. I shivered and scanned the joint and then toward the door. Just as I did, Gia waltzed over to our table.

"Melanie," she said, "some guy came in and said he saw someone hit a white Jeep. Sounds like it was yours. Better go check."

"Crap!" I said as I slid from the booth and into my jacket. "I'll be right back."

"I'll come with you," Jack said.

"You stay here with Rubie," Claire said. "I'll go."

Secretly, I was happy he listened. Claire's husband had insisted she be able to protect herself and their daughter when he was away on active duty, so she is now a second-degree black belt in karate. And if there was a reason for my strong suspicion a moment ago that someone was watching—well, Claire would be more helpful than Jack.

As soon as the door closed behind us, I scanned the parking lot and shivered again, rubbing my upper arms. "You're going to think I'm crazy," I said quietly, "and I probably am, but I'm getting this strong hunch that someone's watching us."

Claire inhaled sharply. "Did you see someone?"

"No. It's a feeling I can't shake."

"Where are you parked?" she asked.

"Right by you and Rubie."

We walked the rest of the way in silence, both vigilant of our surroundings. When we were almost at my car, I zeroed in on something out of the ordinary on my driver's window. I couldn't tell if something was on the glass or if the dim security lights cast shadows, giving it that appearance. But when we got closer, I knew my sixth sense served me well. Written on my window in what looked like red lipstick was the message, *Buzz off or you're third.*

Claire gasped. "The third what?"

"If I had to guess, I would assume the third dead body," I said gravely.

"Looks like you have a problem," someone said from behind us.

Claire screamed and spun around, ready to kick some butt. I jumped and turned around to see the man from the Rest Awhile Motel who'd been ogling Andie Rose. Natalie was standing at his side, her hand looped through his arm.

"Hi ladies," Natalie said, concern etched in her face. "Melanie, who did you tick off?"

It took a minute to register that they were together. "I don't know yet, but I'm going to find out. I won't accept someone threatening me."

Natalie's mouth hung open. "You mean you're not going to take heed of the warning? You need to call the police!" She looked at Claire. "Tell her she needs to call the police."

"You do, Mel. At least call Levi. Or let me call Cole."

I took my phone out, snapped a picture, and then sent Levi a short message. *Someone paid me a visit tonight while I was in Grizzley's with the girls and Jack.*

"What does this mean?" Natalie asked. "What do they want you to keep your nose out of? And the third what?"

I kept my eyes on the man who was within inches of the message, studying it closely.

"This is Ted," Natalie said.

Ted reached out his middle finger and touched one of the letters.

"Don't touch it," Claire said. "It's evidence."

"Of what?" he asked, looking at the red smear on his finger where he touched. "Looks like—" he rubbed his thumb against his finger, "lipstick." He furrowed his brows. "Does that mean anything to you?" he asked, looking at me. "Why lipstick?"

"Melanie and Claire own the hair salon, A Cut Above," Natalie said to him, then looked at me. "Do you think that has anything to do with it?"

"The lipstick, yes, probably just to prove a point," I said. "The message, no." Her eyes looked at me expectantly. "I've been trying to solve a murder. The one from the gym. And the guy outside."

Her eyes grew wide, and her mouth formed an *o*. Finally, she said, "Oh, my goodness. This message is from a murderer? Now I must insist even more that you have to call the police. Here, use my phone." She extended her hand toward me, but I held up my own in answer.

As if on cue, my phone buzzed with an incoming text. *Stay put. Walker's on his way.*

U 2? I sent back.

On my way. But Walker will beat me there. R u safe?

Yes. Claire is here.

I waited for a response, and when I was sure he was done, I said to Claire, "Levi and Detective Walker are on their way. He said to stay put."

"Let's go wait inside," Natalie said. "We'll wait with you."

"Natalie, just curious—Grand Pharmaceuticals. Was that the story you were working on with *Lakes News and Reviews*?"

She frowned and shook her head. "Someone is threatening you, and you want to stand out here and talk about work?" She touched my arm and gently pulled me forward. "Come on. Let's go inside where you're safe. We can talk in there."

"It's okay; I've got Claire here. And our friends Rubie and Jack are inside waiting for us."

"Can't you at least wait inside? For my peace of mind, if nothing else. It doesn't seem safe for you out here." She looked at the message and back at me.

"No, I'm not leaving. I don't want to chance someone taking it off before the police get here."

Natalie tugged lightly on Ted's arm and looked up at him. "We'll wait with you then. There's safety in numbers."

"Okay," I said. "What brings you out here tonight?"

"I'm heading back home tomorrow morning," she said. "I've got deadlines I need to make on a story Jill is helping me with."

"Jill?" Her statement surprised me. "I thought Jill was the receptionist."

"She is," Natalie said. "But she has aspirations of becoming a journalist." She rolled her eyes. "Her daddy is making me work with her since Maggie was—you know. The girl drives me crazy! All she does is talk, talk, talk. About nothing!" She sidled in closer to Ted. "I hate to leave him to go back and listen to Jill."

I was taken back and looked at Ted. "You live here in Birch Haven?"

He nodded and tucked his hands in his front pockets. Natalie still clutched onto his arm. "I do," he said. He must have seen the question in my eyes because he added, "When Nat comes to town, we stay at the motel."

"My sister doesn't know about us," Natalie said. "I'm not sure I'm ready for her to know."

"Why?" I asked before I even realized it. "Oh, uh —" I made a gesture as if erasing the question.

"She's sorry," Claire said, shooting me a look, eyebrow arched. "It's none of our business."

"No big deal," Natalie said with a slight chuckle. "Sonia's a bit old-fashioned. I have no idea where she got it from. Ted's divorce isn't quite final yet, and Sonia would literally kill him if she knew that. Like literally." She chuckled nervously. "She'd be so mad! My dad cheated on my mom, so she's pretty sensitive to that." She gasped and added quickly, "I mean, that all sounds horribly wrong. Ted and I aren't having an affair. I'm not married — in fact, I'm very unattached — and Ted is separated from his wife. And not because of me."

Yeah, right. Visions of my unfaithful ex popped into my head. My phone buzzed with an incoming text, and I looked at the display. Jack. *Did u get lost or what?*

It'll be a bit. 2 much 2 text.

U okay?

Will fill u in as soon as we come back.

I slipped my phone into my pocket. "Natalie, is Sonia married?" I asked.

She laughed. "Sonia married? How to answer that." She seemed to ponder it for a moment. "Yeah, she's on her second time around. And the guy is a loser."

"Do you know a Marco Vega?" I asked hopefully.

She appeared to think, then said, "No, I don't think so. Why?"

"The name has just come up a couple of times lately. With Birch Haven being a smallish town, and with his last name the same as your sister, I just thought…" I trailed off, hoping Natalie would pick it up.

"Vega's a common name," she said. "Like Smith or Johnson." Working with the public, I knew exactly how common those names were. Too many to count. "Wait, how did you know my sister's last name is Vega? I didn't think you guys knew each other when we were at the gym."

"We don't. When you introduced her, you said her last name."

She laughed loudly. "Oh! Duh," she sang.

Ted laughed. "You're such a dunce."

Interesting words coming from a man who had been checking out Andie Rose earlier when he was there with his girlfriend. I got a bad taste in the back of my throat. I doubted Ted was even getting a divorce. But I guess just because my ex cheated on me doesn't mean Ted was doing the same thing. But still. It didn't cast him in a favorable light.

"Is Vega your last name too?" Claire asked.

"No. Sonia and I share the same mom but have different dads. Sonia's dad was a Vega, and she kept her maiden name when she got married both times. Her dad is dead. But I'm pretty sure there are more Vegas in Spirit Lake."

"Yeah. But I didn't see a Marco in the phone listings."

She shrugged. "I don't know of a Marco, but maybe he's Jill's ex. I never met him. But I'm pretty sure he was a Vega."

30

Detective Walker pulled into the parking lot and went up and down a couple of rows before coming upon us. He got out and lumbered over to us. "Melanie, I've seen you more than Levi has lately. It's a small town. People are gonna start talking."

"Somehow, I doubt that," I mumbled. Claire elbowed me. I tried to see the cuteness Andie Rose mentioned, but all I could see was a man who'd investigated me too many times in too many cases. That somehow squashed any cuteness in my head. "Andie Rose thinks Walker's cute," I whispered to Claire, still hung up on that for some unknown reason.

"He is," she whispered back. "Very."

I wrinkled my nose.

"Ladies?" he said.

My cheeks warmed, embarrassed that he may have heard us.

"Fill me in," Walker said.

"Gia came over—she's one of the servers—she came over to our table and said someone reported that they saw a car hit a white Jeep. She knows what I drive, so she assumed it was mine." My eyes grew wide. "Oh geez! With the window incident, I forgot to check the rest of my car." I shined the flashlight on my smartphone and began walking around my vehicle, inspecting it. Detective Walker took his utility flashlight and did the same.

"Not a scratch on this thing," he said.

"That's odd," I said.

"Maybe it was a different white Jeep and not yours at all," Claire said.

"Maybe," I mused, not convinced. "Or maybe someone lured me out here to see my window."

"That'd be my guess," Detective Walker said. He looked around the parking lot, walking to and fro, looking at the other vehicles.

I looked around. "Where's Natalie and Ted?" I asked Claire.

She looked around as well, then shrugged. "Ted wanted to go in."

"I don't like that guy, Claire. He's the one who was checking out Andie Rose today at the Rest a While."

"I figured as much when you started talking about the motel," she said.

Detective Walker came back to Claire and me when Levi pulled up. He got out of his car, wrapped an arm around my waist, and kissed the top of my head.

"Get a room, Wescott," Walker said, chuckling like a teenager.

"It's not my crime scene," Levi said, "it's yours. And I'm not on the clock," he teased back. "I'm just here for moral support." He stepped away from me and toward my car to scrutinize the writing. "Lipstick?" he said, frowning.

"Between the nail polish messages and now lipstick, what is this guy, the beauty products killer?"

Walker laughed along with Claire and me.

"Wescott," Walker said, "sure glad you came back."

Before Levi and I had officially gotten together, he moved to the East Coast for almost a year to be closer to Jackson when Jackson's mother moved him out there. Thankfully, they moved back to Birch Haven, and Levi got his job back on the Birch Haven Detective Team.

"You and me both, brother," Levi said.

The two of them shared what I assumed were theories and conclusions in hushed tones until both fell silent. Then Levi said, "Walker, want me to chat with the server who told Mel about the accident? See who reported it?"

"Nah, I got it covered. Go." He waved Levi on.

"Well, I guess I'm coming in with you ladies," Levi said to Claire and me. "I wouldn't want to impede Walker's investigation." Both men chuckled. "And I can see that Melanie gets home safe."

"I'll bet," Walker mumbled and snickered.

My night just went from great to perfect. Jack and the girls loved Levi, and the feeling was mutual. "I won't argue," I said.

He looked at me, his eyes narrowing. "What's the catch?"

I chuckled. "Why does there have to be a catch?"

"Because you never give in that easy," Claire said warily. "What's up?"

I turned sober. "The fact that this guy knows what I drive tells me he's a little too close." I elbowed Levi gently. "And I've got a wedding I need to be at."

Levi guffawed. "If I can get you to set a date."

***

On the way back to our booth, I swung by Natalie's table, Levi right behind me.

"It's all good," I told her. I placed my hand on Levi's arm. "Natalie, this is Levi. Levi, this is Natalie. She's the one I met at the gym. And Jed," I added, nodding toward him.

"Ted," the man corrected, extending his hand toward Levi.

"You guys have a good evening," I said, smiling at Natalie.

When we were out of hearing range, Levi asked me, "What was that about?"

I shrugged. "Dunno." I looked up at him.

"You do," he argued, amusement tugging at the corner of his lips, his eyes dancing.

"I don't like the guy."

He chuckled. "Never would have guessed."

When we reached our booth, Levi pulled a chair from a nearby table and parked it at the end of our booth. Gia was at our table in a heartbeat.

"Hey, how come you don't come to our table that fast when Levi isn't here?" Rubie asked.

"Are you complaining about my service, Rubie?" Gia asked, laughing.

"Not even a little," Rubie said.

As soon as Gia got Levi's order, a bottled vanilla porter, he said to me, "Why don't you like Ted? Or should I say Jed?" He filled the rest in on my name mishap, and they all laughed.

"Because he's the one who checked out Andie Rose so obnoxiously when we were at the motel. Not only is he dating Natalie, but she is staying with him there. That is so tacky."

"I'd have to agree," Levi said, slipping Gia some bills when she set his beer in front of him. "You can keep the glass, Gia," he said. "I'm a bottle guy."

"Claire filled us in," Jack said, then looked at Levi. "What's your opinion?"

"Someone is feeling a bit of heat and knows too much of what Melanie is up to," he said. "Not only does he know what she drives, but he's using nail polish and lipstick to write his messages. I'd say he's done his homework and knows far too much about her." Levi looked at me. "I don't want you to think I'm controlling, but I don't want you alone until we get this figured out."

As much as I expected the familiar feeling of suffocation at the thought of not having time alone, it didn't come this time.

Jack sat back and straightened his collar. "Well, if the two of you don't mind, I'd like to crash at her house tonight. Driving back to Minneapolis this late isn't appealing."

"I would insist on it," I said. I looked at Levi. "I'm still curious about how Marco Vega fits into all of this. Who is this guy?" I filled him in on what we found out from Natalie. "If Jill's supposed ex was a Vega, maybe they're in this together. Or if she's married to Marco and was having an affair with Connie's husband, that would make total sense that he would have killed Paul."

"Yeah," Claire said, "except you said the picture of Jill and Paul was sitting out in the open by her desk. She wouldn't have it sitting out there for all to see if she was married."

I tipped my head to the side. "Good point. But maybe that's how Marco discovered her affair."

"I don't think so. She still wouldn't have had the photo on her desk," Levi said.

"If she's divorced from Marco, she wouldn't bother hiding it." I thought back to Jill in the office. "But then she looks far too young to be married at all, much less divorced."

"I thought you said she was in her early twenties," Claire said.

"She is."

"Well, you can get married at eighteen in Minnesota, so being divorced at her age isn't too surprising."

"I'll look into Jill," Levi said. He took out his phone and punched in a number, then waited. We all watched him with bated breath. "Walker?" he finally said. "Can you look into the receptionist from *Lakes News and Reviews* from Spirit Lake? First name Jill, unknown last name. It might be Vega. Boss's daughter." I heard the faint rumbling of Detective Walker's voice before Levi said, "Yeah. She could be involved in this somehow. Can you let me know what you find? Yeah, okay. Talk to you later." He ended the call and said, "Well, I don't have to tell any of you what was said since you were all, except for Jack, practically on top of the table listening."

"How do you suppose Grand Pharmaceuticals plays into this?" Rubie asked.

"I looked into the company," Levi said. "It would appear the tentacles reach beyond their own business. They own *Lakes News and Reviews*."

I gasped, grabbed his arm, and my eyes grew huge. "The boss of the magazine is Jill's father. The two murders and the drug company are connected. I know it!"

"It's a likely possibility," Levi said, "but not for certain. There are too many unknowns."

"Well, let's turn them into knowns, then," I said. I slid out from the booth and said, "I'll be right back."

"Where are you going?" Jack asked warily.

"To use the ladies' room," I said. Jack visibly relaxed. "All four of you are sitting right here; what did you think I was going to pull?" I asked him.

"I never know with you," he said.

"Relax and have another beer, Jacky." I grinned at him and headed off toward the restroom. I scanned the room for Ted and didn't see either of them.

Once inside, I primped a bit until Natalie came out of the stall. "Hey, Melanie," she said. She set her purse on the vanity, turned on the water, and squirted some soap in her hand.

"Hey! I thought you guys left."

"Not yet. Ted wants to hang here for a while."

"Natalie, you work at *Lakes News and Reviews*. What—"

She interrupted. "I don't work *for* them, I'm just collaborating with one of their journalists on a story. I already told you that."

"What do you know about Grand Pharmaceuticals?"

She stopped sudsing and looked at me through the mirror. "Who wants to know?"

"I think they have something to do with Maggie's death. And probably Paul's as well."

She finished rinsing and snagged two paper towels, drying her hands slowly. "I stay out of it."

"Why?" I asked. I saw what looked like fear in her eyes. "What do you know?"

"What do *you* know?" she asked, turning to look at me rather than through the mirror.

"I know they're responsible in some way for the deaths, but I don't know how. Natalie, is Jill involved with them somehow?"

"I can't talk about it, Melanie. And you shouldn't either." Suddenly, she gasped. "Do you suppose that's who wrote on your car window? Exactly how involved are you? And I sure as hell hope you're not getting the both of us killed as well."

Fear reflected in her eyes. "I need to find out who killed Paul, Natalie. I need to clear his wife, Connie. She doesn't deserve this."

"I'm begging you, Melanie. You don't know what you're getting into. Grand Pharmaceuticals is far-reaching. Ted will kill me!"

"Ted?" I turned my head slightly and squinted. "How is Ted involved?" When she didn't say anything, merely looked at her hands as she twisted a paper towel, I said, "Natalie, please tell me so I can be aware and not walk in blind. I'm going to find out who killed Paul. Tell me why they're so frightening and how Ted is involved." I stepped toward her and reached for her arm, touching it gently. "Natalie, if I can bring them down, and *them* includes Ted, then you wouldn't have anything to be afraid of anymore." When she didn't say anything, I added, "I'm going to find out with or without you. I'm already well on my way."

My eyes met hers, pleading with her to help me. But in her eyes, the fear no longer resided. Her green-gray eyes turned stormy. She reached in her purse and took out a small pistol. I inhaled sharply.

"You should have kept your nose out of it, Melanie. Connie left well enough alone as she was told to do. You, on the other hand, don't listen so well, do you?"

"But, Ted—"

"Is a great fall guy." She pointed the gun into my rib cage. "Come on. Take a left. We're going out the back door."

"And if I don't?"

She laughed quietly. "Oh, you will." The gun jabbed into my ribs. Women's voices came near the door, and hope surged up within me. "Don't even think about it," she said.

When the voices passed by the door, my hopes fell.

"Go," she said, giving me a slight shove.

I opened the door, hoping one of the many women in the restaurant would be coming our way. Women's restrooms were never empty. Why now?! Natalie assisted in forcing me to take a sharp left down the dimly lit hallway leading out to the back. I had found myself in this very spot a couple of years ago. Grizzley's Tap House was turning out to be as dangerous for me as the gym. I had to find different stomping grounds.

"Why are you doing this, Natalie?" I asked. "How are you involved?" I had to keep her talking. Somehow keep her answering the many questions I had in case I happened to make it out of this alive. Which I was starting to wonder about as she led me around a dark corner. "Are you going to kill me like you did the other two?"

"I didn't kill Paul. Maggie did."

"I don't believe you."

"Why would I lie about that?"

"Oh, I don't know," I said. "Maybe because you're not exactly a stand-up, reliable person?"

"I'm telling you the truth," she said. "I didn't kill Paul. I hired him to keep an eye on Maggie. She was trying to destroy the pharmaceutical company, and they were paying me big bucks. Money talks, ya know?" She chuckled humorlessly and tilted her head. "I knew through Jill that he's a PI. It was the perfect situation, actually, with Maggie coming to Birch Haven to tackle another assignment and all." She laughed at her apparent genius. "I saw Maggie follow and approach Paul. She discovered he'd been following her, they argued, he turned to walk away from her, she picked up a rock and smashed him over the head." She chuckled again. "I didn't know she had that kind of strength. Or that she had it in her to kill someone. Though, I don't think she meant to because she freaked out afterward. But then she went to the gym and worked out like nothing had happened. Tough broad."

"But why was Maggie so threatened by Paul?" I asked as she continued to force me on my way slowly. I wanted answers in case I came out of this alive. Fear escalated, my breaths became quicker. My chances were greater if I could distract her by keeping her talking.

"Paul's an investigator. Maggie's got a deep dark secret Paul threatened to expose if she didn't back the heck off from the Grand Pharmaceutical story. Apparently, she was intent on keeping that secret to her grave."

By now, she'd led me, ironically, back by the dumpsters. The bulb on the light pole flickered. I thought about Levi and the wedding that might never happen. I thought about Claire, Jack, and Rubie and how I wished I'd have listened. I thought about Max and Daisy, the new family I'd been enjoying so much. And then I thought about Nana, and tears welled up in my eyes. "Why did you have Maggie followed?" I asked. *Keep her talking. Just keep her talking.*

"She was going to blow the top off Grand Pharmaceuticals. We couldn't let that happen. She saw me in the locker room and said she knew about me, my involvement, and that she would end me. I panicked, grabbed the first thing I could think of, and well, we know what happened after that. Pure luck when you think about it. A ballpoint pen? It's as if it was supposed to happen." She shoved me again with the butt of the gun. "It didn't have to come to this with you, Melanie. You have yourself to thank."

"Ted."

"Who?" she asked, her voice sharp in the darkness.

"Ted isn't Ted. He's Marco Vega, isn't he?"

"He's Jill's ex-brother-in-law. Now get down on your knees. Face the dumpster."

I thought of Nana again. "Natalie, please," I begged. "Levi will know it was you."

She laughed louder this time. "Levi will know? I don't think so."

"You're wrong." Levi's voice cut through the darkness. "I do know, Natalie. Drop your gun."

I finally exhaled. Levi was rescuing me. Again. In a split second, Natalie's surprise caused her to lose her focus on me; using a move Claire taught me, I jabbed my elbow backward and upward, connecting solidly with her ribs. She squealed and doubled over, crying in pain as Levi cuffed her. I retrieved the papers I'd swiped from Maggie's office from my cross-body handbag I'd been wearing and extended them toward Levi. "Here. Hopefully these will help."

"You won't get away with this, Melanie Hogan."

"Oh, that's where you're wrong, Natalie. I'm not the one in cuffs."

"I'm not in this alone, you know," she said, her eyes hard in the still-flickering light. "You think I'm dangerous? You haven't seen anything yet. The top dogs'll come for you."

My legs shook slightly, realizing she might be right. But there was also the chance that she was bluffing, and she was one of the top players and the key to closing this case; unlikely, but possible. And if that was the case, the house of cards could all come down. But if not...well, I decided I was willing to take that chance. Regardless, I wasn't about to let her see any fear. "I'm not afraid of you or any of the Grand Pharmaceuticals henchmen," I said with forced bravado. "You're all going down."

31

Driving home from Nana's the following afternoon, I held back tears. Dr. Cannon had a cancellation, and Nana's was the first place I thought to go after the appointment. First, I told Nana about the confrontation with Natalie and how Levi had stormed to my rescue. Again. As I'd told her, I realized how close I'd come to not living to see another day, and I felt as though I'd suffocate from welled-up emotion. Then I told her the other news from the doctor that had rocked my foundation as I knew it. My life would never be the same again. I'd gone to the doctor in hopes of getting something to help me sleep and left with mind-blowing news.

I welled up with a fresh wave of tears as I wondered how Levi, Claire, Jack, and Rubie would take the news. Nana was surprisingly strong. Now a river of tears washed down my cheeks and my neck. What was I going to do?

I opened my car window and forced a deep breath, letting the fresh, spring air fill my lungs.

I picked up my phone and punched in a number. "Levi?" I choked out when he answered. "Can you meet me at my house? I need to talk to you."

"Blondie? Are you crying?"

I heard the panic in his voice. "Yeah, I guess I am."

"What's wrong?"

"Not on the phone."

"I'm on my way. I'll be there in ten."

"Please be careful," I said, wiping a cheek with the palm of my hand, then the other cheek. I wiped my nose on my sleeve.

Next, I punched in Claire's number. She would be coming over that evening and said she'd tell Rubie to come by too. I was relieved the salon was closed on Mondays. I wouldn't have been able to go back to work after the appointment. I needed my circle right now, but I would have to tell Jack over the phone and hope he understood.

Levi's car was already in front of my house. I pulled up my long driveway, wondering how I would tell him. Fresh tears poured forth. I turned my car off, wiped my cheeks again with the palms of my hands, and took a long, deep breath. *Here goes nothing.*

Before I got out of my car, the front door opened. "How fast did you drive? You didn't use your sirens, did you?" I asked him across the yard.

"Fast enough." He met me, wrapped me in his arms, then led me into the house. "You've got me worried half to death," he said, the slightest quiver in his voice. He led me to the sofa and sat beside me, pulling me toward him, his arm tight around my shoulders, the other holding my hand. Finally, he pulled slightly back and looked into my eyes, his finger under my chin. "What's going on?"

"I went to see my doctor today."

"I know. After six years. That's what's got me so freaked out."

I took a deep breath and laced my fingers through his with my left hand. I trembled. Why hadn't I married this man already? He was so perfect, and I'd kept putting off setting a date for no good reason other than fear. And now it was too late. A tear escaped and rolled down my cheek. He gently wiped it away with his thumb.

"Melanie, please. What is it?" I gulped fresh air but came up short. Finally, with my right hand, I took his and pressed it against my belly. "What would you say if I told you you're going to be a father again?" His jaw dropped open, and I held my breath, sure he was going to turn and run for the hills. We weren't exactly the age for a baby; he didn't sign up for that. He sat completely still, not uttering a word, only staring at me. "Levi?" I said. My voice was quiet but seemed to echo in the room. I was certain by now I was going to spiral into a full-blown panic attack.

Suddenly, without warning, he scooped me up and held me close, squeezing me a little too tight. I pushed against him to get some air. I looked into his eyes, afraid of what I might read there. He ran his finger softly along my cheek. His eyes danced with—was it delight? Could it possibly be?

"I would say, Ms. Hogan, soon-to-be Mrs. Wescott, that your sleuthing days are over." My lips trembled as he kissed me gently, then pulled back to look at me again. "But how? I thought you couldn't."

"You, me, the doctors, everyone thought I couldn't." I watched him closely as he stared at me. I could almost see the wheels turning in his head. "It appears the powers that be have intervened in getting me to stop the detective stuff. If you don't want to stay around, I completely understand. I wouldn't hold it against you. I would never expect you to stay because of the baby."

"That's offensive." He frowned. Seeing the question in my eyes, he said, "I am not going anywhere. And don't even think about pushing me away."

"I'm just saying—"

"You've just made me a very happy man. And we are going to be superb parents to this little guy."

I laughed softly between sniffles. "Little guy? What if it's a girl?"

"As long as she looks like you and not me."

I laughed, looked deep into his eyes, and touched the side of his cheek. His whisker stubble was rough against my hand.

"How are you doing with all of this?" he asked, his voice so gentle it made me weak in the knees. "This has to be quite the shock for you."

I sat back and rested my head against the back of the sofa. "Levi, this is everything I've ever wanted since as far back as I can remember. It's the reason my first marriage ended. Which was a blessing in disguise." I looked at him. "Just when I'd come to terms with the fact that it was never going to be, and I was finally okay with it, I'm pregnant." I rested my forearm over my eyes then put it back down again. "But I'm forty-three years old! I feel like Sarah from the Bible."

He laughed quietly. "You're a spring chicken compared to Sarah. She was ninety when Isaac was conceived. That said, my dear, she was married. It's time we do this right and make an honest woman out of you."

I giggled, feeling like a giddy teenager. "It's too late for that."

"What did your grandmother say?"

My eyes widened. "How did you know that I—"

"I've been around the block with you, Melanie Hogan. I would have been shocked if you hadn't told her first."

I smiled at him, feeling a warmth spread throughout my body. This man was too good to be true. "I wasn't sure how she would take it. How she would respond. But she was so strong, so—so perfect, as always. And just so you know, she expects us to be married yesterday." I grinned.

"Well, then," he said, standing up, holding my hands, and pulling me up beside him, "We wouldn't want to disappoint her, would we?"

"What exactly do you have in mind, Detective?"

"This weekend. You and me. Here in this house. I'll get the officiant."

"Nana, Claire, Syd, Jack, Rubie, Max, and Daisy need to be here. And especially Jackson. Jackson!" My hand flew to my mouth. "What will he think? Will he be okay with this?"

"Are you kidding me?" Levi said. "He's been asking me for a little brother for a long time now."

Relief washed over me. "And if it's a girl?"

"He'll still be thrilled."

"We need to tell him before anyone else does. I want to tell him with you."

Levi looked at his watch, took out his phone, and punched a number. "I'll call him right now. We can do a video call. It'll be our weekend with him anyway, so having him here for our nuptials won't be a problem."

"What happened with Natalie?" I asked.

He looked at me as though I'd lost my mind. "You want to talk about the case? *Now*?"

I shrugged sheepishly. "Just because I'm pregnant doesn't mean I've lost my curiosity."

He rolled his eyes and snickered. "I'm sure you haven't. She wants to cut a deal. She gives us information on the drug company's shenanigans, and she's released from the charge."

"What?" I managed to get out. "Are you serious? She gets off scot-free? That won't happen, will it?"

He shrugged, regret reflected in his eyes. "Not my call to make. It won't be completely dismissed but will likely be a much lesser charge if she cooperates." He shrugged again. "Usually, in high-profile cases such as this one that could potentially have a lot of fallout, it's worth offering a lesser to the low man on the totem pole if it means getting the people at the top." He looked deep into my eyes and put his hand protectively on my back. "The charges for what she did to you will stick. She can't weasel out of those."

***

I took Nana shopping with me to find something to wear. I wanted casual, which set Claire and Rubie on alert and insisted on going with as if they didn't trust me not to wear a pair of blue jeans and black boots. They did, however, consent to me wearing white jeans with black and white sandals. High-heeled, of course. I wouldn't know how to walk in anything else. I even let Rubie talk me into wearing a cold-shoulder top with floral-patterned lace, a keyhole on the front—in pink. When I agreed to the pink part, I thought both Claire and Rubie might pass out. Nana even looked pleased, her eyes tearing up a bit.

"Child," she'd said, "I don't think I've ever been happier except when I married your granddad."

"Nana," I'd told her, as I held her shoulders gently, looking into those twinkling eyes, "you say that every day."

Her smile broadened even further. "I suppose I do, dear, I suppose I do. But today, I especially mean it."

Jack was still flabbergasted that I was pregnant.

"How?" he'd asked incredulously when I'd told him. "I mean, not that I'm not elated, but *how*?"

"Oh, Jacky," I'd said, laughing into the phone, "I'm not the one to tell you about the birds and the bees."

Connie came back when she'd heard the news about Paul's killer, and as a thank you for sticking up for her, she agreed to come back to the salon until we found someone to replace her. I'd promised her the going away party of the century for going through everything she had with me the past few years. Today, she and Babs were running the place and would meet us as soon as they could for the celebration at Grizzley's. Levi reserved the party room.

"No restroom trips, little mama," he'd said. To which I only laughed. Obviously, he didn't know what it was like to be pregnant.

Now, I descended the stairs as quietly as I could after sending Claire and Rubie down earlier. I told them I needed a few moments alone. I stood at the base of the stairs watching everyone I loved so dearly. People for whom I would walk through fire. I watched as Levi and Nana conversed off to one side, both smiling warmly at one another. Jackson stood close by his father, grinning up at Nana, who was dressed so beautifully in a light blue dress, her silver hair in a loose bun at her nape, compliments of Claire. Claire, Sydney, Cole, Rubie, Scott, Max, Daisy, and Jack were in a circle laughing and ribbing one another. Claire positively glowed in a bouncy orange miniskirt, white top, and orange headscarf. And Rubie? A puff of pink from head to toe. I could smell her Loves Baby Soft waft through the air. The officiant, who was the chaplain at the police department, stood by himself in front of the large picture window, Bible opened in his hand. He appeared to be reviewing the ceremony he'd planned.

I glanced again at Levi at the exact moment he looked my way, and my heart stopped as our eyes met. He was in his black jeans, black jacket, and black boots, his head cleanly shaved and shiny, his tiny earring glinting off the white lights Claire and Rubie strung throughout the house. I'd never seen him look so dapper. And sexy. This man, the father of my child, love of my life. Jackson looked like a mini-Levi but with black curly, tousled hair. Levi walked over and stood in front of me, taking my hands in his, our eyes never wavering. "Ready?" he said, his voice low.

"Ladies and gentlemen," the chaplain said, though I barely heard him. All I could hear and see was Levi. "Can we please take our seats? Let's have a wedding!"

Nana's Goulash

1 lb ground beef
Green, red, yellow peppers (1/2 of each)
1 medium yellow onion
1 small can diced tomatoes
1 cup beef broth
1 can Campbell's tomato soup
1 ½ cups elbow macaroni (any pasta will do)
1 cup shredded cheddar cheese (optional)
Salt/Pepper/Garlic
(Oregano & Basil are optional for a slightly altered flavor)

Combine ground beef, onion, and peppers--fry until ground beef is no longer pink; drain
Season with salt, pepper, & garlic
Add diced tomatoes, beef broth, tomato soup; stir and simmer
Cook elbow macaroni to desired tenderness (Nana likes to keep her macaroni on the firm side)
Add cooked macaroni to ground beef mixture, stir, and let sit on medium-low heat for 5-10 minutes.
Stir in cheese and remove from heat

Nana's Chocolate Chip Walnut Banana Bread

½ C butter or margarine

1 C sugar

2 eggs (beaten)

3 mashed bananas

2 C flour

1 tsp soda

Desired amount of dark chocolate chips

Desired amount of chopped walnuts

(Nana uses ½ cup of each chips and walnuts)

Mix in order given. Grease pan and bake at 350 for 1 hr.

Dear Reader,

Word of mouth is the best promotion for an author. Please consider leaving a review on Amazon and Goodreads. A sentence or two is all that is needed. By doing this, it helps me, as the author, as well as other readers.

I would love for you to connect with me at:

Website: rhondablackhurst.com
Email: rhondablackhurst@gmail.com
Facebook: www.facebook.com/rjblackhurst
Twitter: @rjblackhurst
Instagram: rhonda.blackhurst

You can sign up for my newsletter at shorturl.at/ltwCH or by visiting my website for the latest information on upcoming books, giveaways, call-outs for recipes, and other valuable information.

Also, as a certified life coach, I would love for you to sign up for my private Facebook group, Live Your Best Life, to get tips and ask questions on how to live *your* best life.

Best,
    Rhonda

Acknowledgements

So much gratitude and appreciation go to the following people, whether you have walked this journey with me, been an important part along the way, motivated and inspired, or simply just did *you*, making my writerly journey so beautiful. I value each and every one of you.

Rachel Olson (No Sweat Graphics & Formatting) — for your creativity in designing my covers and formatting my words. Thank you for taking my vision and making it beautiful.

Jessica Cornwell (Jessica Cornwell Author Services) — for your expertise in taking my story and making it shine.

Tim Anderson, Kelli Anderson, and Sandy Hilger — for your willingness and your time to make this book better.

Francelia Belton, Karen Whalen, Pat Breslin, Jamie Birzer, Sara Jonas, Sandy Delgehausen, Brenda Tagtmeier, Bridget Dyson, Lisa Steffan, Roger Cielinski, Melanie Notsch, Kerri Keprios, Becky King — each of you have supported me on my journey in your own special way.

Sisters in Crime (National, Colorado Chapter, and Guppies) Colorado Authors League, Northern Colorado Writers, and Rocky Mountain Fiction Writers — for the sister/brotherhood of other creatives.

My dad and mom — for your never-ending belief in me, encouraging me to live my life's dream.

Clint—my one, my person, my biggest supporter, and my go-to for police procedure. Even though I veer off track a bit "for the sake of the story"—which I know drives you crazy—you still love me. It's an honor to share life with you.

Ben, Yvette, Alex, Jennifer, Glen, Zoey, Olivia, Emilia, Annabelle, Benny, Morgan, Jayden, Cassidy, Cody, Spencer, Caity—for being my whole world. You're my sun on cloudy days, and my rainbow in the rain. Thank you for far more than I could ever say.

And, always, my Lord and Savior, for the unending, underserved GRACE You continually bestow upon me.

About the Author

Born in northern Minnesota, Rhonda now resides in Colorado with her husband and her very spoiled Pomeranian, Roscoe.

Her love of writing took flight at the tender age of four when she was caught writing with her crayons on the knotty pine walls of the family home. In her teens, she tested her hand at journalism by writing an article or two for the city newspaper about school events. She completed a Journalism/Short Story Writing course and was a stringer for a local newspaper.

She is also a certified life coach who specializes in teaching people how to live their best life with a program called Rising from Victim to Victor. You can learn more at her website: www.rhondablackhurst.com

Recently retired from the District Attorney's Office, she can now be found hibernating in coffee shops or her home office creating characters, settings, and stories, emerging occasionally for coffee and dark chocolate.

www.ingramcontent.com/pod-product-compliance
Lightning Source LLC
Chambersburg PA
CBHW072121250626
47159CB00007B/2522